KU-033-636

Acclaim for Sheila O'Flanagan's novels

'A thoroughly enjoyable read' *Ireland on Sunday*

'Engaging characters and flowing dialogue . . . an eventful, compelling and ultimately satisfying journey' *Irish Independent*

'Easy, witty and feel-good' *U* magazine

'Another fine read from Ireland's leading lady in fiction' *Belfast Sunday Life*

'Well written, down to earth and honest' *Woman's Way*

'Hugely enjoyable' *Best*

'Chick lit at its very best' *Irish Examiner*

'Well written and very readable . . . a refreshing change from the usual stable of women's contemporary fiction' *Publishing News*

'Sheila O'Flanagan is one of the blinding talents on the female fiction scene . . . she never strays far from the top of the bestseller lists' Scottish *Daily Record*

Also by Sheila O'Flanagan
and available from Headline Review

Suddenly Single
Far From Over
My Favourite Goodbye
He's Got To Go
Isobel's Wedding
Caroline's Sister
Too Good To Be True
Dreaming of a Stranger
Destinations
Anyone But Him
How Will I Know?
Yours, Faithfully

P2 GAVE UP

CONNECTIONS

Sheila O'Flanagan

headline
review

Copyright © 2007 Sheila O'Flanagan

The right of Sheila O'Flanagan to be identified as the Author of
the Work has been asserted by her in accordance with the
Copyright, Designs and Patents Act 1988.

First published in 2006
by HEADLINE REVIEW
An imprint of HEADLINE PUBLISHING GROUP

First published in paperback in 2007
by HEADLINE REVIEW

5

Apart from any use permitted under UK copyright law, this
publication may only be reproduced, stored, or transmitted, in
any form, or by any means, with prior permission in writing of
the publishers or, in the case of reprographic production, in
accordance with the terms of licences issued by the
Copyright Licensing Agency.

All characters in this publication are fictitious
and any resemblance to real persons, living or dead,
is purely coincidental.

ISBN 978 0 7553 3028 7 (A format)
ISBN 978 0 7553 2345 6 (B format)

Typeset in Galliard by
Palimpsest Book Production Limited,
Polmont, Stirlingshire
Printed and bound in Great Britain by
Clays Ltd, St Ives plc

Headline's policy is to use papers that are natural, renewable and
recyclable products and made from wood grown in
sustainable forests. The logging and manufacturing processes
are expected to conform to the environmental
regulations of the country of origin.

HEADLINE PUBLISHING GROUP
A division of Hachette Livre UK Ltd
338 Euston Road
LONDON NW1 3BH

www.reviewbooks.co.uk
www.hodderheadline.com

Author's Note

The number one question I'm asked by readers is 'Where do you get your ideas from?' For this collection of short stories, I'm able to answer that!

I was lucky enough to stay in a lovely hotel on a Caribbean island some time ago. It was an extremely popular wedding location and one evening I noticed a bride-to-be having a heated discussion with her partner. My imagination started to run away with me as I wondered what on earth they were arguing about and suddenly I was making up stories about the wedding couple and everyone else who stayed there – *Connections* is the result!

Additionally, many readers have asked me about sequels to some of my novels. I don't generally like sequels myself, but from time to time I've thought about characters I've created and wondered what might have happened to them. So I've included two stories here with characters from *Isobel's Wedding* and *He's Got To Go*. I hope readers who have asked about Isobel and Bree will be happy with how things turned out for them! You may also pick up references to a couple of other characters from previous novels. I hope you'll enjoy recognising them too.

I'd like to thank Ciara Considine for insisting that I write

Sheila O'Flanagan

more short stories and editing these so meticulously; Breda Purdue and Ruth Shern for being so unfailingly positive about my writing; and Carole Blake for reminding me to take time out to walk along the beach.

A special thank you to my family who are so wonderful – particularly my lovely nephews David, James, Hugh and Oisín.

And again, to all my readers, thank you for your support. I hope you enjoy this collection and that, no matter where you are, it transports you to tropical climes! As always, you can contact me on www.sheilaoflanagan.net if you have any comments on any of my books.

Contents

Room 404 (Corinne)

Jennifer Jones sat at the table on her balcony.

No, thought Corinne, that's too boring. It doesn't say anything, doesn't let people know where she is. Or what sort of person she is. Or what might be about to happen to her.

Jennifer Jones watched the crystal-clear water from the chair on her balcony.

But what's she doing sitting down? Corinne asked herself. Why is she sitting around like a lame-ass when she's somewhere gorgeous and exotic? And when she's supposed to be gorgeous and exotic too? And especially when she's supposed to be a sassy action heroine? She shouldn't be sitting anywhere just looking at the sea like a feeble pensioner. (Though pensioners don't have to be feeble. Note to self: how about a pensioner heroine for a future novel? Mightn't that be interesting? Or is that too Agatha Christie? Miss Bloody Marple, of course. Nobody can do a pensioner like Miss Bloody Marple, can they?) Corinne frowned as she looked at her revised opening sentence again. I haven't even said that it's the sea she's looking at, have I? Crystal-clear water could be a lake. I'm still not giving any information about what's going to happen to her at all.

Jennifer Jones . . . Jennifer Jones . . . Corinne stared at the open laptop in front of her. Oh bloody hell, she thought. What the hell *is* going to happen to her? *I've* no damn idea. She pushed the laptop away from her in disgust and stared out over the blue and white wooden rails of the balcony of Room 404. She sighed deeply. Bloody Jennifer Jones. She loathed the woman. Detested her. Hated her. Abhorred her. Corinne pulled the laptop towards her again and clicked on the thesaurus. Abhor. Abominate. Deplore. Detest. Dislike. Execrate. She frowned. Was execrate a verb? She wasn't sure. She'd never heard of it before. But it would do. If it meant what it was supposed to mean, then she absolutely totally and utterly execrated Jennifer Bloody Jones.

Corinne snapped the laptop closed and got up from the table. She walked back into the air-conditioned bedroom and picked up the pile of books on her bedside locker. They all had a black jacket with the silhouette of a tall, extremely thin woman etched on the front. The silhouette was in various colours. Vivid green. Pillar-box red. Shocking pink.

Jennifer Jones and the Jealous Journalist by Corinne Doherty. The Number 1 Bestseller. A new and exciting addition to the slick-chick genre. *Jennifer Jones and the Jade Jester* by Corinne Doherty. Further Adventures of Europe's Sassiest Private Eye. *Jennifer Jones and the Jellybean Jackpot* by Corinne Doherty. Ms Jones Rides High!

Why in God's name had she called the woman Jennifer Jones? It was getting harder and harder to come up with clever titles – not that the ones she'd come up with before were all that clever, but the publisher loved the alliteration – and it was becoming even more difficult to think of a half-decent plot to go with them. How many murders could one woman solve, for heaven's sake? How many times could her heroine save the day? Heroine, hah! Jennifer Jones wasn't a heroine to Corinne. She was a bloody weight around her neck.

But Jennifer Jones was apparently a beloved heroine to loads of other people. What had started out as a kind of niche private eye caper had turned into an unexpectedly big seller and had, astonishingly, been bought by readers of the darker kind of crime novels too, propelling Jennifer Jones towards the top of the charts and fostering a clatter of Jennifer Jones fan-sites on the internet. (Corinne worried about some of Jennifer's fans. They seemed to know more about her than she did herself!)

Of course she hadn't expected anything like that to happen. When she'd tentatively sent off the first novel to an agent and had waited, with fingers crossed, to hear back from him, she'd loved the idea of her long-legged, bean-pole-bodied supermodel private eye. And she'd loved the plot of the Jealous Journalist too, a plot that had come to her all of a sudden as she sat in the bath, so that she jumped out, towelled down and started writing straight away. But she hadn't intended to write a damn series. The whole concept was a one-off as far as she was concerned. She hadn't (if she was really truthful with herself) even expected the book to ever hit the shelves at all.

She flopped across the queen-sized bed and closed her eyes. When Arnie, her agent, had called to tell her about the publishing deal, she'd almost collapsed with the excitement. And when he'd told her that Dagger Press, the publishers, wanted a second book about the private eye from her, she'd barely hesitated before agreeing. After all, she reckoned, the Jealous Journalist had been easy to write. And even though she hadn't intended another novel with Jennifer, well, she could manage it. So she did. The Jade Jester had been a bit more difficult to put together, but she'd suddenly found a cracking plot and, of course, Jennifer did her exotic thing the whole way through. That book had sold even more than the first. And then – well, everything should have been perfect. Most people would have said it actually was.

Arnie had called her, barely containing his excitement, to say that Dagger Press wanted more of Jennifer Jones. Lots more. And so did the reading public. They loved her. She was becoming a guaranteed bestseller. Dagger Press wanted to keep Corinne and Jennifer Jones on their list. Other publishing companies wanted her too. She was hot property. And – Arnie had paused for dramatic effect here – the TV people were interested. They loved comfortable crime, he told her. Or glossy crime. Particularly for Sunday nights. Stuff like *Midsomer Murders*, where nothing was too gory or horrible but where there was a ridiculously high body count and an engaging sleuth. Jennifer Jones would fit that bill perfectly in a modern way. She would update the whole vista of Sunday-evening viewing. She was more than slick-chick territory – she could nab the older viewer too.

Corinne had always wanted to be hot property, although she'd never expected that it would really happen. And the idea of her stories being used as Sunday-evening TV was very exciting. But she felt a nervous flutter in the pit of her stomach.

'I've only written two books,' she told Arnie anxiously. 'They can hardly make a series out of two books.'

4

'What we're talking about is adapting the books,' he said. 'Three- or four-parters. They can do the first two and by then you'll have produced the third. After that we'll see how to progress. There's a lot of mileage in Jennifer Jones. You can do more books but the TV could equally be stand-alone, just using the character. You don't have to write the TV stuff, of course.'

'But . . .' Corinne looked confused, 'how can they do something when we don't know what's going to happen to the character? I mean, what if Jennifer Jones decides to get married?'

Arnie looked at her sternly. 'Don't do anything stupid like marry her off,' he said. 'The great thing about her is the chemistry between herself and the people she's investigating. You can't marry her off. And be careful who she sleeps with too. You don't want to alienate anyone.'

Corinne blinked.

'The public love her,' said Arnie, a little more gently. 'They've invested time and interest in her. You don't want to piss them off.'

'She's *my* detective,' said Corinne defiantly. 'I can do what I want with her.'

'Not when we sign this deal,' Arnie told her. 'She'll become a brand name. You can't mess with a brand name.'

Corinne hadn't wanted Jennifer Jones to become a brand name. But when Arnie told her the amount of money involved for another three books, she took out her special contract-signing fountain pen and scrawled her signature straight away before the honchos in Dagger Press changed their minds. The money meant that she could pay off all of her debts (and put an end to those letters from her credit card company reminding her about the necessity to make the minimum payment every month); buy a new car and put a deposit on a lovely apartment; pay for her mother's hip operation and her father's glaucoma one; and give her adorable, but totally hopeless younger brother some cash towards setting up his own plumbing business. Although as she wrote out the cheque for Bill, Corinne couldn't help thinking that it was money down the drain. Literally.

'You're the best, sis.' His eyes were bright as she handed him the money. 'I'll make you so proud of me.'

She wrote *Jennifer Jones and the Jellybean Jackpot* in a haze of delight, thinking of all the great things she could do for her family with the money she was going to bring in over the next few years. But *Jennifer Jones and the Jellybean Jackpot* didn't sell quite as well as *Jennifer Jones and the Jade Jester*. It made a quick appearance in the bestseller charts but was then bumped out by a plethora of books about the Holy Grail (thanks a lot, Dan Brown, she thought miserably) and the novel that had been selected for the latest TV book club. As far as Corinne was concerned, *Model Murder*, written by a stunning former catwalk model, was a rip-off of Jennifer Jones. Only – according to the critics – grittier. She was enraged that a grittier rip-off of her book was being paraded as a must-read for millions of TV viewers, and even more enraged when the interviewer on the programme told them that *Model Murder* was the best piece of crime fiction she'd read in years and that it was a definite number one.

Corinne had thought about making Jennifer Jones grittier herself but had been persuaded against it. She kept having wonderful ideas about her private eye getting hooked on designer drugs (after all, she moved in circles where recreational drug use was perfectly acceptable. As were uppers, downers and appetite suppressants), or taking a lesbian lover, or developing bulimia; but when she mentioned this to Arnie he'd nearly had a heart attack.

'Jennifer Jones is a role model,' he'd hissed at her. 'Role models don't have drugs issues or lesbian lovers. And they certainly don't have bulimia.'

'Princess Diana did,' Corinne pointed out.

'Yes. And she's dead.'

Sometimes, thought Corinne, Arnie could be ruthlessly businesslike.

'What about this *Model Murder*, though?' asked Corinne. 'Everyone thinks it's brilliant. Rowena Roselli has taken over my spot!'

'Don't be ridiculous.' Arnie snorted. 'She's a one-hit wonder. I have it on good authority that her next book is a crock of shit and the publishers are tearing their hair out over it.'

'Yes, but she was on all the TV programmes,' wailed Corinne. 'Flaunting her jail sentence.'

Rowena, the author of *Model Murder*, had served a few months for supplying drugs. She'd been on *Parkinson* and *Jonathan Ross* and a whole range of other TV programmes talking about her 'lapse' and how it had made her a better person. When she told her story on daytime TV everyone whooped and cheered and agreed that she deserved a second chance.

'It's a selling point, that's all,' said Arnie.

'Well maybe I need a selling point too!'

Corinne had thought long and hard about what her selling point could be, but she couldn't actually come up with anything. She'd led an unfortunately blameless and boring childhood. It was disgraceful, in fact, how boring her childhood had been, and now it had become a real drawback because it was so damn competitive out there – people wanted to read novels by authors who'd been abandoned by their parents or overcome some awful disease or done something really extraordinary in their lives (as though serving a jail sentence for drug-pushing was anything to be proud of, Corinne thought bitterly); it just wasn't enough to have written a damn book any more.

'You're being paranoid,' said Arnie when she wailed all this to him. 'Stop thinking like a fool and get on with it.'

But she couldn't get on with it. All she could do was think about Rowena Roselli and the huge feature article about her in the *Sunday Times* magazine, which pictured her draped in nothing but diamonds and smoking a cigar. The diamonds had given Corinne an idea about her own potential childhood problem. If she revealed to everyone that she was a reformed kleptomaniac, surely that would get her a few column inches in the papers?

The only slight flaw in the plan was that she'd never actually stolen anything in her life. Except the Cadbury's Creme Egg from the display in the local Spar a few years earlier. And that wasn't actually stealing. She'd picked it up and meant to pay for it along with the newspapers, magazines and birthday cards that she was buying and somehow she'd just managed to put it in her pocket before the sales assistant had rung it up on the till. She only realised it after she'd walked out of the shop and then she'd gone straight back in and paid for it.

All the same, she'd thought as she mulled over the idea, it was a possibility. When she'd been interviewed a few days later by someone doing a piece for the local paper about the sudden surge of crime-caper writers, she'd almost said something about the kleptomania. But in the end she'd chickened out. Her mother would go berserk if she read that Corinne had been robbing things from local shops, and in the end people would find out that she'd been lying anyway. Although maybe she could say that she was a pathological liar instead?

She rubbed her eyes in despair. She had to stop thinking like this and start thinking about her novel. But it was much harder than she'd expected. She hadn't even managed to come up with a title, although that was the first thing she normally did. It was actually very difficult to think of titles for someone called Jennifer Jones, which was why she couldn't start writing until she had the right one. Why on earth hadn't she originally called the woman Brenda Byrne? she wondered. There were hundreds of brilliant titles that would go with Brenda Byrne. *Brenda Byrne and the Battered Body*. Basic Burglary. Breathless Beauty. Oh yes, thought Corinne miserably, *Brenda Byrne and the Breathless Beauty* would have been fantastic. She could have set it even more firmly in the supermodel world where Jennifer Bloody Jones was supposed to be plying her trade and it would have been miles better than *Model Murder*. It could have been an exposé of all the bitchery and back-stabbing that went on. (Back-stabbing, thought Corinne. *Brenda Byrne and the Backstabbing Bitch*! Brilliant!) Maybe, though, for someone called Brenda Byrne, which wasn't a very glamorous name, she could have set it in the more prosaic world of catalogue modelling instead. She knew a bit about that. She'd done some work for catalogues in her early teens, before she lost her cheeky grin. That was why she'd made Jennifer Jones a model in the first place, moulding her on a simply gorgeous-looking woman who'd once been involved in catalogues too. Of course Jin Corcoran hadn't stayed in modelling. Nor had she become a detective. She'd just got married to someone incredibly rich.

Corinne sighed deeply. She'd picked modelling because she was supposed to be writing about what she knew. Not, of course, that she knew a whole lot about gruesome murders either, but she'd once been introduced to a really nice Irish detective at a conference and Siobhán Farrell had become her sounding board for the criminal activities that went on in her books. Corinne was very grateful to her journalist friend JoJo for introducing her to Siobhán in the first place. She'd dedicated *Jennifer Jones and the Jellybean Jackpot* to both of them. They'd been thrilled, but a lot of good that did when it hadn't reached number one on the bestseller lists.

Jennifer Jones and the Jamaican Jerk. It had eventually come to her in the middle of the night and she thought (with an overwhelming sense of relief) that it was a good title. The publishers agreed.

So it became the title of the book she was supposed to be working on. That was why she was on this Caribbean island. (OK, so it wasn't actually Jamaica, but she'd been there before on a last-minute cheap deal with two of her friends from the travel agency where she'd worked before becoming a best-selling crime-caper novelist, so her location didn't really matter.) She'd decided to come to White Sands because she'd heard about it from another author at an awards ceremony to which she'd been invited even though she hadn't actually been nominated. The ceremony had been excruciatingly awful. Rowena Roselli was up for best newcomer, though thankfully she hadn't won. Corinne rather thought that there would have been a real-life murder if she had, because she wasn't sure that she wouldn't have stabbed Rowena there and then. Which could have been a good selling point too, she supposed later. Maybe *Jennifer Jones and the Jellybean Jackpot* would have scorched through the charts if its author was in jail for the attempted murder of a rival novelist. But White Sands sounded a good deal better than jail. The ideal place, she thought as she packed a couple of sarongs and half a dozen swimsuits, to soak up some atmosphere for writing *Jennifer Jones and the Jamaican Jerk*.

If only she could come up with a plot. Her mind was a complete blank as far as Jennifer and the Jerk were concerned and she was terrified that she had writer's block. Most writers she knew said that there was no such thing, that it was just an excuse for not sitting at the computer. But Corinne had sat at the computer for weeks back home, playing solitaire over and over again and googling her name on the internet (she had to stop doing that, it was far too depressing), without even the tiniest edge of a plot coming to her. So now she was convinced that writer's block was real and that she had it and that she'd never be able to write another word again.

She looked at the words she'd typed on the computer and deleted them all. They were rubbish. She was rubbish. She simply couldn't do this any more.

She sat up again and checked her mobile. No messages. Nobody was looking for her. Well, she'd told them not to. She'd said that she was going to the Caribbean to work. She'd implied that she'd be totally out of touch (except, of course, with her muse. She'd have to be in touch with that. Whatever it was. Wherever it was).

'Have a lovely time,' her mother had said. 'How lucky you are.'

'I'll be working,' she reminded her.

'I'd love to be working in the sun,' said Lillian Doherty.

'Yeah, you're right.' Corinne felt guilty. Guiltier still the day she'd left when the rain had been bucketing down out of the lumpy, leaden grey skies.

Jennifer Jones and the Jamaican Jerk. Maybe if she took her laptop down to the beach it might help.

Most people had already settled in to the morning routine. Loungers had been pulled into preferred locations along the narrow crescent of fine white sand. Holiday-makers were sleeping or reading, usually with a brightly coloured cocktail on the wooden tables beside them. Corinne scanned the reading material to see what was popular.

Three people were reading *Model Murder*. She bit her lip and tried to clamp down on her feelings of jealousy. After all, she told herself, it's not like I don't sell. It's not like I'm a struggling author who hasn't sold anything. It's just that – she shivered in the warmth of the afternoon sun – it's just that I'm afraid I can't do it any more. And if I can't do it any more, then what the hell *can* I do?

The latest celebrity kiss-and-tell autobiography of a glamour model was the top non-fiction choice. Glamour modelling, mused Corinne, maybe that's something that Jennifer Jones could get involved in. *Jennifer Jones and the Glamour* . . . only she couldn't have Glamour in the title, it began

12

with the wrong letter. She'd have to think of something else. Besides, Arnie wouldn't want Jennifer Jones to be involved in glamour modelling. He'd think it was seedy, even if Corinne managed to persuade him that Jennifer was going under cover. She giggled to herself. Hardly under cover when you were talking about glamour modelling. There was something in that, surely. She'd met a guy from Amazon once who told her that the books that got the most hits on the site had the word naked in the title. *Jennifer Jones Naked* might be a good title, despite the lack of alliteration.

Nobody was reading Jennifer Jones on the beach. It didn't matter what Arnie said. It didn't matter how many books they told her they were selling. It was all going horribly wrong. She wasn't required beach reading material. She was a has-been. A total failure.

She sat down on the nearest lounger, close to a man on his own. She'd seen him around the hotel before; he seemed to be alone with his young son, which Corinne thought was lovely. She liked the whole idea of a father–son bonding thing going on. Her useless brother, Bill, had a son of his own but he hardly ever got to see him. When Bill's girlfriend Debbie had discovered she was pregnant, she'd told him that it was her problem and she would deal with it. Bill insisted he would take responsibility for his child, but Debbie's idea of Bill's responsibilities was for him to transfer a huge chunk of his salary every month to her account to support them. Which would have been fair enough, thought Corinne, except that she then moved house so that she was now a four-hour drive away which meant that it was difficult for Bill to see his son regularly. She was sure that Bill would have loved to come to the island with Hal for a bit of male bonding. Perhaps, if she ever managed to write this damn book, she could pay for them to go.

Corinne shivered again. She peeped over the top of the computer at the man on his own, who was staring, unseeingly, across the water. He looked worried, thought Corinne. She wondered why.

Stop wondering, she told herself firmly. Stop wondering about people around you and start bloody writing. The people in your head matter more right now than the people on the beach.

And then she bit her lip as she remembered Niall's parting words as he walked out on her after two years together. 'You care more about the people in your head than you do about me. And that Jennifer Jones creature is appalling. Why you think anyone could possibly find her remotely interesting is beyond me.'

Well, she'd had the last laugh there, hadn't she? Even though it hadn't seemed like it at the time. Niall had been really rude and horrible to her. But she still missed him. People in her head were one thing, but she missed having a person in her bed too. And she'd been working too hard over the last couple of years to find someone new. For some reason people thought she lived a totally glamorous and exciting life. But how glamorous could it be when she didn't even have a casual bloke in it?

Anyway, it had taken more than a year to get over Niall. At the time she'd been writing *Jennifer Jones and the Jade Jester*. It had been an edgier book than the Jealous Journalist. Jennifer had become involved with a really murky character in it and had almost fallen into a criminal situation herself. Even though the book had been harder to write than the first, Corinne knew that it had ultimately been better. Because she'd poured more emotions into it. More bitterness. More unhappiness. And, as she'd felt her heart mend, more feistiness.

God, she thought, what on earth can I put into this one? More pina coladas?

She closed the laptop again. It was too hard to read the screen in the sun. Bringing it down to the beach had been ridiculous. Attention-seeking. But maybe she'd wanted some attention. Maybe she'd been tired of being a single woman on her own in a place full of couples.

Actually, she thought, as she leaned back on the sun-lounger and closed her eyes, there seemed to be more than one woman on her own here. There was the old dear who went for a swim every morning before breakfast wearing a staid bathing suit and an old fashioned swim-cap festooned with brightly coloured plastic flowers. She used an economical breast stroke to go out as far as the jetty before returning – a swim longer than Corinne could possibly do herself. Corinne had also noticed an efficient-looking woman who (she knew because she'd heard her talking about it) was the private secretary to some hotshot businessman who paid for her winter break. And there was an olive-skinned girl with dark hair who had been on her own at first but who now seemed to be with a bloke whom Corinne had first seen with a different woman at the manager's cocktail party (that had given her some food for thought; she'd wondered if there was an affair going on and whether or not she could work that information into a Jennifer Jones storyline. After all, murders were often crimes of passion. But it had all seemed a bit passé. Jennifer needed more exciting plots than that). The man and the woman were on the beach now, sitting beside each other on the sun-lounger, the girl dressed in shorts and a T-shirt and obviously going home on the afternoon flight, while he wasn't yet ready to leave.

As she watched, the man stood up and took the woman by the hand. Corinne could see the chemistry spark between them. She watched as he leaned towards his companion and kissed her on the back of the neck. Crikey, thought Corinne, it's a turn-on just watching them! She chewed on the inside of her lip. She wondered if she could have some kind of plot with a couple who were on holiday on the island and the woman being seduced by the Jamaican Jerk and then somehow getting involved in smuggling . . . drugs? diamonds? back to Europe. And Jennifer Jones would obviously have to uncover all this. Although how was a mystery to her.

'Can I get you a drink?' One of the white-shirted waiters stood in front of her, beaming broadly. She ordered a pina colada. Maybe a cocktail would help her think.

As she sipped her drink she noticed a stunning-looking girl walking along the water's edge. Her long dark hair cascaded in a whirl of curls down her back and her white swimsuit set off an even tan. Corinne knew that this was Sahndhi Jeffries, from *Pop Princess*, the reality TV series. Sahndhi had been the runaway winner and her name and picture had been plastered all over the papers, though Corinne wouldn't necessarily have recognised her, because she didn't have time to read the papers or watch TV these days. The reason she did recognise Sahndhi was because the girl had been having her photograph taken all week, a team of photographers and journalists seeming to track her every move.

She was alone now, though, her single file of footprints being washed over by each gentle wave. She was murmuring under her breath, rather like Corinne herself did when she walked along the beach trying to work out dialogue in her head. She'd been doing that every morning, her auburn hair tied into a knot on the top of her head the way Jennifer Jones wore her own dark tresses, so that she felt in character. Not that it had done any good, of course, because she hadn't managed to come up with anything. But still, at least she could watch the Pop Princess and not think she was totally demented. She supposed that Sahndhi was practising songs in her head.

Maybe the Jamaican Jerk could be a man on a pop star jury. And he could be asking sexual favours in return for saying that the contestants were brilliant. And one of them could murder him . . . Corinne blinked a few times as her eyes followed Sahndhi's progress along the beach towards Coco Villa. He could be staying in an exclusive hotel and they could track him down . . .

'Hello, dear.' The elderly woman broke her train of thought. Corinne checked the feeling of irritation at being interrupted just as perhaps she was getting something going for the Jamaican Jerk.

'I hope you don't mind me disturbing you, but I wondered if this lounger was taken?' She indicated the one recently vacated by the dad on his own.

'I don't think so.'

'Oh, I'll just plop myself so.' She sat down. 'I can't manage to drag another one into the shade.'

Corinne smiled absently at the woman, her mind still on the possibility of murder at Coco Villa. It wasn't at all a bad idea, she thought. She was perfectly certain that many of the contestants on those TV shows wanted to murder the presenters. And if she made the Jamaican Jerk a really horrible character with absolutely no morals whatsoever . . .

The elderly woman took a copy of *Model Murder* out of her beach bag. Corinne nearly choked with rage.

Perhaps she could be the mother of one of the contestants, Corinne thought. Maybe her daughter was one of the girls who was asked for the favours. And she found out about it and murdered him. She snorted under her breath. The thought of this little old dear murdering anyone was outrageous. She was a novelist, she told herself, but she had to get a grip. Sometimes she allowed her imagination to run too far away with her. Still, she had to explore every possibility.

Murder-sex-contestants, she wrote. *Possibly granny murderer? (Too far-fetched, but you never know!)*

By the time she'd been on the island for almost a week, she'd managed to write five words. They were, quite simply: *Jennifer Jones was in Jamaica.*

Corinne thought that it was a better opening than having Jennifer staring at lakes or oceans or vast tracts of water, but it still didn't get her very far. She'd set herself a target of writing ten thousand words while she was at White Sands. She had a day and a half left to do it and today she hadn't bothered to open her laptop at all. Instead she sat on the beach and watched one of the many wedding ceremonies at the resort. As the bride walked along the promontory, her long white veil floating in the gentle offshore breeze, Corinne wondered if Jennifer Jones could be the guest at a society wedding. The bride would be murdered. There'd be red blood all over the white dress. The husband would be the suspect. But of course it wouldn't have been him. Or maybe it would. She could twist and twist the story so that nobody would know who it was. And – she suddenly sat up straight on her lounger – all of the guests at the wedding could have some dark secret to hide.

Like, perhaps, the group of people who were currently sitting together talking loudly about the upcoming nuptials of the girl called Suze and her future husband, Kevin. Perhaps there could be a secondary murder. Suze's friend, a girl whose name Corinne didn't know, kept looking daggers at another bloke in the group. It was potentially very interesting, thought Corinne. She could imagine the girl killing this bloke, only she didn't know why. Not yet anyway.

And then the society wedding could have family problems too. Corinne had seen two elderly people with a woman who was obviously their daughter wandering around the place, and she was intrigued by them. She couldn't understand what the daughter was doing with them, since she seemed utterly miserable. At first she'd thought that she was a nurse, because both the elderly people seemed to have mobility problems, but then she'd heard her refer to the man as 'Daddy', a word which seemed too childish for her to use. So maybe the daughter was frustrated by the parents and would murder them at the wedding too.

Was there something wrong with her, she wondered, that every time she set eyes on someone she thought of them as a potential murderer? That lovely old lady. The guests at the wedding. The elderly parents and their daughter. Couldn't she just sit here for five minutes and not think about death and destruction? She was the kind of person who couldn't kill spiders, for heaven's sake.

She couldn't do this any more. She really couldn't. She'd lost it completely. She got up from her lounger and walked into the Caribbean sea, loving the way the soup-warm water wrapped itself around her. She swam halfway to the jetty and then flipped over on to her back and floated, eyes open, staring up at the sky.

'Ahoy!'

She flipped over again when she heard the man's voice. She looked up and saw a fair-haired guy in a pedalo.

'Want a lift?' he asked.

She recognised him. He was one of two men who spent their days lying on the loungers near the pool.

'Hi,' she said, treading water. 'Where's your pal today?'

The man grinned at her. 'He overdid it a bit on the cocktails last night,' he told her. 'So he's taking it easy. Which means there's room on the boat. Like I said, want a lift?'

Corinne nodded. She hauled herself on to the pedalo and flopped into the seat beside him.

'My name's Matt.' He extended his hand and she shook it.

'Corinne,' she told him.

'So – are you liking it here, Corinne?'

She nodded. His accent was American.

'Steve and I come here every year,' said Matt. 'We just love it. Everyone in the hotel is so nice, and the guests . . . well, a lot of them come back year after year too. This your first visit?'

She nodded again.

'What do you do?' asked Matt. 'We've seen you with your laptop. Steve thinks you're a federal agent.'

Corinne laughed. 'As if. I write.'

'No, really!' Matt looked at her wide-eyed. 'Should I have heard of you?'

Corinne hated that question. If she said yes and the person hadn't heard of her she'd feel like a complete fool. If she said no they would be bitterly disappointed that they'd met someone who wrote books but who wasn't famous. Fortunately, though, because Matt was American it didn't matter.

So she shook her head and explained that Jennifer Jones hadn't crossed the Atlantic yet, even though Arnie was pushing hard to get her an American deal. (It was their dream to crack America, but Arnie had warned her that the market was cut-throat. Worse than Ireland and the UK.) She tried not to think about the fact that Rowena Roselli had signed an American contract for a breathtaking sum. God, she muttered, make me the kind of person I was before. Ordinary. Not a complete lunatic who gets overcome by jealousy and paranoia and sheer despair every time I think about my life.

'Jennifer Jones?' Matt's eyes widened. 'The detective chick?'

'Um . . . yes.'

'You're Corinne Doherty?'

Corinne looked at him hesitantly. 'Yes.'

'This is so coooool!' cried Matt. 'Me and Steve have both read your books and love them. We got them off Amazon. A friend of ours in the UK told us about you.'

'Really?' Corinne felt a surge of pleasure run through her.

'Hell, yes.' Matt grinned at her. 'Jennifer Jones is such a gay icon.'

Corinne's look was a mixture of puzzlement and enthusiasm. 'Gay icon?'

'Oh, come on, Corinne. Sure she is. A sexy, sassy woman who kicks ass. We love her. Steve and I have ordered your book for our book club and we so want to see you in the States.'

'You and Steve are partners, then?' Corinne had guessed as much but she hadn't wanted to give in to her stereotyping instincts when she'd seen the two good-looking, immaculately dressed men together.

'Yes. I own a bookshop in Seattle. Corinne, we absolutely want to have you come to our store. I'm gonna talk about you to a publisher I know. She's the best. We'll make you big. It's such an honour to meet you.'

'Oh, look, it's not that big a deal.' It was nice to feel wanted, but she didn't want Matt laying it on too thick. That made it unbelievable.

'Maybe not for you. But for me! Steve will be so thrilled, he really will. You'll join us for dinner tonight? He'll be better by then. Come on, honey. What's the next book about? Give me the lowdown.'

He looked so eager that she didn't want to disappoint him. She mentally ran through all of the ideas that she'd rejected and bit her lip.

'Have you got a title yet?' asked Matt.

Well, at least she could tell him that.

Jennifer Jones and the Jamaican Jerk.'

'Love it,' said Matt. 'You have me hooked already.'

She couldn't help smiling.

'So, come on, what's the big murder in this one? And

does Jennifer ever get to buy the Gucci bag she lusted over in the Jellybean Jackpot?'

Corinne laughed. 'I haven't decided yet.'

'So are you going to tell me anything about the plot?' asked Matt. 'Or is it a deep, deep secret?'

'I usually keep them a secret,' said Corinne.

'I understand.' Matt nodded at her knowingly. 'But it'll be brilliant. *You're* brilliant.'

She didn't believe him. She wasn't brilliant. But there was a germ of an idea forming in the back of her mind.

'There'll be a murder,' she said slowly.

'I kinda guessed that.' Matt grinned.

'You know . . .' she looked at him, 'I really should get back. I need to work on it a bit more.'

'Absolutely.' Matt pedalled harder. 'And will you join us later?'

'I've a target number of words,' she said. 'If I reach it – then yes.'

She didn't actually reach the target for *Jennifer Jones and the Jamaican Jerk* by dinner time. But her fingers had flown over the keys when she got back to the room as she wrote about the murder of the top-selling Jamaican novelist at the Booker Prize awards. The chief suspect was his big rival for the award, but what nobody knew was that the victim had previously trashed another author in print, calling her work 'light and frothy' and saying that it was entirely inappropriate to consider it literature. And so the novelist had hatched a plot to kill him. She was perfectly justified, Corinne decided, because the Booker nominee had actually pinched her plot for his own work, only he'd made it dense and unreadable and filled it with all sorts of flowery and unnecessary language to show how clever he was. Suddenly Corinne was enjoying herself immensely as she wrote, the words tumbling from her head in a torrent, not having to stop to think but simply filling the screen while the little word-count icon at the bottom of the page clicked higher and higher.

It was cramp in her hands that finally made her call a halt. She closed the laptop and sighed in relief before showering and changing for dinner. It's all OK, she told herself as she walked into the bar where the guests at White Sands were having pre-dinner cocktails. I can do this again. I know I can. And it doesn't matter about Rowena Roselli and *Model Murder*, because I know that this time I've really cracked it. And even if I haven't – hell, I'm working on a Caribbean island and I'm surrounded by interesting people and it's a good life really.

She looked around for Matt and Steve, her glance flickering over the other guests. She'd weave them into the plot, she thought, as she watched a grim-faced man and his younger companion walk into the bar. There were lots of possibilities for extra plot lines at White Sands. Maybe she could have the Booker ceremony moved to a Caribbean hotel. Make things more exotic!

She caught sight of Steve and Matt and waved at them. They ordered her a vodka martini from the bar. It was Jennifer Jones's favourite drink. And Corinne's too. Jennifer Jones was a great character, decided Corinne, as she sipped the drink. All she needed was for Corinne to do her justice. *Jennifer Jones and the Juicy Justice*. Excellent. She even had the next title in the bag. Why had she been worrying about writer's block? Everything was going to turn out just fine.

Hopefully.

If she could keep it going.

Which she could.

Maybe.

Oh hell, she thought as she took another gulp of the vodka martini. I got a lot done today. I achieved something. And I can always panic about it again tomorrow.

Room 217 (Bree)

I don't think I'm really a holiday sort of person. Especially not a lie-all-day-in-the-sun holiday person. I like travelling, definitely, but that's a completely different sort of thing. I love going to new places and having new experiences and getting out of Ireland as often as I can. After all, I've lived and worked in the US and Europe and I've usually avoided touristy sort of places like Florida or the south of Spain or the Italian coast. Anyway, the jobs I normally got weren't touristy sort of jobs like waitressing or working in a bar or – God forbid! – selling timeshare. I'm a mechanic and so I got work in garages. I've fixed engines in places like Dakota and Seattle as well as Valencia and Lombardy, and everything worked out fine for me. A piston is a piston after all.

In fact, until this week away with Declan, I've only ever been on one holiday which fell into the sun, sand and surf variety, and that was with my two sisters, Cate and Nessa. Even then, holiday is probably not exactly the right word for it. We'd never gone away with each other before – and we haven't gone away with each other since! It was supposed to be a get-away-from-it-all sort of holiday because we'd all been going through a bit of a bad time. What we forgot is that you can't really get away from it all. You usually end up bringing it with you.

But in the end it turned out OK and I learned a lot about my sisters – and myself. It was after the week in Spain that I became the sister with the boyfriend nobody expected. Probably least of all me.

I was remembering the get-away-from-it-all holiday and its aftermath as the 747 circled the island in the sun. I'd allowed Declan to choose it for us (well, he'd insisted on choosing but he'd told me that he'd find the perfect place) and he picked this all-inclusive resort on a Caribbean island, showing me the brochure with undisguised glee, rather like a dog who's just brought you the newspaper but chewed it up en route. I tried to be as upbeat and cheerful about it as I could, but in all honesty, if someone had sat me down and asked me to pick the worst holiday I could ever imagine, it would be an all-inclusive resort on a Caribbean island. And it didn't matter that as I looked out of the aircraft window the tiny disc of land was a vibrant finger-print of green in the middle of the turquoise sea, or that dotted between the emerald and jade of the foliage were red-roofed houses and tropical multicoloured flowers. It didn't even matter that a ring of pale golden sand circled the entire island. What terrified me was the idea of being marooned with Declan for a whole week and nothing to do.

And there would be nothing to do. At least, nothing interesting to do. Apparently that was the whole point of the ultra-luxurious White Sands Hotel. It made a lot of the fact that pretty much all you would want to do was to spend the whole day lounging on the beach and the entire evening lounging in the bar, thus chilling out completely.

Windsurfing was the only available watersport (they didn't want to disturb the marine ecology with jet-skis, which was fair enough); the whole emphasis, according to the endlessly glossy brochure, was on renewal and relaxation. And if the sun and the sea weren't renewing and relaxing enough for you, there was always the luxurious spa which was attached to the hotel and which offered every possible pampering treatment known to man.

Cate would love it. Of the three of us, she's the one who's totally into the whole body-wrap and moisturising thing – despite having an adorable but time-consuming kid she still looks like an elegant stick insect. She maintains that her massages and her aromatherapy and all that sort of stuff help her cope with being a working mother, so I couldn't help feeling that the week at White Sands was much more her sort of thing than mine.

Yet I hadn't the heart to say this to Declan. When he told me that he wanted to bring me away so that we could spend a little time on our own together, I jumped at the idea. But I thought that he meant a city break where we'd be on the go the whole time! I hadn't for a second imagined this.

The plane thundered on to the runway and the engines screeched into reverse. Declan looked at me with suppressed excitement and I grinned back at him. It wasn't that I hated the idea of the holiday with him. And it certainly wasn't that I didn't love him or want to be with him. It's just that I'm hopeless at sitting around doing nothing and I was afraid that chilling out was beyond me.

I felt a bit better when we got off the plane, mainly because the airport – despite calling itself an international airport – was small and compact and the luggage carousels were far too small for the amount of bags that were feeding through, so that everything was mildly chaotic. A girl stood to one side of the mêlée, clutching a wedding dress and looking both abandoned and anxious. Apparently White Sands specialises in weddings and sends a limo to meet wedding guests, but she'd still have to find her luggage first. I think it was the fact that it seemed an impossible task that might have been getting to her. From what I could see, retrieving your luggage was a kind of adventure sport. I chuckled to myself. Maybe if chaos reigned everywhere things wouldn't be so bad after all!

And then Declan spotted our luggage, pounced on it with all the skill of a hunter moving in for the kill, and whirled us outside.

We climbed into a taxi along with four other people. The driver sprinted away from the terminal building, scattering the few locals standing in front of him and waving at other drivers as he went. I yawned widely. We'd been up at the crack of dawn that morning to get the connecting flight from Dublin to London and then the transatlantic flight to the island. And although I normally stay up till about midnight and my body clock was now telling me that it was only around ten in the evening, I was knackered.

Declan didn't seem to be tired at all. But then, Declan never does! He's nearly twenty years older than me and he's the sort of guy who would make Margaret Thatcher and her four-hours-a night look like a complete sloth. Declan can stay up all night and still be alert the next day. I think it's because he's a barrister and he spends his time poring over detailed briefs written in incomprehensible English, the kind that would send any normal person to sleep instantly. So he's had to get used to staying awake no matter how tired or bored he is. Which meant that while I yawned my way along the twisting, pot-holed road from the airport to the banal-sounding White Sands, he kept poking me in the side and pointing out another bougainvillea-covered house or another glimpse of the sparkling blue sea.

I tried to look enthusiastic as he pointed out the fourth pink-painted house with green shutters at the windows and purple flowers cascading down the walls. I knew it was all gorgeous and enchanting but all I wanted to do was sleep. I felt terrible for feeling terrible.

The driver whirled us around a sharp bend and down a gentle slope. I saw a discreet pastel-pink sign that said White Sands Hotel, although the building itself was almost hidden behind tall palm trees and glossy green bushes. We careered over the speed ramp and shuddered to a halt outside the doors. Actually, there weren't any doors, I realised, just a canopied entrance leading directly into a high-roofed reception area where a dozen ceiling fans languidly stirred the warm air. The floor was sandstone. Glass-topped tables and comfortably padded wicker chairs were dotted around the expansive lounge. Further through the reception hall I could see a bar and then – again with no doors – the exit to a sun terrace beyond which sparkled the ever-blue sea. It was idyllic. If that was your idyll.

'Why don't you sit down while I check us in?' suggested Declan.

I nodded, yawned again, and sank into one of the chairs. A waiter dressed in black shorts and a multicoloured shirt appeared with a tray of cocktails. I chose a tequila sunrise and leaned back in the chair again. The drink was helping to chill me out after all. I hadn't realised how stressed I was feeling and how guilty I was feeling about feeling stressed when everything around me was so determinedly stress-free. A black and white cat strolled across the tiled floor, jumped delicately on to the table nearest me and then settled down beside me on the wicker chair. I smiled and rubbed it gently behind the ears. The cat purred in satisfaction.

I like cats. They're independent sorts of creatures. And I like the way that they force humans to feed them and cosset them and that the only thing they give in return is a gentle purr.

'Bree?' Declan's voice broke into my thoughts. 'Are you ready?'

I drained the cocktail and stood up, much to the cat's disgust. A further flurry of activity, this time caused by more new arrivals (including the tense girl with the wedding dress I'd seen in the baggage reclaim hall but who was now cheerful and smiling), caused him to stalk out of the reception area and along a wide passageway signposted 'Spa'.

Declan took my hand as we followed a porter through the tropical gardens and to our room. The brochure had described the layout but I hadn't quite managed to fix in my mind the concept of a hotel where all of the rooms were actually built away from the public areas. At White Sands the rooms were arranged in little blocks of four or six or eight, dotted along the hillside that led down to the beach with its eponymous white sand.

'Isn't it gorgeous?' Declan squeezed my arm as we stopped outside a pale-blue-painted door and I realised that our room was in a block of four with a breathtaking view of the gardens beneath us.

'Yes,' I said in agreement. 'It is.'

The room was fantastic! In fact it was nearly as big as my entire flat in Dublin. It had a queen-sized bed with lockers and dressers and all that palaver; and then, down two steps, a small lounge area with a table and a couple of those comfortable wicker chairs. The patio doors led on to one of the biggest balconies I'd ever seen in my life. I went outside (welcoming the warm air after the chilly air-conditioning of the room) and looked out. From the balcony I could see over the gardens, past one of the hotel's three swimming pools and down to the sparkling sea. If there was a more picture-postcard-beautiful place on the whole of the planet, I'd yet to find it.

'Well?' Declan followed me on to the balcony. 'Do you like it?'

'It's absolutely beautiful,' I said truthfully.

He wrapped his arms around me. 'I'm so happy to be here with you.'

I turned to him and kissed him. I love kissing Declan. He's a good kisser. He's good at all of the physical stuff. He led me to the bedroom and we made love on the queen-sized bed where – despite my tiredness of earlier – I was an enthusiastic participant.

I yawned again afterwards, though, and he kissed me gently on the forehead.

'Sleepy-head.'

'C'mon,' I protested. 'It's night-time at home. I've every right to be tired.'

'Why don't you have a nap while I unpack?' he suggested. 'Then we can go down to dinner, have a nightcap and come back to bed.'

I looked at him warily. 'It'll take ages to unpack and I'm not hungry. Why don't we just go to bed now.'

'We can't!' His tone was aghast. 'It's only five o'clock here. Dinner isn't for two hours. Besides, we have to unpack!'

'We could skip dinner,' I said mildly.

'It's all-inclusive,' he told me. 'We've already paid for it.'

'Declan Morrissey!' I regarded him as sternly as I could. 'You're rolling in money. Missing one meal here or there isn't going to break you.'

'That's not the point,' he said sulkily (he always gets sulky when I point out that he's loaded). 'We have to have dinner together on our first night here.'

'I thought the whole idea of a holiday is that you don't *have* to do anything,' I said mildly.

'Well, of course, not like that. It's just that – I expected . . . it's simply . . .'

He looked so woebegone that I couldn't help relenting. 'Well, sure,' I said. 'I'll probably be hungry by then anyway. The only thing more sure about me than my ability to sleep is my ability to eat.'

'Y'see!' He perked up considerably. 'I knew that, Bree.'

'Oh shut up.' I curled up in the wicker chair and let him loose on the unpacking.

I couldn't fall asleep. I watched him through my half-closed eyes as he took his carefully folded short-sleeved shirts from the case and placed them neatly in the chest of drawers. Everything he did, he did carefully and logically. Shirts in one drawer, jocks in another, shorts neatly pegged on hangers . . . Declan is a fastidious man. Suddenly I didn't want him opening my case and seeing the higgledy-piggledy way I'd stuffed my clothes into it. I snapped open my eyes and told him that I was awake again now and that I'd get on with my own unpacking.

'I don't mind doing it,' he said, as he brought his toiletries into the big bathroom.

'Naw, I'll do it myself.'

'Honestly, Bree. If you want to chill out a bit longer, it'll only take me a few minutes anyway,' he called.

'It's fine, really it is. I'll do it.'

'I left you space on the left-hand side of the sink,' he told me, re-emerging into the bedroom. 'That's where you prefer stuff to be, isn't it?'

He was right. But honestly, I thought – that he noticed in the first place was a bit scary!

At this point you might have the impression that I'm fed up with Declan. I know I've been harping on the downside of things. But I'm not. It's just that I'm uneasy at the way we've slid into couple-dom. Scared at how easily he seems to have taken to it. Fearful about what it might mean.

Of course Declan had the experience of being part of a couple. He's a widower, whose wife died a few years before I met him. From what I knew, Declan had been fantastic throughout her illness and had looked after their three children singlehandedly after her death. In fact I got to know him because I'd been dating his son, Michael. The thing with Michael would never really have worked out, although to tell you the truth, I fancied him like crazy at the time. (He's an incredibly good-looking guy, having inherited Declan's quite stern features but softened by the genes of his Spanish mother.) For a very brief moment I'd wondered whether Michael Morrissey would be the bloke who'd become a real boyfriend to me instead of the hopeless fuck-ups I'd managed to pick up until then. But it hadn't worked out, and now I couldn't imagine having dated Michael at all. Dated is probably the wrong word – we'd gone out a few times but we hadn't even kissed properly. When I realised that it was Declan who had a greater emotional hold over me, I was very relieved that we hadn't – it was hard enough to allow myself to go out with the father of an ex-boyfriend in the first place, without having had both of them kiss me too. That would surely have messed with my head!

Declan has two other children besides Michael, his daughters, Marta and Manuela. My relationship with them is still a bit fraught. Neither of them was happy with the idea of their father seeing anyone again after their mother died. And the fact that he was seeing me, someone only a few years older than them, made things worse.

Sometimes it all gets to me a bit. Other times I forget everything other than the fact that Declan is the most wonderful, thoughtful man I've ever met, and he's great in bed too!

It took me about ten minutes to unpack, using the drawers that Declan had left me and forcing myself to fold things properly – of course if I'd done what he'd done and folded them when I was packing, it would have made things a lot easier.

'A shower before dinner would be the thing,' he said as I finally put away my shoes (I'd lost one, not realising that I'd accidentally kicked it under the bed, and had gone crazy looking for it). 'Freshen us up – wake you up.'

'I *am* awake,' I lied (I was feeling even more exhausted after the enforced neatness of putting things away).

'They've supplied some really nice shower soap,' he told me.

I gave in. Besides, he was right. A shower would perk me up a bit.

Actually it was just an excuse for us to make love again. And the shower soap supplied by the hotel was fabulous – lots of lovely lather and a nice musky smell that did it for both of us. I have to hand it to Declan. Sometimes he knows me better than I know myself.

Despite cavorting in the shower we were still among the early arrivals for dinner. I looked around the elegant dining room and wished that I'd changed into something a little more suitable than another pair of jeans and a loose T-shirt. Declan was wearing a crisp white short-sleeved shirt with a pair of light trousers and he fitted right in, but I felt as though I stuck out like a sore thumb. I knew Declan had told me that the Green Garden was less formal than the hotel's other resturant, Mariner's Reef, but his idea of informal and mine were clearly different. I wish he'd actually said something to me earlier instead of obviously biting his tongue and letting me turn up underdressed. I noticed, as more people arrived for dinner, that nearly all the women were wearing strappy dresses and high heels.

The head waiter showed us to a lovely table overlooking the sea, where underwater lights illuminated the aquatic world beneath. The menus were leather-bound and exotic. The wine list was extensive. The hotel was officially five-star. To me it was all that and more.

The only problem was that I get uncomfortable with five-star. I'm not good with fine dining or sommeliers pouring reverent glasses of wine or waiters shimmying in and out to clear away plates the moment I'm finished. It's not that I don't appreciate it. It's just that I can't seem to act naturally when someone else is wiping the crumbs from my crusty roll off the table.

But Declan is brilliant. He does the wine-tasting thing really well (he's a bit of an expert) and it never fazes him when waiters bustle around.

'Really excellent,' he told the head waiter as we left, an hour later.

'Thank you, sir,' he replied. 'It's our pleasure to serve you again.'

I supposed that they always said that. It sounded like a line that you learn in waiter school.

Declan wanted to stop for a drink in the bar after dinner but I persuaded him that since I was now fed to the gills with wonderful food, I was sleepier than ever and absolutely had to get back to the room. I said that I really didn't mind if he wanted to have an after-dinner brandy or something but I honestly couldn't keep my eyes open. He looked at me as though he was going to try to make me change my mind. Then he shrugged and said that I was probably right, and that he was tired too – maybe a bit overtired. He stopped at the bar anyway, ordered a brandy, and then knocked it back in three swift gulps.

'Help me sleep,' he said sheepishly as I looked at him in astonishment. 'And besides – it seemed the right thing to do.'

Maybe he was more jet-lagged than I thought. But his behaviour seemed out of kilter to me. As though now we were here, he was just as worried as me about how it would all turn out.

He was awake first the next morning, sitting at the table on the balcony reading a leaflet about the hotel spa.

'Morning, sleepy-head,' he said as I wandered out to join him. 'You're late for breakfast.'

I peered blearily at my watch. 'It's only eight o'clock,' I protested. 'And we're supposed to be on holiday.'

'Breakfast starts at seven,' he told me. 'I've been watching everyone heading to the restaurant. There'll be nothing left.'

'You can't seriously be telling me that people get up at seven for breakfast!' I looked at him in disbelief.

'Here they do,' he said. 'It's bright and it's warm. That's why there's an early-to-bed, early-to-rise culture.'

'I guess I did my bit for the early-to-bed last night anyway,' I remarked. 'And to me, eight o'clock is early to rise!'

He laughed. 'Come on. Let's get you fed and watered and head for the beach.'

I surprised myself by packing away a breakfast of bacon and potato bits, waffles, banana bread and fruit. After dinner the previous night I hadn't expected to be able to eat a thing, but I was ravenous again. Actually, I'm always hungry. Cate despairs of my diet. But I'd eaten lots of fruit as well as the bacon and waffles so maybe I wasn't totally overloading my heart. As we walked back through the gardens to our room, I suggested to Declan that perhaps we needed to go for a long walk to burn off the calories.

'Maybe later,' he told me, a kind of suppressed excitement in his voice. 'We have to go to the beach first. Get a nice spot and wait for them to come and bring us a cocktail.'

I didn't see the big urgency for the beach, although when we got there, I was utterly beguiled by the texture of the fine sand and the silkiness of the warm water.

'So, you wanted to do things,' he said as we sat side by side on a pair of loungers which he'd dragged beneath the shade of a straw umbrella, telling me that this was a great location, not too near the watersports and not too far from the bar. 'Which treatment would you like?'

'Treatment?'

'In the spa,' he said patiently. 'Come on, Bree. This hotel is as famous for its therapies as it is for its cooking. What about this?' He reached into his rucksack, pulled out the glossy brochure and pointed to the apricot scrub followed by the orange blossom and mango wrap and the body silk moisturising treatment.

'It sounds more like a dessert than a body treatment,' I told him. 'I'd probably start licking it off! Maybe I'll book in for a massage later in the week.'

'Oh, but you must get a treatment,' he said, sounding shocked that I didn't want to be lathered in apricots. 'Everyone gets a treatment.'

'I'll check it out at some point, don't worry.'

'You have to book now to get what you want,' he said. 'The spa is always busy.'

'Surely not,' I said idly. 'After all, this is the lowest of the low season. The week before Christmas. The hotel isn't that full.'

'But everyone books them,' he said darkly. 'You'll be disappointed.'

'For heaven's sake!' I looked at him in amused irritation. 'I'd swear you were running it yourself. I didn't realise you were so up to the minute on women's beauty stuff!'

'I just . . . well . . . don't you think . . .'

'It's like you've done all this before,' I muttered as I picked at a bit of dry skin on my heel. 'Or that . . .' I looked up, my attention caught by a fleeting glimpse of guilt on his face at my statement, and frowned. 'You haven't been here before?' I asked. 'Have you?'

I didn't really expect him to say that he had.

'Well . . . yes,' he admitted.

'When?'

'It was a good while ago.'

The penny dropped. 'With . . . with Monica?'

'Yes.' He hesitated and then rushed on. 'We used to come here a lot.'

I stared at him. 'A lot?'

'Every year.'

'For how long?'

'Five years. Until she got too sick.'

I felt a dull thud in the pit of my stomach. I was OK with the fact that Declan had been married before. I could even cope with the fact that his wife had (according to Marta and Manuela) been the most wonderful woman who'd ever walked the earth. But that was because we were totally different people with totally different interests and I wasn't trying to take her place.

'You stayed in this hotel?'

'Yes,' he repeated.

I looked along the beach, half expecting to see Monica's ghost walking by. But the only person walking along the shoreline was a raven-haired woman in a bright swimsuit and patterned sarong who seemed to be carrying a laptop computer under her arm.

'Every year for five years?'

'Yes.'

'And now you're here with me?'

'It's a beautiful place,' he said. 'You told me to go ahead and book something, and I wanted to bring you somewhere special. This is a very special place.'

I stared at him in utter disbelief. 'And did Monica lie on

the beach and go for treatments every day?' I asked eventually.

'Don't be silly,' said Declan mildly. 'Of course we lay on the beach together. And she had some treatments. That's what everyone does.'

'So on your first day here with her I guess you sat on your sun-loungers and discussed what peels and massages and stuff she'd get.'

'Like I said, the spa is always busy.'

'And I suppose you always went to the restaurant for something to eat as soon as you arrived so that you didn't waste the all-inclusive dinner?'

He stared at me. 'Sure, we went to dinner. Not just because it was paid for. Because we were hungry.'

'And you had a brandy in the bar afterwards?'

'I like a brandy after a meal.'

'And did she let you do all the unpacking?'

'I'm a methodical person,' Declan said. 'I like unpacking.'

'I'm going for a walk,' I told him. 'Don't follow me.'

I strode along the beach, not certain where I could actually walk to. The beach was quite small and crescent-shaped, bordered each end by smooth rocks. It took less than five minutes to reach the end. I glanced back. Declan was still sitting on the lounger, staring after me. The girl with the laptop was pulling another lounger past him. I clambered over the rocks and out of his sight.

'What the hell are you doing!' A female voice wafted down to me. I glanced up. A young woman, in her early twenties I guessed, was glaring down at me from a balcony set higher into the rocks.

'Going for a walk,' I called back.

'Well this part of the beach is private,' she shouted. 'Didn't you see the sign? Coco Villa. Private.'

I hadn't seen the sign, but I was perfectly prepared to take her word for it. Her voice was laden with anger and suspicion.

'Keep your hair on!' I shouted. 'I'll move on.'

'Yes, do,' she retorted. 'You're not welcome here.'

Stupid cow, I thought, as I sprinted along the narrow strip of beach which was obviously her private domain and legged it over some more rocks. What's her problem?

The next strip of beach was deserted, but as I walked further, I found myself on another beach, obviously attached to yet another luxury hotel. It was less extravagantly expensive in appearance than White Sands – the loungers were plastic instead of wood, the mattresses were thin instead of luxuriously padded and the gaudy parasols on the beach weren't half as classy as our straw ones. I walked along that beach too, wondering if it was possible to circle the entire island by going from beach to beach. After my third hotel beach, and on another deserted stretch of sand, I sat down and starting picking at my heel again.

How could he have brought me here? To a place where he'd come with her so many times already? I'd never had any hang-ups about Monica before, and Declan rarely talked about her. As far as I'd been concerned she was in his past. A tragic part of his past obviously, but one he'd dealt with. Now, though, I wondered if he'd dealt with it at all. I mean, surely common sense would have told him that I'd be uncomfortable coming to a place that had been their favourite holiday destination? Not to mention common sense telling him that this wasn't my kind of holiday in the first place?

I pulled viciously at a loose piece of skin and yelped in pain as it came away, leaving a tender patch on my heel. There was a whole week of this to go. Of Declan wanting to do Monica things with me. Of me wanting to do almost anything else. I didn't know what I was going to say to him. He'd been so upbeat about this holiday and the great time we were going to have, and I'd got so caught up in his enthusiasm that I'd almost come to believe that I could spend a whole week on an island doing very little. But now I wondered if he'd been excited about the trip because it was revisiting a place that he'd loved so much with her and not because he really wanted to be with me. Was he trying to recapture something of their relationship? Did he think that by coming here I'd become more like Monica? Did he want me to be another Monica? And what would being more like Monica mean?

I knew some things. I knew that she was incredibly beautiful. There was a picture of her on the sideboard of the family home in Donnybrook. It had been taken long before the cancer and its treatment had thinned her cheeks and made her lose her hair. In the photo she was vibrant and healthy, rather like a young Bianca Jagger, looking teasingly at the camera. I knew that in a million years I'd never be able to look like that. I always look terrible in photographs because I hate having them taken. I look away at the last minute so that I appear like a mutinous child. But Monica looked out from her photo as though the camera was her friend. Maybe that's why Declan had brought me. Maybe he thought that a whole week of exfoliation and massage and wraps would turn me into the kind of woman who could tease the camera and who fitted in with exclusive five-star resorts and the kind of life he used to lead.

She wouldn't have come down to dinner in jeans and a T-shirt on her first night. She would have realised that there was an unspoken dress code. She would have sat with him in the bar afterwards and drunk whatever it was that she drank while he indulged in his brandy. She would have complemented him, not irritated him.

I had thought that somehow we complemented each other. It seemed that way at home in Ireland, where I had my own life and where, on the rare occasions that I accompanied him to some fusty old function, we spent the time giggling like kids and making outrageous remarks about everyone else under our breath. I thought he enjoyed that. But maybe he didn't really. Maybe deep down he wanted to be like Arthur McCormack, SC, the senior barrister who looked like he would explode under the weight of his own pomposity. I could see Arthur in a place like White Sands, discussing the wine list and ordering the lobster simply because it was the most expensive dish on the menu (and an extra to the all-inclusive!). But Declan – well, with Declan I always thought that it would be a more light-hearted thing. And yet it seemed like I was wrong.

Either he'd brought me here to turn me into Monica, or he'd come here to recapture something of his life with her. Neither of those alternatives was very appealing to me.

But why did he want me to be someone else? I didn't want him to be anyone else. I loved him exactly the way he was – good in bed, good in the kitchen, good at his job and (at least when we were at home) good about giving me personal space. Because he was so busy he wasn't able to be with me all the time. But that suited me perfectly, because I hated it when men tried to muscle in on my life. I needed to be able to do my own thing.

Because of Declan I'd stayed in Dublin even though I'd been having thoughts about heading off to the States again for a few months. But when we'd discovered each other and fallen in love I hadn't wanted to go. It was the very first time a man had ever influenced one of my major decisions. But knowing that Declan was there for me (even though his children complicated things a little) made me feel so much easier in myself. Suddenly Dakota or Minneapolis held no appeal for me whatsoever. Amazingly, I wanted to stay put.

I got up and began walking back towards the hotel. I didn't know what to do, what to say to Declan. I thought I'd known him, but I suddenly realised that I hardly knew him at all.

A catamaran had pulled up on to the beach. The captain, tall and rangy, in ancient grey shorts and a bright red top, was trying to persuade people to come on a trip.

'How 'bout you, girl?' he asked me after he'd rounded up a few customers. 'You walkin' along the beach all on your own? Why don' you come with us? We only need one more person.'

'I don't have any money with me,' I told him. 'I'm staying at White Sands.'

'No problem,' he told me in his lilting Caribbean accent, making me believe that it really was no problem at all. 'You pay me when we get back. I pull up at White Sands to let you off and you can go get your money.'

I smiled at him. 'How long are we going out for?'

'Coupla hours,' he said. 'This is a mornin' trip. You be back after midday, girl, no problem.'

What the hell, I thought. I nodded at him and climbed on to the boat. Then we pushed away from the beach and headed out to sea.

We sailed past the White Sands beach. I looked hard at it to see if I could spot Declan, but we were too far away to make out individual people. The captain hit a button and reggae music blared out. People started to dance. I did too, even though I'm a crap dancer.

'Beer for all!' he called, lugging some cool bags on to the deck. 'It's included in the price,' he told me as I looked doubtful. I took a beer and chugged it back. I always prefer beer to cocktails.

It was wonderful out on the sea. The breeze was warm, the people were nice and the captain made sure that we were all having a good time.

'Are you on your own?' A guy, his face a little too sunburned for comfort, looked at me.

'Today at any rate,' I said.

'Lee,' he told me, extending his hand. 'Pleased to meet you.'

'Bree,' I said, grasping it firmly. 'Nice to meet you too.'

'Hey, you guys!' he called to a mixture of men and women. 'It's the Lee and Bree show.'

It kind of was. We danced together on deck, shouting words of encouragement to each other when we tried to limbo our way under the pole that the captain had stretched out for us. Lee was fun and uncomplicated and nice to know. He was from Michigan. I knew that a few years ago I probably would have slept with him after the morning on the boat. But when it pulled in to the beach in front of his hotel and he asked me to drop by later, I told him that I wasn't sure I could. His eyes narrowed at that.

'I'm with a friend,' I said uncomfortably. 'Look, maybe I'll see you around.'

We moved away from the shore and turned northwards,

towards White Sands. The hotel beach was almost deserted, probably because it was lunchtime and lunches at White Sands were part of the all-inclusive package.

I hopped off the catamaran, into waist-deep water.

'Won't be long,' I told the captain.

'You take your time,' he said easily. 'I ain't goin' nowhere.'

I might not have wanted to be on a Caribbean island for my holiday, but I was beginning to think that the Caribbean temperament was ideal for me. I walked up the beach, past the two sun-loungers which Declan had dragged into position earlier in the day. They were still covered by our bright blue towels. I supposed that Declan was in the restaurant along with everyone else, having his all-inclusive lunch.

I hurried along the path to our room. It wasn't until I was almost at the door that I realised that I didn't have my key.

'Shit,' I muttered. I hadn't brought any money down to the beach that morning and my purse was locked in the room safe. I made my way back to the hotel dining room and reception areas. I could see the catamaran bobbing gently on the waves. There was no sign of Declan in the dining room. I bit my lip and looked around me in frustration. Maybe he'd moved to one of the pools. There was a pool at the far side of the complex, one on the way to our room (though I hadn't seen him there as I passed it by) and one higher up the hill. I'd have to check them all.

I went back to the beach to explain it to the captain of the catamaran.

'Hey, don' worry,' he said, uncurling himself from his position on the boat. 'Tomorrow I come again. You pay me then.'

I looked at him in complete astonishment. 'Wouldn't you

prefer the money now?' I asked. 'After all, what if I'm not here tomorrow?'

'Then I come the next day.' He grinned at me. 'You honest, girl. I see it in you.'

'I'll be here tomorrow,' I promised. 'Call on your way out for the trip.'

'Sure thing.' He pushed the boat back along the channel. 'See you then.'

'Yes,' I said. 'See you.'

I walked the few steps to our sun-loungers and sat down. I realised that Declan had left the beach bag with our lotions and books underneath his lounger. I sprayed myself with some Factor 15 and took out the death and detection thriller I'd bought at Gatwick. That had been the first niggle, I realised as I opened the pages. Declan had needed to buy another book because he'd realised that my reading material consisted almost entirely of car and bike magazines and I hadn't brought anything to share with him. (I was still riding my wonderful Yamaha YZF-R6 and there was an article about them in the latest monthly bike mag.)

'We'll be there for a week,' he'd said in shock. 'You must want to read something other than magazines.'

'Nessa gave me a book,' I told him. 'Some womany, relationship sort of thing. I can't really see you wanting to read that. She said I'd enjoy it. But to be honest, I'll probably stick with the magazines.'

'I thought we'd share books,' he said. 'That's why I only brought a couple. I'll have to get something else.'

WH Smith were doing a special offer – buy one and get another for half-price. Declan chose the latest John Grisham.

'Busman's holiday,' I remarked.

He laughed. 'You're no different, bringing all those car mags.'

'OK, OK, for your second book you can get something for me,' I told him.

'What would you like?' he asked. 'Since you've already got the womany book.'

I grinned. 'Something with cops and corpses,' I told him. 'There'll be more than enough gorgeousness where we're going. I could do with a few gruesome murders and a slick private eye.'

The tall bloke with the horn-rimmed glasses who'd been standing beside us leafing through the paperback edition of what was labelled the Booker Prize-winner glanced at me and then moved away cautiously. Declan caught my eye and the two of us giggled.

He bought me a thin thriller, black cover with a pink silhouette, which he said had been a top seller that year and which was a mixture of death, destruction and feminine wiles. The private eye was a woman, he told me. And since I'd done a bit of detecting in the past (well, I'd followed my brother-in-law around to find out if he'd been cheating on my sister), he hoped I'd relate to it.

You see, that was how things normally were with us. There were differences but we made fun of them. He never made me feel inferior because I hadn't gone to college, or because I didn't spend my time with my nose in a book like his Manuela, or because I was the kind of girl who enjoyed getting her hands dirty. In fact, I'd always thought he liked it.

Now I thought that I'd been wrong.

I opened the book. It was fun and pacey and I loved the female private eye. I'm a slow reader but I'd made it to page fifty before I sensed someone behind me. I looked up. It was Declan.

'Nice lunch?' I asked.

'Fine,' he said. 'Where did you go?'

I told him about my walk along the beach and my trip on the catamaran.

'You know that they tell you not to go on casual trips like that,' he said. 'Often they're more expensive than the organised tours, and some of the boat owners don't have insurance.'

'Oh, for heaven's sake!' I flung the book down and glared at him. 'I didn't have the money to give him and he's coming back tomorrow to get it from me. It's hardly the action of a Caribbean pirate! What the hell's got into you, Declan? It's all the price of this and the cost of that and an obsession with doing things a particular way – the way you did it with Monica! We'll I'm not bloody Monica and I never will be, and I can't for the life of me understand why on earth you thought I'd like to come here and play second fiddle to a goddamn memory!'

I got up off my lounger and stomped away from him. This time I stopped at the swimming pool. I still didn't have our room key.

The only other people at the pool were a group of three people (a family, I thought, even though the daughter seemed older than me. Christ, I muttered to myself, coming away with Declan was bad enough. I can't imagine what going on holiday with my parents would be like). The patriarch looked at me with ill-concealed irritation. I wasn't sure where to go now, although I knew I wouldn't stay here. But I was still only wearing a swimsuit with a short sports skirt over it. And I'd left my flip-flops at the beach.

Paradise Island. That's what Declan had called it when he'd shown me the brochure. And that's what it had been for him with Monica. Now I'd destroyed those memories by fighting with him. I felt deeply sorry for him, but even sorrier for myself. I'd thought that I'd found a good relationship, but really it had just taken me a bit longer to realise that, like my other relationships – Gerry, the spaced-out hippie, Fabien, the womaniser, Terry, who'd been wanted by the UK police and who'd skipped off to join the Foreign Legion – Declan was a weirdo too. I hadn't thought he was a weirdo because he was a barrister, which was a serious kind of job, and because he had three kids and because he was a widower. But I was wrong. He was probably the most disturbed of them all. He hadn't really got over Monica's death, and he was obviously grooming me to take his dead wife's place, and if that wasn't being a weirdo, well, I didn't know what was.

My stomach rumbled. It was four o'clock and I hadn't had anything – other than a few beers – since breakfast. There was a bowl of fruit in the bedroom. But Declan had the key to the bedroom.

I walked back to the beach. He was lying on the sun-lounger again, reading his John Grisham. I asked him for the key. He handed it to me wordlessly. I took it and went back to the room, where I ate two bananas and an apple. I still felt hungry. I wondered if it was possible to get a room service sandwich. But room service sandwiches probably weren't included in the all-inclusive. I opened the fridge and chuckled in a kind of manic way at the sight of a Snickers bar which I unwrapped and ate voraciously.

It was dusk before Declan returned to the room, his face glowing from the sun. He had to knock on the door to be let in and he walked straight past me and into the bathroom where I heard him run the shower.

I sat on the end of the huge bed and pointed the remote at the TV, flicking my way through about a hundred different home shopping channels being beamed directly to us from the States. But I wasn't really listening to the patter about genuine gold-plated bracelets or diamante earrings. I was wondering what the hell I was going to do now.

It was obviously over between Declan and me. I didn't want to be his substitute wife, and if we couldn't even speak civilly to each other on the first day of our holiday, we'd end up totally hating each other by the last. I wondered when I'd be able to get a flight home. And, without wanting to seem like a miser after all my criticising of Declan over his desire to eat his way through everything, I wondered whether I could actually afford it. Declan had wanted to pay for the entire holiday but I hadn't let him, even though the price for the week was astronomical and probably more than my total holiday spend for the past ten years combined. I was pretty sure that the price of a one-way ticket out of Paradise would stretch my credit limit to breaking point.

Declan walked out of the bathroom, a towel wrapped around his waist. His wet hair stuck up in spikes on his head. He looked cute and vulnerable. He opened the wardrobe and took out another crisp shirt and a pair of trousers.

'Are you coming to dinner?' he asked.

I had to go to dinner. The fruit and the Snickers had only barely taken the edge off my hunger earlier and I was ravenous again. Even though I was already starting to feel inadequate at the idea of the elegant dining room and the women in their strappy dresses.

'Sure,' I replied.

'Are you having a shower?'

'Yes.'

'I'll wait on the balcony.'

I went into the bathroom and had my shower. When I came out I took my own (only) strappy dress out of the wardrobe and put it on. I brushed my face with the bronzer that Cate had recommended for me a few months earlier, dabbed on some eye shadow (again from Cate) and slid a pearly-pink lipstick over my lips.

I still didn't look anything like Monica.

'Ready,' I told Declan.

He looked at me as he walked in from the balcony.

'Suits you,' he said.

I didn't know whether he meant the dress, or the make-up. Of course I'd worn dresses and make-up going out with Declan before, I'm not a total loss. I just didn't get done up very often. I simply prefer jeans and a T-shirt.

We walked in silence to the restaurant. The air was humid and the cicadas were going nuts in the trees around us. The moon shone down from a clear sky, reflecting dizzily off the gently lapping sea. It was beautiful. It really was. Why was I such a fool?

We were shown to the same table in the restaurant. I thought that the waiter treated me with a bit more respect than the previous night, although that could have been my imagination. I blinked a couple of times as I looked at the menu. My memories of the night before were hazy, but everything seemed completely different.

Declan studied his menu for a moment and then put it to one side. I spent ages looking at mine, terrified of having to put it down and sit in silence opposite him. Eventually, after the waiter had hovered around us for the third time, I closed it and selected a starter and main course at random.

'Difficult choice?' asked Declan.

'It all looks lovely,' I said.

'But not what you want?'

I shrugged. 'I'm so hungry I could eat a horse.'

'Don't think that's on the menu.' He half smiled.

'No.'

We sat in silence until the waiter returned with our starters. I couldn't even remember what I'd chosen. It turned out to be tiger prawns.

'This was a mistake.' Declan didn't speak until he'd finished his starter. I was still eating the prawns. I swallowed one whole and had a coughing fit. He watched me, a flicker of concern in his eyes as I struggled to catch my breath.

'I'm OK,' I said, as I eventually regained my composure. He filled a glass with water and handed it to me.

'What was a mistake?' I asked when I'd taken a sip. 'Choosing the prawns?'

This time he smiled. 'No. Coming here.'

Funny, I'd been thinking the same thing ever since we arrived, but now, hearing Declan say it, I wanted to cry.

'You were right, of course.' He folded his napkin into a neat square and put it beside his plate. 'I chose it for selfish reasons. Because it had good memories for me. I hoped that it would give us both good memories in the future.'

'You're an intelligent person, Declan,' I said shakily. 'I don't know how you could possibly think that bringing me somewhere you'd enjoyed with your wife was a good idea.'

'I didn't think it would matter,' he told me. 'I thought to myself, well, it's just a place. It's so beautiful that I thought you'd fall for it too.'

'It's very beautiful,' I agreed. 'And maybe I would fall for it. But by doing my kind of thing. Hiking around the hills or something. And that's the problem, Declan, isn't it? I want rough and ready and you want sleek and sophisticated, and it just won't work.'

'How come it works in Ireland?'

'We do our own thing there,' I said.

'We also do a lot of things together,' he reminded me.

'But you want to do more Monica things.' I looked at him unhappily. 'You want to do the things you did with her. You want to cosset me and send me to luxury spas because that's what she liked. You want me to dress up for dinner every night. You want me to lie out on the beach all day. You want a different sort of woman to me.'

'I thought you'd enjoy it. Something different,' he said.

'Parts of it,' I agreed. 'But not all week. And not in the order that you did things with Monica. Rushing down to the beach – I bet that was the spot you usually picked with her. And if it wasn't, you were probably looking at the spot you normally picked with her.'

'I didn't want it to be exactly the same,' he told me. 'I wanted it to be our holiday. But when I got here, I suppose I felt that it had all worked so well before and why should it be different now.'

Suddenly I wasn't hungry any more.

'I need to be on my own,' I told him. 'I won't wander off, don't worry. I just need . . . some time.'

I really wasn't getting value out of the all-inclusive, I thought as I walked through the gardens. Another pre-paid dinner gone to waste!

I clambered into the hammock which was strung up between two huge coconut trees. I lay there with my eyes open and gazed up at the stars. Nessa loved looking at the stars. Of course she was an astrology freak rather than an astronomy freak, always checking her horoscope to see what the next day would bring. We used to tease her about it, and deep down I think she knew it was total rubbish, but she enjoyed it all the same.

I'm a Sagittarian. I'm supposed to be fun-loving and philosophical. And in many ways I am. I was trying to be philosophical about what had happened between Declan and me, but I was finding it difficult. The thing was, I loved him. I'd never really loved a man before.

I loved Declan because of all the things that had driven me mad in the last two days. I loved him because he was methodical and organised. I loved him because he made me feel cherished and protected. I loved him because he'd had a tragedy in his life but it hadn't made him bitter or miserable.

But the tragedy had come back to haunt us. And I realised that he didn't really love me. He might have loved having me around, but he really wanted to have Monica. He wanted her here to have the spa treatments and let him run her life. Instead he was stuck with me. And I'd lashed out at him.

Damn it, I thought miserably. Why does it always have to go wrong?

'I'm going back to the room.' His voice, coming out of the darkness, startled me, and as I tried to sit up, I tipped out of the hammock.

'Bree! Are you all right?'

'Yes, fine.' I dusted down my strappy dress. 'You gave me a fright.'

'Sorry.' He looked at me apologetically. 'I thought you

heard me coming along the path. Anyway, I'm going back to the room. There's a movie on the TV.'

'I thought we only got shopping channels,' I said.

'No, there's a movie channel too,' he told me. 'They put up the schedule on the noticeboard every day. This is an Al Pacino one. He plays the devil.'

'Sounds good.'

'Do you want to join me?'

'Oh, Declan.' Suddenly I was crying. 'I don't bloody know.'

He watched me, his expression uncomfortable. I don't cry very often and I guess my sudden weakness surprised him.

I wiped at my eyes with my fingertips.

'Here.'

Naturally he had a damn hanky.

'Did the two of you watch movies too?' I asked.

'No.'

'Why not?'

'Because we usually stayed for all of dinner and I had a brandy in the bar afterwards, remember?'

I nodded.

'Come and watch the movie.'

I didn't know what he wanted from me. I didn't know what I wanted from him. I shrugged and followed him back to the room.

I don't remember a thing about the movie. I wouldn't imagine Declan does either because he fell asleep halfway through. But I, who can normally sleep at the drop of a hat, well, I couldn't sleep at all.

*   *   *

He was still sleeping at seven in the morning when the restaurant opened for breakfast. I left him there and went down myself, hungry again. He didn't appear in the restaurant even though I waited for ages. I went down to the beach and sat on a sun-lounger. I'd brought the dizzy detective book with me although the words seemed to spin on the page and I hadn't really got a clue what was going on.

I'd been there an hour when the catamaran pulled in, a new group of people on board. The captain waved at me.

'How you doin', girl?'

'I'm OK. I've got your money.'

I rummaged in the bag I'd brought with me while the captain jumped into the water and walked up the beach.

'Have you a full load?'

I spun around at the sound of Declan's voice. It was creepy the way he could suddenly appear behind me and I never seemed to hear him.

'Today, man?' The captain looked at him. 'I have my minimum number. I can always take one more.'

'How about two more?' asked Declan.

'Sure.'

'Two more?' I looked at Declan enquiringly.

'You had a good time without me yesterday,' he said. 'Least you can do is show me what it was like.'

'On the catamaran? You want to go on the catamaran?'

'Why not?' he asked.

'I thought you got seasick?'

'Nah. I say that so's I don't get hauled on to things, but . . . I'll be fine.'

'It's . . . it's not a cruise,' I said. 'Look at it. It's very casual.'

'I *am* casual,' protested Declan. 'I'm in shorts and a T-shirt. And bare feet.'

I giggled. The captain laughed.

'Two?' he asked.

Declan was looking at me. There was hope in his eyes. But love and affection too. He waited for me to speak.

I handed the money over to the captain.

'That's for yesterday,' I told him. 'And for the two of us today.'

We got on to the boat. Declan put his arm around me. And as we moved away from the beach, he kissed me.

Which was a damn good start to the rest of our lives.

Room 403 (Esther)

What Esther liked best about the Caribbean was the climate. It was hard to imagine that back in Ireland her friends were wrapped up in their heavy winter coats and battling with rain-soaked, wind-swept streets when she was sitting on the balcony of Room 403 wearing a light T-shirt and a pair of Bermuda shorts, enjoying the feel of the tropical breeze around her shoulders. She'd bought the Bermuda shorts ages ago because she'd known that she'd be coming to the White Sands Hotel for ten days in December this year. She'd booked it months ago, exactly three weeks after Jim's death.

Esther knew that her four children were very concerned that she'd decided to make this trip on her own. Each of them had called or visited her in turn, telling her they were thrilled that she was ready to get on with her life so quickly but wondering wasn't the trip across the Atlantic alone just a bit taxing for a woman of her age? She'd wanted to snap at them all that just because she was seventy-one it didn't mean that she'd lost her marbles, and that she was perfectly capable of getting on a plane by herself. She did, in fact, point out to Kathryn (her youngest daughter) that once she was on the plane it made no difference how far it was going, all she had to do was sit there.

'Well, not just sit there,' Kathryn had said anxiously. 'You have to get up and walk around, Mum. There's always the danger of deep vein thrombosis.'

Esther had sighed at that and told Kathryn that she'd bought a pair of flight socks from Boots.

'What if you're delayed?' That had been Derek's question. At forty-two, he was the eldest of her children. Maybe that was what made him the most anxious, always worrying about something, always looking for the downside. Esther thought it was quite unusual in a man but she admitted to herself that it was hard to make sweeping generalisations. After all, her only experience of men was Jim and she'd never really known what he worried about. If anything. She told Derek that if she was delayed she'd simply sit at the gate until the flight was called. And if it was delayed for ages she'd go and get something to eat but keep an eye on the screens.

'How will you manage your luggage?' Naomi, two years younger than Derek, had demanded.

'Quite well, I expect,' said Esther as she regarded her daughter over her mug of frothy cappuccino (they'd gone shopping together – it was on this trip that she'd bought the Bermudas while Naomi had looked at her in astonishment; she'd never known Esther to wear shorts or trousers before). 'I'm sure there'll be plenty of porters at the airport jostling for business. I can manage. Besides, I'm not you or Kathryn. I won't be bringing my entire wardrobe with me. Just a few light things for the beach and some dresses for the evening.'

'Won't you be lonely?' This, over the phone, from Philly who lived in London. Esther got on better with Philly than all her other children and she had a feeling that was because she only saw her a couple of times a year. Philly had a pressurised job in a City firm and mainly kept in touch with her by e-mail because she spent so much time on the phone during the day and rarely felt like talking on it again when she was at home.

'I won't be lonely,' Esther assured her. 'It's only for ten days and there's plenty to keep me occupied. Sure, I'm often a damn sight lonelier here.'

'Are you?' Philly sounded anxious. 'Would you like to come and stay with me for a while?'

'Don't be daft,' said Esther briskly, thinking that there'd be nothing more awful than spending time on her own in Philly's soulless apartment. 'And the loneliness passes.'

'I'm sure it does, but . . .'

'I'll be fine,' said Esther. 'Please don't fret. And tell your brother and sisters not to fret either.'

She knew that they weren't really fretting. But that they needed to reassure themselves that it wasn't a heartless and unfeeling thing to allow a seventy-one-year-old woman to jet off to the other side of the world without someone by her side. She didn't know why it was that children had to feel in some way responsible for their parents once they'd passed retirement age. As far as she was concerned she was perfectly capable of looking after herself. But they'd never really known that. Because Jim had always been there before, and they'd always assumed that Jim was the one who looked after her and would always look after her.

Well, she thought, as she gazed out over the clear blue water at the catamaran which was heading out to sea with its latest contingent of happy tourists, nobody lives for ever. It was funny how people didn't want to accept that these days. The Sunday papers were always full of the latest medical advances which held out the promise of life expectancy of around 120 or 130 as though this was a good thing. Esther wasn't so sure about that. She wondered who'd be worrying about her travelling on her own at 120. Her own children, who'd be older than she was now? Her grand-children? But wouldn't they be worrying about their parents? Great-grandchildren? Great-great-grandchildren?

Esther thought it was very selfish of people to want to live to such old ages. She had to admit that personally she didn't actually want to die right now, but she accepted that she was in the last . . . well, what? quarter of her life? Maybe less. Maybe this time next year she too would be lying in that graveyard outside Cork city, not caring that the rain was beating down on the shiny stone chippings while the sun shone on the clear water of White Sands Bay. She hoped not. She hoped that this time next year she'd be back here again.

So far it had exceeded her wildest dreams. She was loving every minute of the fuss that they made over her because she was on her own. She loved the exquisite food, the brightly coloured cocktails and the ever-present sun. She loved the cheerful hotel staff and their laid-back accents. She loved the tropical gardens and, of course, the white sands. The brochure had called it Paradise Island. The brochure, Esther thought, was dead right.

She discovered that the hotel ran a loyalty programme for repeat visitors. If she came back next year she'd be en-titled to a free massage at the luxury spa. The year after that, she'd get an upgrade on her room. On her first evening she'd met an American couple who'd been coming for the same week in December for the past eleven years. They'd been upgraded to the magnificent Coco Villa for their stay the previous year as a special thank-you for their ten-year anniversary. Of course the villa was occupied this time and so they couldn't have been put up there again anyway, but Amanda had told her that the hotel had put a limo at their disposal for the duration of their holiday this time, as well as arranging free treatments in the spa. That was what Esther liked so much about the hotel. They made every guest feel special.

Esther always sat on her balcony in the afternoon. She made it known to other guests that this was what she liked to do, so that they wouldn't worry about her. Really it was a bit of a nuisance having to worry about other people worrying about her, but she knew that they looked out for her – every morning at breakfast, after her swim, people would nod and smile at her, ask her how she was, had she spent a good night and what she was going to do for the day ahead. And she always replied the same way: that the night before had been perfect and that she was going to sit at the beach until lunchtime and then go to her balcony afterwards. But she didn't mind that all of the days were the same. She was perfectly content with that.

She supposed that having a very set routine was in some way symptomatic of being an older person. Sometimes she wondered whether she shouldn't get up late one morning and do things in reverse; or go on one of the many trips organised by the hotel for the amusement of the guests. But any time she'd been on holidays with Jim they'd done every single organised tour, and she wanted this holiday to be different. Besides, she hadn't come to the island to look at the wreck of the pirate ship or the English-built church. She'd come to escape the miserable Irish weather. She was perfectly happy to sit around all day, revelling in the December warmth and reading her books or doing the crossword in the English paper which she bought every day from the hotel gift shop.

She liked watching the other guests too. She especially liked watching the weddings – there'd been two so far this week – always overcome by the hope and joy on the faces of the brides and grooms, as though things would be this good for ever. She wanted to believe that things would always be good for everyone who married here, but she wasn't truly convinced of that. Time on the island was time out from how things normally were – people resting, like her; hoping, like the newlyweds; or escaping from something else in their lives. She rather felt that there were a number of people at White Sands who were indulging in a bit of escapism. She wondered in particular about the young girl in Coco Villa who, having been photographed almost every day since Esther had arrived, now seemed to be on her own. Apparently she was quite famous, having won some talent show back in England, but almost everyone at the White Sands Hotel was scathing about her fame and her talent.

'It's all manufactured,' Dee Bradford told her at breakfast one morning. 'She may have a decent voice but how on earth would you know? I saw the show. If you ask me, the reason that she won was because she was practically naked singing her song. According to the papers, every boy under the age of eighteen voted for her – and probably a lot over that age too.'

Esther had laughed at that as she buttered a perfect slice of toast. Dee had chattered on and on about the girl and Esther nodded from time to time, although she wasn't really listening. She put Dee into the escapist category. The other woman was on her own too. She was in her forties and worked as the PA to some very famous businessman whose name Esther couldn't remember (senility, she muttered to herself, as she tried to recall it). The businessman paid for Dee's winter holiday every year while he took three weeks off to be with his family. From what Esther gathered, it was the only time he actually spent with his family. Dee chattered every day about how good Mr – Mr – not Branson, that was the airline guy, Esther knew, but something like that – anyway, Dee was always going on about how fantastic he was to work for and how well he treated her, but Esther couldn't help feeling that it was an easy thing to do to pay for a holiday for your PA when she'd given up absolutely everything to be at your beck and call all the time. Dee didn't seem to have time off other than this particular three weeks and Esther thought that it was a bit much for a forty-year-old to have to try and find a life in a mere twenty-one days.

Other guests invited Esther to join them for lunch or for dinner. Sometimes she accepted and sometimes not – though she always categorised them. And, of course, the French owner of the hotel – Jean-Jacques Remy – always came over to her at dinner to ensure that everything was to her satisfaction.

Of course it was. How could it be any other way?

The American couple, the Kingstons, were in the bar when she arrived down for her pre-dinner drink that evening. Eleven years in a row. Esther wondered what the odds were of her even living another eleven years. She looked towards them, not wanting to intrude or make them feel that they had to include her in their conversation. But Amanda Kingston's blue eyes lit up at the sight of Esther and she waved at her.

'Well, hello there!' She smiled broadly. 'Do join us. How was your day?'

Tony Kingston stood up and offered his seat to Esther. Really, she thought as she sat down and he pulled up another padded wicker chair for himself, Americans do have the nicest manners.

'I had a lovely day,' she told them. 'I did absolutely nothing.'

'We went shopping.' Amanda smiled conspiratorially at her. 'The jewellery shops. Oh, my – they are so fantastic.' She extended her hand and Esther blinked at the enormous diamond which sparkled in the lights.

'Beautiful,' she said, although if she were to be totally honest, it was a little too brash for her liking.

'Big,' said Amanda in satisfaction. 'I like my rocks big.'

Esther glanced at the thin gold band with its three tiny diamond chips on her own engagement finger.

'Oh, honey.' Amanda squeezed Esther's arm. 'I didn't mean to imply that your beautiful ring wasn't good enough. It's a symbol, isn't it? Of you and your poor husband who passed away.'

Why was it that so many people hated the word 'died'? wondered Esther. They much preferred to talk about crossing over or passing or slipping away, as though any of those phrases actually changed what had happened.

'Oh, that's all right,' she said. 'It was all we could afford at the time.' She twisted it around on her finger.

'Comes to us all, I guess,' said Tony gruffly. 'Passing on.'

Esther noticed him flexing his muscles, as though reassuring himself that he might be in his sixties but he was in as good a condition as a man half his age.

'Well, that's life,' said Esther prosaically. 'Jim had a bad heart so it wasn't entirely unexpected.'

'And you're doing OK by yourself?' asked Amanda.

'Not a bother on me,' said Esther.

'Well, I guess that's a good thing,' said Amanda. 'And of course, these days seniors can do so much more, can't they?'

Seniors. Esther mulled over the phrase. She supposed it sounded better than old folk, which she'd always hated. But she wasn't convinced. She wished that someone could come up with an expression that encapsulated how she actually felt about her age. Which was pretty much that her body had wrinkles but her mind didn't. And that she wished she'd known half as much aged twenty as she did now.

'Maybe I'll have a spa treatment,' she said. 'Knock a few years off my senior look.'

'Oh, you should!' cried Amanda. 'I had a sea salt exfoliation yesterday. It was wonderful.'

'I'd be afraid they'd exfoliate the skin off me,' observed Esther.

'Not at all,' Amanda assured her. 'They do absolutely wonderful things to you there. You must definitely book something.'

Esther nodded, although she wasn't sure that she would. The treatments were unbelievably expensive. She frowned mentally. So what if they were? She hadn't gone on any of the trips, had she? She'd saved money on all of the things that she normally would have done with Jim. Surely that would cover the cost of an exfoliation? Though maybe a massage might just be enough for her. Something pampering anyway. She smiled faintly at the thought of being pampered even more.

'The restaurant is open,' remarked Tony. 'Shall we go in to dinner? Esther, will you join us?'

Although she enjoyed eating on her own, Esther was happy to join the Kingstons for the evening. They talked about their families and Esther filled them in on her children before asking about theirs. Tony and Amanda's eldest son was in the US military and had done two tours of service in Iraq. Now he was home again.

'I'm glad he's back,' said Tony. 'And out of the army. But it's changed him, and now I worry about him even more.'

Esther nodded.

'I'd have gone crazy if anything had happened to him,' said Amanda. 'We have friends who lost sons over there. And some whose kids came back injured. It's horrible.'

'Yes, well, my belief is that the whole thing was a monumental mistake,' said Esther.

Tony frowned. 'I can't believe so many Europeans didn't support us.'

'It's not that we didn't support you,' said Esther. 'But many of us thought it was the wrong thing to do. I still think it was wrong. But I admire your son for going.'

Tony said nothing, but stabbed a piece of beef with his fork.

'We can disagree without it causing an international incident,' remarked Esther mildly.

Amanda smiled, but Tony continued to eat in a moody silence.

After dinner he went to get drinks while Amanda and Esther sat on the terrace.

'I'm afraid I've spoiled your evening,' said Esther. 'I'm sorry.'

'It's OK,' said Amanda. 'I think Tony has his own doubts about things, but he'd never say. His dad was in the military too, and he's just so proud of Brad. He wanted to join himself but he has asthma. He's never quite gotten over it.'

'I was insensitive,' said Esther. 'I'm afraid that living on your own makes you shoot your mouth off a bit more than you mean to.'

Amanda nodded. 'I understand.'

When Tony came back, Amanda turned the subject to shopping opportunities and the atmosphere between them lightened again. But when she'd finished her drink, Esther excused herself and said that she was going to have an early night.

'It was lovely to meet up with you this evening,' she told them warmly. 'Thank you for sharing dinner with me. I'm sure we'll be talking again.'

She picked up her bag and walked back along the footpath to her room. She wished she hadn't said what she'd said about America and Iraq because she wouldn't for the world have upset Tony. But she hadn't been able to help herself. It wasn't her fault. She'd been tongue-tied for the past forty-five years, but now it sometimes ran away with her. It wasn't always a bad thing, but she really needed to take a little care, because one day it might run away with her far too much for her own good.

She opened her bag and took out the room's key card, which slid through her fingers and fell to the ground. She cursed softly. Bending down wasn't her best thing these days. Her knees made dreadful cracking sounds and of course, getting up was so much harder. But as she sighed deeply at the thought of having to pick up the card, the dark-haired girl from the adjoining room turned the corner and instantly bent down and retrieved it for her. Apparently the girl was a very successful crime writer. You'd never think it to look at her, thought Esther. She looked far too meek and mild to think about crime.

'Thank you,' she said.

'No problem.' Corinne Doherty smiled back at her. 'Would you like me to open the door for you?'

'No thank you,' said Esther. 'I can manage.'

She watched as Corinne made her way to her own room. She didn't want to get too friendly with her. She didn't want Corinne to start using her as research material.

She let herself into her room and opened the fridge. She took out the bottle of rosé and poured herself a glass, bringing it out on to the balcony where the temperature was significantly more pleasant than in the air-conditioned room.

She drank very little when she was at dinner or in the bar because she was actually afraid that she might talk too much. That the alcohol might loosen her tongue and she would simply blurt out the whole story, and that would be a disaster.

Because it might be that these people wouldn't understand what had happened. That they'd see it all from their own perspective and make judgements based on some of the facts, not all of them. They might look at her and blame her for how things had turned out. They'd think she'd been wrong to do what she did. Esther was afraid that all of the people who were so nice to her now would change their tune if they really knew her. Maybe, in their place, she'd condemn herself too. But she hoped not. Because she wasn't a bad person, really she wasn't.

At home, most people had considered her to be lucky. They'd seen the façade, of course. They'd seen the happily married couple with four wonderful kids. They'd seen her look after the home while Jim had looked after everything else. They'd seen him bring her on holidays every year. She knew that some of her friends had envied her. Only what was there to envy really? The fact that he took her on holiday, because that was what he wanted to do himself? The fact that he'd never allowed her money of her own, had doled out cash from his pay packet and demanded that she account for every penny? The fact that he mocked her at every opportunity, criticising her hair, her clothes, her weight; telling her that she didn't know how to make the best of herself but that at least she was good for the housekeeping? The fact that he had hit her with the back of his hand on more than one occasion when she'd argued with him?

Women were told to walk out in those circumstances, but how could she have walked out in the 1960s, with two children and nowhere to go? When the local priest had told her that Jim's anger was a cross she had to bear? When other people thought that if your husband gave you a thump he had a damn good reason?

And the thing was, Jim wasn't the worst of them. Most people wouldn't have called him abusive. The slaps were few and far between and only when he was angry. The money – well, times were tough and the head of the family had to look after every penny. As for her looks – truth was, Jim wasn't so wrong about that. She hadn't lost the weight she'd put on after the children and she hadn't had the time or money to spend doing herself up. Which was, of course, why he'd found his fancy woman. It had gone on for five years until Yvonne herself got pregnant. Even in the 1970s that wasn't an option for an Irish girl. She'd headed off to London and stayed there. Esther wondered if Jim had really loved Yvonne or whether she'd just been a diversion. As far as she knew there hadn't been anyone else, but that was probably because no girl in her right mind would give a tinker's curse for Jim Egan any more. He had a few bob all right; the creamery business had done well for him and he'd got out at the right time. But despite his nagging at Esther over her weight, he was no oil painting himself, having developed a gut that hung over the belt of his trousers and with a red face that gave away his fondness for the drink and his blood pressure problems.

But nobody here knew all that.

It wasn't Jim's fault either, Esther thought. He was a product of his time. She could think this now that he'd 'passed away', but she hadn't thought it then. She hadn't thought it the times that he'd slapped her or mocked her or sighed in despair at her. And she hadn't thought it when she'd found out about Yvonne Baker and the baby that was Jim's.

Eventually people had suspected that everything wasn't right. They didn't know everything, but they knew that there were problems between Jim and Esther Egan. But nobody talked to her about it even though sometimes she wished they had. The children had known that there were sometimes arguments over money and other things, but Esther had always been very careful to gloss over it all because she didn't believe that their lives should be upset due to the fact that she'd married a boor by mistake. She never, ever told them about the times he'd slapped her. There was always the chance that Derek might have gone for him or that the girls would have begged her to leave. And in the end, she hadn't been able to do that. She hadn't been able to turn her back on the feeling that she'd made her bed and had to lie in it, no matter how things in the country had started to change and the tide had turned against men who bullied their wives just because they could.

She used to say to herself that one day he'd leave her, although as time went by she realised that he had no interest in leaving at all. So sometimes she'd daydream about him walking under a bus or falling into the stream at the back of the house. Because she wanted him to leave. She'd had enough. Only she didn't know how to leave herself. There were the children to consider, after all, and the fact that she wasn't qualified to do anything and that she hadn't got any money of her own . . . leaving was an utter impossibility. Which was why she dreamed of him dying instead and then felt incredibly guilty about it.

And then the doctors had diagnosed Jim's angina. They'd told him to lose weight and he'd made the effort, even though Esther knew that if she baked an apple pie or rhubarb crumble he'd eat the whole lot given the opportunity. Her dreams turned to killing Jim by feeding him saturated fats and too much salt, but she hadn't had the nerve. (Although she had once insisted on him finishing up the last piece of the pie and cream and had then been in a state of high anxiety in case it would actually kill him.)

The day he'd had the heart attack he hadn't eaten anything at all. He'd woken up feeling unwell and had snapped at Esther over little things. It wouldn't normally have bothered her, she'd become used to it, only that day had been her seventy-first birthday and she'd been feeling a bit miserable herself. Because it had occurred to her that she was, actually, getting old, and she had never lived life the way she wanted it to be lived. She'd been feeling that way because she'd heard the girl on the radio singing that terrible but beautiful song about the woman who realised she'd never drive to Paris in a sports car with the warm wind in her hair. And the woman in the song was only forty-seven. If forty-seven-year-olds were feeling like that, well then, Esther thought, what hope had a seventy-one-year-old?

And so when she'd come downstairs and Jim had turned around to her, a panicked expression on his face, she'd stared silently at him as he'd slid to the floor, gasping for his tablets. You wouldn't let me go to Paris, she remembered. When the ladies' club was going. Ten years ago. You wouldn't give me the money. We would have been in an air-conditioned coach, not a sports car, but it would still have been Paris.

'Tablet,' he wheezed as she looked at him. 'Tablet.'

She knew where his tablets were. On the top shelf of the cupboard. High up, out of her reach. He put things on the top shelf because he liked her to have to pull out the step ladder to get them. He told her that it helped to keep her fit.

'Hurry, Esther,' he rasped.

It would be quicker to stand on a chair to reach the shelf, but Jim had always complained if she stood on the chairs. He'd ask why she didn't use the perfectly acceptable step ladder in the utility room and point out that the chairs were expensive ones, for sitting on, not standing on.

'Esther . . .'

She could see that he was in serious trouble. She could see that he needed the tablets quickly.

'Hurry,' he said again.

She walked out to the utility room. The step ladder was against the wall. The ironing board and Jim's set of golf clubs were in front of it. The last time she'd picked up the golf bag she'd dropped it and the clubs had spilled out on to the floor. He'd raged at her then and she'd thought that he was going to hit her. But he didn't hit her any more. He didn't really need to. She could feel the sting of the blow without him ever touching her. She moved the golf clubs carefully and propped the bag in front of the far wall. Then she moved the ironing board and placed it equally carefully beside them. She lifted the step ladder and carried it into the kitchen.

He was stretched out on the floor now, his breath coming in jerky gasps. She opened out the step ladder and climbed it. She took the tablets from the top shelf and came down the step ladder again.

He'd stopped breathing. Her hands were shaking as she struggled with the child lock of the cap. It took her a few attempts to open it, and then the cap popped off and she dropped the bottle. The little tablets spilled out, scattering across the tiled floor. She picked one up, blew nonexistent dust from it, and placed it in Jim's mouth. Then she went to the phone to call Dr Marks.

Esther got up from her balcony chair. In the first few days, when she remembered how Jim had died, her hands would shake again. She expected people to blame her, for Dr Marks to wonder out loud how it was that she hadn't reached Jim in time. But he hadn't. Everyone talked about Jim's angina and his heart problems and how he always did too much. Everyone sympathised with her on her great loss.

The children clucked around her and offered to have her stay with them. Everyone worried about her even when she told them that there was no need to worry about her any more. She was fine. Honestly.

She cried at the funeral, of course, as his coffin was carried out of the church. But she remained dry-eyed at the graveyard. She heard one of the neighbours comment that she was very composed.

She hadn't really felt composed. She'd been in shock. Shock that he was finally gone. Shock that she had a life without him. Shock that she could do exactly what she wanted from now on. And when she thought of these things she wanted to laugh out loud. But she didn't, of course. She thanked everyone for coming to the funeral, and for their kind words and deeds, while she planned her holiday to a place where Jim had always refused to go.

Her hand was perfectly steady as she picked up the phone in her room and dialled room service.

'How can I help you?' asked the voice at the other end.

'Can you send up a bottle of champagne?' asked Esther. 'The best that you have.'

'Certainly,' replied the waiter. 'Room 403? Mrs Egan?'

'Yes,' said Esther. 'Mrs Egan. And I'll only need one glass. Thank you.'

She replaced the receiver and went back out on to the balcony again. The breeze was still warm, even late at night. The sound of the calypso band wafted towards her. She recognised the tune. It was from the James Bond movie *Dr No*. She'd wanted to go to see that at the cinema but Jim had refused to take her. He'd told her it was nonsense. But she'd loved it when she finally saw it on the TV. And she loved the tropical tune too.

She hummed along under her breath until she heard the knock at her bedroom door.

The bottle of champagne was an extra, of course, but she didn't care.

Room 105 (Jennifer)

We nearly missed the flight. Our connection from Dublin had been delayed (I'd warned Harry that could happen, but of course he immediately told me I was being paranoid); then, because we had to check in again at Gatwick, and because there'd been some kind of problem with the computer system, we found ourselves at the back of a barely moving queue which snaked halfway around the airport and out of sight. I looked at the numbers in front of us, did a quick calculation based on allowing a very slim check-in time of three minutes for everyone ahead, and announced that we'd make it about ten minutes after the flight was due to depart.

'Don't be so silly,' Harry told me, although I could hear a faint flicker of anxiety in his voice. 'There's buckets of time.'

Well, of course there wasn't buckets of time. We shuffled along the queue with me trying desperately not to show my increasing anxiety, while Harry tried, equally desperately, to appear ultra-nonchalant about the minutes that were ticking inexorably by. It wasn't a good start, I thought, as I shot him looks of ill-concealed rage, despite also trying to convince myself that it was hardly his fault. But I wished he'd done what I wanted and travelled from Dublin to London the night before, when we would have been able to avail ourselves of the late-night check-in facilities and avoid the morning mêlée around us.

I flexed my shoulders as we moved forward again. The weight of the dress which I was carrying over my arm was monumental. It was coming with me as cabin baggage, even though I knew it would take up a vast amount of space. But it was my fairy-tale wedding dress and it had cost almost as much as the trip itself. There was no way I was letting it out of my sight.

Everything would be OK once – if – we got on the plane and were on our way to our perfect wedding location. I couldn't begin to imagine how I'd feel if we missed the flight. I'd been looking forward to this week for the past twelve months.

The brochure had been absolutely compelling – Weddings in Paradise, it had proclaimed, and I was instantly beguiled, even though a lot of people were saying that Caribbean weddings were a bit naff these days and the chic thing to do was to go totally traditional in your local church or get married in the snowy wastes of Siberia for that authentic all-white look.

It might be naff, but it was going to be perfectly naff if you know what I mean! I had visions of me walking barefoot along the white sands in my white dress and looking elegantly shipwrecked and beautiful with my sun-bleached hair falling in very careful disarray around my face. OK, I know that I would actually look my normal mess (also, I'd bought oyster white Prada shoes, so barefoot wasn't actually an option), but it was a nice image all the same.

The original plan had been for just the two of us to go.

After all, as I pointed out to Harry, much of the reason for heading off to the sun instead of staying in Dublin was to avoid the whole frenzy that the wedding would generate at home. He'd done it once before and I'd seen the photographs. It was my nightmare wedding from hell, a vast crowd of friends and family all jostling for position around the church door, leaving the bride looking a little overwhelmed beside Harry's mother, an overtanned woman in an extravagant purple suit and matching purple hat with a peacock feather rising from the back of the crown. As I looked at those photographs I could see why the marriage had gone up in smoke. No bride likes playing second fiddle to her mother-in-law's hat.

Harry's first marriage lasted three years. I was hoping that ours would last for ever. I was sure it would. I loved Harry. He was The One. He was kind and thoughtful and funny and he treated me like a precious jewel. Honestly. Most of the time anyway. All my friends loved Harry too. He was impossible not to love (well, unless you were Karen – wife number one – who'd once left a message on his mobile phone calling him a self-centred, self-obsessed, selfish bollocks. Karen had a good line in invective and, unfortunately, a good line into Harry's monthly salary, because she'd managed to negotiate a great deal for herself on the back of maintenance for their daughter). However, despite the constant demands on his time and wallet from the woman he'd married by mistake, Harry never let it get him down. The thing is, Harry always looks on the bright side. He's the life and soul of any party and has a good word to say about everyone. He likes being surrounded by friends, and despite the fact that his brother and sister don't seem to be around very much, he cares about family too, which is why he never got riled by Karen's rantings. I knew that Harry was also devoted to his mother (his father died a few years before I came on the scene). I'm making him sound a bit too perfect, maybe, and obviously that was never the case, but he was perfect for me. After all, despite his love of socialising, he understood that I couldn't spend every night out and about – I'm a nurse, and so my shifts mean that I can't always go on the complete lash because obviously I don't want to poison a patient by mistake owing to the fact that I'm still out of it the next day. Unlike my previous boyfriend, Carl, who called me a prissy cow who was a walking party-pooper. I wasn't. I'm not.

I allowed my tiny private wedding to turn into a massive party, didn't I? That's not the actions of a party-pooper. To be honest, I wasn't exactly mad about that particular idea. After all, the reason for going to the Caribbean in the first place had been to indulge in a private romantic idyll; but as Harry talked to everyone he knew about it, it became obvious that he was keen on the idea of having people around for the big day.

'We don't need anyone else,' I told him.

'No, absolutely. But it would be nice, don't you think? After we've done the business and drunk the coconut milk on the beach or whatever, wouldn't it be just fantastic to have our closest friends around to celebrate with?'

He had a point. It did seem a bit of a downer to do the whole wedding thing and then just sit down for a meal on our own. The reality was that it would make it all much more memorable if there were people to share the moment with us. I wasn't sure whether too many people would really be able to make it – travelling to the Caribbean just before Christmas mightn't be their idea of how to spend their time and money – but in the end I was happy to invite them. I knew that if anyone came along it would be Harry's friends. Mine wouldn't be able to afford it. Harry's mates seemed to be somewhat better-off, although maybe it was because they were all in jobs that paid well whereas my friends had gone into careers that were big on caring and short on cash (not that there's anything wrong with earning money; I wish I had more of it myself!).

We didn't plan on asking family though. Mine is huge and you know how it is, if you leave someone out you've insulted them for life, never mind the fact that they probably wouldn't really want to come anyway, especially when it was such a distance. But the whole question of asking people was a minefield and I just didn't want to go there. I talked it over with Mum and she was perfectly happy with our desert island plan – she's done four weddings already with my sisters and brothers so she was easy-going about missing this one. Besides, I've a younger sister planning to do the big family wedding thing so there's plenty more opportunity for her.

Harry was a little more concerned about his mother because he felt that she'd like to come along. But as I pointed out, it wouldn't be much fun for Gloria being the only parent there among all of our friends. She might feel awkward and uncomfortable (although I wasn't actually so sure of that – like Harry, Gloria is a social animal even though he frets about her being home alone too often). But since this was a second wedding for Harry, I thought she'd understand the lower-key nature of things even though she probably felt slightly miffed out about losing an opportunity to wear a fancy hat again. (She has delusions about herself and her hats. She once won Best Dressed Lady at the annual horse show – a reasonably prestigious prize in the circles in which she moves, so she considers her taste in fashion to have been proved impeccable. I know I sound bitchy here but, well, the phrase mutton dressed as lamb was kind of written for her, and although it's unfair to judge her solely on her love of glitzy clothes and make-up, I can't help it!)

Much to my surprise, after Harry had spoken to his wide range of close friends, about a dozen people elected to celebrate with us. Then we discovered that our hotel, the beautiful White Sands, offered a special rate on the rooms if we were going to take a minimum number of them, and so, in the end, it worked out that two of my own friends, Sarah and Deirdre, were able to tag along too because spreading the cost between everyone made it more affordable. I was delighted about that because, much as I like Harry's gang, I was beginning to feel outnumbered.

So that was the travelling party, although we weren't all flying together. I knew that some of Harry's mates would be on our flight but it had been amazingly well-booked and the others, as well as Sarah and Deirdre, were coming on a different one with a different airline later in the day.

But Rob, Ken, Dave, Winston, Emily and Brigitte were with us in the never-ending queue.

'Don't worry,' said Emily as she saw me check my watch for the hundredth time. 'They won't go without us.'

They nearly did. But thankfully we weren't the only people caught in the snaking line and a squadron of airline employees began walking up and down, checking where everyone was travelling, and fast-tracking those of us whose flights were due to depart in less than an hour. So suddenly we were bumped up to the front and we were at the check-in desk and Harry was smiling at me and telling me that he'd told me all along that there was no need to worry.

I like the fact that Harry is an optimistic person whereas I'm always looking for the snags in life. It balances us out. I can't help myself, of course. I want to be as laid-back and cheerful about things as him but it's just not in my nature. I reckoned that this was what drew us together. My half-empty glass and his half-full one. Oh, look, I'm not that bad really. I just feel that life has a habit of hitting you in the face just as you think it's time to peek over the parapet. So I like to be prepared for the worst, even though secretly I do believe and hope that the best will happen.

The worst happened at the boarding gate. The stewardess took one look at my gorgeous dress and told me that it would have to go in the hold. I told her that it would end up there over my dead body. She said it wouldn't fit in the overhead bin. And, she added, even if it did, it'd get crushed by the hand baggage of the other passengers. We looked defiantly at each other for two full minutes before I agreed to allow her to hold on to the dress. This was because she promised to bring it up to the plane when everyone had boarded and ask the steward to find a place for it in the cabin.

And then, after me getting really upset about everything and imagining my beautiful dress being dumped into the hold while we were sitting in row 64, I was totally surprised when the steward came down and told us that there was a space for us in the premium cabin where my dress was waiting for me.

'You see,' said Harry as we sat down in the wider seats with more leg room and took up their offer of free champagne, 'there was no need to worry about anything.'

It was a great flight though I wished we'd been on our own because Rob and Brigitte and the rest of them kept coming up to us and slagging us about our upgrade and our upcoming nuptials and I couldn't help thinking that some of the other people in the premium section were getting a bit fed up about our slightly raucous friends.

'It's just that they're a bit . . . well . . . over the top,' I explained to Harry.

'They're happy. They're fun. They're looking forward to a great week.'

'Me too,' I said, and then I freaked out because I discovered that Emily had somehow managed to spill champagne on to the bottom of my dress which had a seat all to itself. (It was swathed in cellophane and covers but the hem just peeked out.) We were coming in to land when I spotted it and so I didn't really get to see the island as the green speck in the sea that everyone apparently oohed and aahed over because I was having quiet hysterics. But by the time we landed I'd been comforted enough by Harry to feel that maybe things weren't so bad. All the same I clutched the dress to me as he and the others piled into the baggage hall to retrieve our luggage, and I was more than relieved when we were finally alone in our gorgeous room with its huge balcony overlooking the fabulous Caribbean Sea.

'This is the life, eh,' he said as he stretched out on the luxurious bed with its muslin canopy. 'Couldn't you just live here for ever?'

I nodded.

'Though I suppose you'd get fed up with it after a while,' he said.

'Rubbish.' I smiled at him as I lay down on the bed beside him. 'How could anyone get tired of Paradise?'

'Indeed,' he remarked as he slid my T-shirt over my head and found my left boob with his lips. 'Total paradise.'

Paradise was fan-bloody-tastic. Really it was. Blue skies, blue seas and the gorgeous white sands. Even though I felt a bit overwhelmed by being in a gang (I'd only ever gone on holiday in a group of four until now), it was fun. I'd have preferred a bit more time alone with Harry, but, as he said to me as we danced to the calypso band on the second night, we had our whole lives to be alone together. This was celebration time and we should live it up to the max.

It was nice to have Deirdre and Sarah with me when I went to the spa to book some beauty treatments ahead of the big day. A stunning local girl named Marilou was going to do me up. She was absolutely lovely to me and promised to make me her best bride ever. I presumed she said that to all of her brides (and so far there'd been a wedding every bloody day – I hadn't realised quite how many people were actually forsaking trendy Siberia for the sun!), but she beamed so widely at me that I wanted to believe her. As I left the spa I smiled at a tall girl with caramel and honey hair and a flawless complexion who I immediately identified as another bride. We exchanged conspiratorial winks and I left her to Marilou's tender mercies while I went back to the beach to top up my own tan. I was going to be a gorgeous bride (hopefully). This would be the best wedding ever. I was the luckiest girl in the world.

The bombshell dropped the following evening. We were all in the Green Garden restaurant, our tables grouped together and surrounded by tropical plants. Winston (one of Harry's nicer friends and an up-and-coming barrister) was giving us the inside track on the celebrity trial of the year – a top Irish pop star had been sued by her driving instructor for sexual harassment and had won the case, though apparently the whole truth had most certainly not come out in court. Winston told the story in a very funny way and I couldn't imagine him being ferocious and horrible to his adversaries, although apparently he was. Deirdre was chuckling beside me and Sarah was laughing helplessly when suddenly Harry stood up and cried, 'Mum!' in a voice which carried right across the restaurant.

I didn't, obviously, think he was actually calling his mother, since Gloria was safely tucked up in her gorgeous Glenageary home, but I did wonder what on earth he was going on about. And then I followed his eyes and my jaw dropped. Because there she was, standing at the entrance to the Green Garden, wearing a blue silk dress which clung to her incredibly lissom body. Gloria is sixty-two but she doesn't look a day over twenty-two. Well, obviously that's a complete lie because she does – it's just that (in addition to the hat fetish, and what I neglected to mention earlier) Gloria is a nip-and-tuck aficionado. She's had 'work' done to her eyes and her forehead as well as some freaky collagen injections to her lips. (Not quite trout pout, but gosh, I wouldn't have liked to be Mr O'Hara with those lips coming at me. So maybe just as well he'd popped his clogs.) However, from a distance, she looks relatively young. Up close, of course, her crêpey hands give her away. As do her gleaming teeth, which clearly aren't nature's own.

'What the . . .' I stared as she sashayed her way across the room.

'Oh, Mum!' Harry gave her a bear hug and lifted her off her feet. 'I'm so chuffed to see you.' He turned to me. 'Well, Jen,' he said. 'What d'you think?'

I was still staring. 'What are you doing here?' I asked.

Gloria laughed. It was a silvery laugh, the kind of laugh that you imagine she learned from watching black and white movies. 'How could I stay away?' she trilled. 'I wanted to be here when my baby married the love of his life.'

There was an amused chuckle around the table and she looked archly at everyone. 'I know you all think I'm far too young to be his mother,' she began (and I swear to God there wasn't a drop of irony in her voice), 'but I couldn't stay away.'

I frowned. 'But . . . but . . . you never said anything!' I looked accusingly at Harry. 'You never said anything either.'

'Of course not,' he said. 'Mum wasn't sure she could come. She's been in hospital, you know.'

Well, I did know. Gloria had been in for a chemical peel. Actually, now that I thought about it, her face still looked a bit raw.

'I didn't want to come unless I could do justice to your big day,' she said grandly. 'And now I can.' She plopped into the chair that Harry had dragged from an adjoining empty table. 'Oh my Lord, you guys, I'm so-oo jet-lagged.' She stretched her elegant (I have to admit this) legs out in front of her and allowed her high-heeled shoes to slip from her feet.

Now, the thing is, I love my mother. I really do. But I'd freak out if she arrived into a gang of my friends and tried to be one of us. She's my mother, for God's sake. Not my friend. And it's probably very childish and anal of me to want my mother to be a mother when there's a conspiracy out there to try and make everyone look the same and act the same no matter what their age, but I can't help that. Anyway, my ma is older than Gloria O'Hara. She always looks OK for her age. But she sure isn't a kind of ancient sex-symbol.

I'm not ageist. When I'm sixty-two I want to look good for my age. I want people to think that I could be anything from thirty-five to fifty-five. Preferably thirty-five, of course. But I certainly don't want to look like a flipping teenage prom queen. In fact, close up, Gloria was just a little bit scary, with her wide-awake eyes and peeled face.

'I didn't realise you were thinking of coming at all,' I said blankly.

'I was at his first wedding,' said Gloria. 'To that silly, silly girl. The least I can do is to support him in the marriage which I hope will be for ever. Which I know will be for ever, dearest Jennifer, because I know you're the exact right girl for him.'

Emily and the other girls cooed. But I knew that Sarah was looking at me with mute enquiry in her eyes.

Harry waved expansively at the wine waiter and asked him to bring us a bottle of champagne. Gloria rested her feet on his lap. And I wondered why it was that he'd obviously invited his mother and never said a word to me.

I didn't get a chance to ask him straight away, and we stayed up late that night. Despite Gloria's jet-lag she managed to quaff a good quantity of champagne, and when the calypso band had finished for the evening Harry played the piano while she sang in the manner of Shirley Bassey without the range. Actually, she wasn't bad. But her rendition of 'Diamonds Are Forever', while grabbing me by the hand and caressing my engagement ring, was totally scary.

It was nearly two in the morning before Harry and I were alone in Room 105 and Gloria was safely locked away in 212. I'd been terrified that her room would be next door but thankfully it was further down the hillside and well out of casual hearing distance. I wanted her out of the way because I was afraid that there'd be a certain amount of shouting in Room 105 that night. And not shouting in the throes of sexual passion.

'What the hell do you mean by asking your mother to come along and not telling me?' I demanded as soon as I'd slammed the door closed behind us.

Harry looked at me in astonishment. 'And what's the matter with you?' he asked. 'Why are you getting your knickers in a twist?'

'Harry!' I cried. 'She's your mum. We decided against asking our families. It was friends only.'

'Crikey, Jen, keep your hair on.' Harry looked at me in surprise. 'It's different for you. You've got both parents, four sisters and two brothers – at least three of whom seem to be at your house at any given time. I've got one brother and one sister but I'm the only one who sees her regularly. I couldn't leave her out.'

'But you didn't tell me!' I wailed. 'I wasn't expecting to see her. It was a surprise.'

'Sure. But a nice surprise.'

I said nothing. Harry and I didn't talk about his mother much. I admired his sense of responsibility towards her. There are loads of blokes who wouldn't bother to call in to see their mum on the way home from work every evening, knowing that she was home alone (even though as I said before, she didn't actually stay in alone. She went to bridge nights and out with 'the girls' and was in the local musical society, which seemed to be a hotbed of social activity). But I sometimes felt as though Harry bent over backwards to look after her. After all, as I told him once, she was a good-looking woman with a life of her own. She didn't really need him. He'd looked at me darkly and told me that though Gloria was without a doubt an attractive woman for her age, and although she did go out from time to time, she was still on her own. And he was her only family within calling distance. So he'd be there for her whenever she needed. But, he'd added, Gloria never, ever asked him to call to see her. Once we were married and had established a routine of our own, he added, I didn't need to worry about Gloria. Because, he said, he felt that I might be getting a little bit worried over nothing. He was wrong about that. I'd begun to think that maybe it was more than Gloria's hat that had upstaged Karen.

But then Karen wasn't a very nice person. I'd heard her on the phone to Harry a couple of times and she was bitchy and unpleasant. If she'd been bitchy and unpleasant about Gloria I could understand why things had deteriorated between them. It would be different between us. I could get to like Gloria even though she freaked me out most of the time. And I would certainly be understanding about Harry's loyalty to his widowed mother.

So that night I just shrugged and told Harry that I must be feeling a bit jet-laggy myself, or that maybe wedding nerves were getting the better of me. And I said that I was sorry for shouting at him and that I couldn't wait to get married in two days' time and that I was pleased and delighted that Gloria was going to be there.

* * *

'She's a fucking horror.' Deirdre was the one who said it to me the night before the wedding. It was barbecue night at the hotel and we were walking back to the restaurant, plates loaded with chicken wings and burgers. 'You want to keep well away from her.'

'I don't see her that often,' I told Deirdre. 'I know Harry has to, because she's on her own, but she doesn't really impinge on our lives that much,'

'She's a cross between Bet Lynch and a drag queen,' said Deirdre. 'And if you give her a couple of years she'll be a candidate for the awfulplasticsurgery.com site.'

I chuckled.

'No, seriously,' said Deirdre as we sat down at the table. 'Where's she going in that get-up?'

I watched as my future mother-in-law tottered towards the barbecue wearing spiky heels and a leopardskin dress. It was a tasteful leopardskin dress . . . well . . . it wasn't a mini or anything like that. It had a long layered skirt and fairly decent chest cover. Gloria's blonde hair was caught up in a stylish chignon, secured by a brightly coloured clip in the shape of a flamingo which she'd bought in the hotel shop that morning.

'She's not so bad really,' I murmured. 'Over the top, but, hey, she's colourful.'

'That's true,' said Deirdre drily.

Gloria kept us entertained all evening. Her stories, like her singing, weren't at all bad. It was just that it seemed somehow inappropriate to me that she was the star of the show. I told myself not to be mean and bitchy; she was Harry's mother and she was a widow and, hell, maybe if I was her age and looked that good (whether by nature or by design) I'd want to be the star of the show too. I could see where Harry got his party-loving nature from. Though I was a bit creeped out when the two of them did the tango together. Fortunately Gloria then danced with all of Harry's male friends which gave me the opportunity to grab him in a clinch myself.

'I love you,' I said, as the band's singer segued into a slower number and Harry tightened his grip around me.

'I love you too,' he told me. He was looking over my shoulder as he spoke and he chuckled.

'What?' I asked.

'Mum and Dave are looking very smoochy together.'

'What!' I tried to turn around.

He chuckled again. 'All in fun, sweetie. All in fun.'

I feel bad about saying that I was beginning to hate Gloria. But the woman was a walking menace. On the beach she wore more leopard-print stuff and blinged herself up with gold chains, earrings and rings. She had a toe-ring too, which she'd bought in one of the jewellery stores in town. And that day before our wedding, she made me feel as though she was the young fun-loving person whereas I was a boring middle-aged crone. That was because I refused to go on the Pirate Cruise around the island. I was trying to spend the day quietly, drinking lots of water instead of cocktails so that my skin would be gorgeous and lustrous for the following day.

'Maybe you're right,' she said eventually. 'You probably do need some extra work on your looks.'

OK, that was going too far. I know that my castaway-beauty image would never happen but I'm not that bad. And I wasn't taking being lectured by someone who couldn't even frown properly!

'Oh, sod off, Gloria,' I said narkily. 'Nobody asked you.' And I got up and went back to the room. I poured myself a large glass of water and took it out to the balcony, where I stretched out on my sun-lounger with a copy of *Jennifer Jones and the Jealous Journalist* by my favourite author, Corinne Doherty, which I'd brought with me but which I'd hardly had a chance to read because everything had been so fun-filled and party-ish. I waited for Harry to join me. He'd been there when Gloria had made her jibe and I'd seen him wince.

Half an hour later he still hadn't come. I was beginning to get annoyed. An hour and I was starting to worry. After an hour and a half I stomped back to the beach.

Sarah and Deirdre (neither of whom had been around when the Pirate Cruise was being discussed) as well as Winston were sitting at the water's edge. There was no sign of Harry, Gloria or the others.

'They went on the Pirate Cruise,' Winston said uncomfortably. 'Gloria so wanted to go and Harry gave in.'

I gritted my teeth and avoided the sympathetic glances of both Sarah and Deirdre.

'What time are they due back?' I asked.

'Not till six,' said Winston.

I got up again. 'I'm going to the spa,' I said. 'I need a relaxing treatment.'

Although they were always busy I thought that maybe they might be able to give me a wrap. There'd been one in the brochure, mango and orange blossom or something, which sounded absolutely fantastic. I felt as though I needed something absolutely fantastic to take my mind off the fact that my fiancé had given in to his mother's demands to go on some ridiculous beer-fest (which for sure was what the Pirate Cruise had to be) on the day before our wedding. I enquired about the wrap at reception but Marilou looked at me regretfully. They were totally booked up on the wrap scene, she told me. But I could have one the day after tomorrow.

'And you should.' A girl wearing a towelling robe looked at me with enthusiasm. 'I wasn't mad keen on the idea but my boyfriend made me do it. And it was absolutely wonderful.' She grinned at Marilou. 'Thanks again. I'll tell Declan that I'm converted.' And she wafted out of the spa in a perfume of fruit essences.

'Samantha could give you a massage in half an hour.' Marilou was consulting her book. 'She only has thirty minutes but that should be enough to relax you.'

'I don't need relaxing,' I snapped and then realised that of course I did.

So I stayed and had the relaxing massage and I did feel a lot better, and then I headed back to the room and sat on the patio lounger, reading my book and drinking bottles of water to help with the lustrous look. By the time I made my way back to the beach, the Pirate Cruise ship was offloading its passengers on to the wooden jetty.

Gloria was wearing a bandanna around her head and a patch over one eye. Maybe she needs it, I thought acidly. Maybe the botox has worn off.

'Hey, there you are!' she cried as she flounced on to the beach. 'You should've come with us. We missed you.'

'I was in the spa,' I told her with dignity. 'I had a treatment booked.'

'I didn't know that,' said Harry as he arrived beside her. 'I thought you'd been plucked and prepped already.'

I made a face at him.

'Anyone for cocktails?' Gloria waved at a passing waitress. 'How about rum punch for everyone?' And before I had time to say that I was sticking to water she'd given the order and a large jug of punch was brought down to the beach.

Everyone was having a good time. Gloria was telling funny pirate stories (and to prove I'm not biased against her I did laugh). Harry watched her proudly.

'You'd never think it, would you?' he murmured to me as she did her Keira Knightley *Pirates of the Caribbean* impression.

'Think what?' I was thinking lots of things about Gloria.

'You know. That she was a mum. That she'd had a hard life. That Dad died and left her on her own.'

I wanted to say that lots of women had hard lives and were left on their own but I didn't. In many ways he was right. Gloria was an amazing woman.

I'd planned to spend a couple of hours with Deirdre and Sarah that evening, but as the sun was sinking in pink-orange flames beneath the horizon, Gloria announced that she'd booked a table for 'the girls' in the Mariner's Reef that evening. The girls were me and her, Emily and Brigitte, Sarah and Deirdre. I was beginning to get seriously pissed off with this woman. She was taking over my whole wedding. But I was afraid to say anything to Harry because he seemed to love the idea of his mum being one of the girls.

We met in the restaurant at eight. The girls (thankfully with the exception of Deirdre and Sarah) seemed to agree with Harry that Gloria was wonderful. They discussed her nip and tucks (which, let me tell you, is a totally gross conversation to have over dinner) and got the name of her favourite surgeon. There was a big debate over the issues of boob jobs (the one procedure that Gloria hadn't apparently had done yet) and liposuction (which she had).

'Though really what makes the most difference is the cosmetic stuff,' she proclaimed. 'Look, I had my eyelids tattooed. Means I don't have to worry about eyeliner ever again.'

I shuddered.

'So,' I asked eventually, 'looking as great as you do, Gloria, is there any chance that you'll get married yourself one day soon?'

Silence descended on the table. Gloria looked at me, the laughter gone from her eyes. 'I really don't think so,' she said icily. 'My husband and I had a wonderful marriage for over thirty years. I have no need for another man.'

'Use it or lose it,' I told her. (I'd broken with my water-only regime and had knocked back a couple of glasses of champagne that Gloria had ordered.)

'Really, Jennifer.' This time her look was one of disgust. 'I don't think that's the sort of thing we want to hear.'

Wasn't it? I'd have thought she'd be up for a bit of sexual conversation.

'C'mon, Gloria,' I said. 'You get tarted up like a dog's dinner every day. Surely it's not all for your own benefit?'

For once Gloria seemed lost for words. Unfortunately I wasn't.

'I mean,' I continued, 'what's with the leopardskin motif if not to attract them and pounce?'

Beside me Deirdre stifled a snort of laughter. I could see that Emily wanted to giggle too.

'You're great for a woman of your age,' I continued blithely. 'But it must be such an effort every day.'

'I beg your pardon.' I could hear the fury in Gloria's voice. 'I'm lucky to have naturally good bone structure. All my procedures have been minor.'

'Minor liposuction?' I asked in disbelief. 'I thought lipo meant shoving a tube into you and sucking out all the fat. I'd hardly call that minor.'

The girls weren't stifling laughter now. They were looking at both of us in tentative horror.

'I have never been so insulted in all my life,' snapped Gloria. 'After all the trouble I went to tonight . . . I don't know what my Harry sees in you.'

She got up and swept from the room, although the effect was ruined a little when she stumbled at the top of the steps and had to be helped back on to her precarious heels by the waiter.

'Crikey, Jen,' said Sarah. 'I think you've blotted your copybook with the ma-in-law.'

I bit my lip. I hadn't originally set out to insult her, but . . .

'I'll talk to Harry if you like,' offered Brigitte. 'Tell him you had a bit too much to drink.'

'I haven't had too much to drink,' I lied. 'I'll sort this out myself.'

The men were having their own dinner in the Green Garden. I didn't bother interrupting them but headed back to the room, where I stretched out on the big bed and was asleep almost immediately.

It was nearly midnight before I woke again, and that was to the sound of the door opening. I blinked as the light was switched on and sat up in bed.

'Hi,' I said as my eyes focused on Harry. Then I saw the time on the clock and frowned. 'It's late.'

'Yes. Well.' He looked at me and I could see he was angry. 'I had to spend some time talking to Mum. She's very upset, you know.'

'Upset? Why?'

'You surely aren't so sozzled that you don't remember being extremely rude to her?' he said.

I rubbed my eyes and ran my fingers through my hair. 'I'm sorry about that,' I said. 'It's just . . . well . . .' I couldn't think of what to say.

'She's very sensitive,' said Harry.

Personally I thought Gloria O'Hara was as sensitive as a rhino. If she was all that sensitive she surely would have realised that showing up here and taking over my wedding wasn't the thing to do.

'Look, I know you think she's tough and gorgeous,' said Harry, while I blinked at him. 'But she's not at all really. And it's been hard for her since my dad died.'

'I understand that,' I said. 'It's just . . .' I still couldn't think of what to say.

'She only has me really,' Harry continued. 'Helen doesn't get home very much and Luke isn't good for dropping by either. She depends on me.'

'I know,' I said. 'And I think it's great the way you do so much for her. I . . . well . . . I find her a bit over-whelming, that's all.'

'Oh, Jen, you find everything overwhelming!' He laughed. 'You know what you're like. Hate going to parties, hate dressing up, hate having to be nice to people . . .'

'That's not true!' I cried. 'I don't hate any of those

102

things. I just have to fit them into my life. I thought you understood that.'

'I do, I do,' he said hastily. 'But you've got to realise that Mum is like me. She enjoys life and socialising. But she also feels very strongly about the people she loves.' He looked at me, his dark eyes soulful. 'So you've got to cut her some slack.'

'I did have a bit too much to drink,' I admitted.

'That's my girl,' he said. 'Now all you have to do is pop down to her room and tell her you're sorry and everything will be fine.'

I had a headache the next morning, probably from too much champagne the night before. My eyes felt gritty too and I couldn't help thinking that all of the treatments over the past four days were such a damn waste when I felt like shit. I sat at the basin in the hairdressing salon and tried to relax as Samantha massaged shampoo into my hair.

I'd gone to Gloria's room after Harry had returned and apologised to her like he'd asked, and she'd been amazingly nice, hugging me and calling me her new daughter and telling me that we were going to be a great family. Then she asked if I'd like to see her wedding outfit, which she'd intended to be a great surprise but – all girls together – she'd love to show it to me. I was quite honestly terrified at what she might produce but it wasn't too bad actually – magenta silk, rather low cut, and I could imagine her non-enhanced boobs still looking pretty good in it, but stylish all the same. The hat – of course there was a hat – was magenta too – a small crown with a wide brim to shade her eyes and an arrangement of netting at the front. It could've been worse. Once again she planned to wear shoes with staggeringly high heels because, she told me, they flattered her legs.

'I'm really looking forward to this,' she confided. 'And I think you'll be so much better for Harry than that Karen creature.'

'I hope so,' I said.

'Absolutely,' she told me. 'She had no idea about marriage. She gave Harry such a hard time.'

'Did she? How?'

'She nagged him constantly. Of course she got pregnant straight away and basically tried to tie him to the house. She freaked out every time he called to see me.'

I couldn't actually blame her. I wondered whether or not Gloria would think I was a horrible nag in a few weeks' time. I had to escape. I told her that her outfit was gorgeous and that the wedding would be wonderful and I got back to the room, where Harry was already asleep.

But I didn't sleep, which might also be part of the reason why I felt so horrible today. I shifted my neck on the cold ceramic of the basin. My heart was thumping away in my chest, which was really weird, because I wasn't in the slightest bit nervous about the wedding. Maybe it was just the excitement. It was hard to believe that the day was finally here.

I'd booked time in the beauty salon for everyone but, of course, had forgotten about Gloria. Nevertheless she arrived about fifteen minutes after the rest of us and gave instructions on what had to be done to turn her into a goddess. When we were done, we all signed the chits for our rooms, except me, because my bridal do was on the house. Gloria signed her name with a flourish and I noticed, because I was standing behind her, that she'd filled in Room 105 for the bill.

'That's our room number,' I pointed out to her.

'Oh, sorry,' she said. 'Still, makes no difference.'

It did make a difference. I didn't want to pay for Gloria's facials. I said nothing. I felt terrible for suddenly being overcome by meanness. I might not be a party animal or a full-blown optimist and I have to look after the pennies a bit because my salary is crap, but I'm not really a mean person. So I said nothing and hurried back to our room. Harry was moving out – only for the preparation time, of course, but he was taking his stuff to Bob's room lower down the hillside. He whistled appreciatively at my hair-do.

'You look good enough to eat,' he said.

I grinned at him. 'But not now. You'll mess my hair.'

'It's fabulous,' he said. 'You'll be the absolute belle of the ball.'

'Well, after your mother,' I told him.

He laughed. 'Does she look cracking?'

I smiled noncommittally. Then, before I could stop myself, I mentioned to him that she'd charged it to our room.

'Well, that doesn't matter,' said Harry.

'I know, I know,' I said. 'It's just . . . well . . . so's you know I didn't have extra hair-dos or whatever.'

'That's OK,' he said. 'Anyway, since we're looking after Mum I'd have known what was what.'

I frowned. 'Looking after her?'

'Her room,' he explained.

I looked at him in puzzlement. 'How?'

'How d'you think, Jen?' His expression showed that he thought I was a complete idiot. 'The bill, of course.'

I stared at him. 'We're paying the bill for your mum?'

'Of course.'

'But . . . but . . .' I was gobsmacked. Last night Gloria had ordered half a dozen bottles of non-house champagne which was not covered by our all-inclusive deal. I'd been touched by the gesture and told myself that she was a generous woman at heart. It's not that I begrudge spending money on champagne (though I guess I wouldn't have splashed out that much!), but I would've liked to know I was doing it.

'What?' he asked.

'Well, it's just . . . if we're paying for your mum, why aren't we paying for mine too?' I asked.

He laughed. 'It's a totally different situation,' he said.

'I don't see how.'

'I told you before,' he said patiently. 'My mum is on her own. She depends on me. I want her to feel happy. Besides, you didn't want your mum here. I did want mine.'

What could I say? He was right. It had been me who'd been against asking anyone at all and that was because of my non-party-animal nature. I had to learn to compromise.

I shrugged. Harry smiled and kissed me. Harry is a great kisser. Soon we were doing more than kissing. And I wasn't really worrying too much about my hair.

But afterwards, while I was waiting for Sarah and Deirdre to come up to the room (they were going to act as bridesmaids), I started to worry again. Back home, Harry's devotion to Gloria was somehow touching. But here his relationship with her was over the top. Not, I hasten to say, in a Jerry Springer I'm In Love With My Mother Oedipus Complex sort of way – God, no. Just – she could do no wrong in his eyes. He wanted everything to be perfect for her. And, well, I was beginning to think that she mattered to him more than I did. I hadn't ever felt like that at home – I'd been annoyed a few times when he'd had to call round to fit a plug or check a blockage in the plumbing for her (can't everyone fit a plug these days?), especially when these things often happened on the evenings I wasn't working. But it didn't really bother me.

This, though. This inviting her and not telling me, paying for her without telling me either (we were sharing the cost, after all); this all bugged the hell out of me. And although I kept telling myself I was blowing it up out of all proportion and it was just because I was terrified about the cost, I couldn't help feeling panicky. I told myself that money didn't matter when you were talking about your wedding day. And I'd been perfectly prepared to blow a fortune on my dress.

I looked at my watch. Half past three. Half an hour to go. Sarah and Deirdre would be here any minute. I sat on the edge of the bed in my gorgeous dress (the hotel had succeeded in removing the stains from the champagne that Emily had spilled on the hem) and wondered, for the very first time, if I was doing the right thing.

I stood up and the skirt of the dress knocked Harry's mobile phone off the locker. I picked it up. He has a much flashier phone than me. I switched it to camera mode and took a photo of myself. Then I looked in his phone book. Karen's name was there. Just Karen. No surname. I couldn't stop myself. I dialled the number.

She sounded harassed when she answered.

'What?' she demanded.

I blinked.

'What?' she demanded again, and then I realised that she thought Harry had phoned her. Still, she didn't have to be so rude.

'Hello,' I said. 'I'm Jennifer Wright.'

'Who?' she said. 'Harry? Is that you?'

'Not Harry.' Was the woman completely stupid? I didn't sound like Harry, did I?

'Jennifer,' I repeated. 'Harry's fiancée.'

'Oh,' she said. I could almost see her frown. 'Why are you ringing me? Is something the matter? With Harry?' There was an anxious tone in her voice now and suddenly I wondered whether she still loved him despite everything. But no, I thought. She left him. She wouldn't have done that if she loved him.

I told her nothing was the matter and she asked why I was calling.

'Well, you see . . .' I really wasn't sure where I was going with this conversation.

'Hold on,' she said. I heard the receiver being put down and her say 'Go back to bed' to someone in the background. I'd forgotten, of course, that it was five or six hours later at home. 'I'm telling you,' I heard her say. 'Bed now or Santa won't come.'

I stared out at the blue sky and couldn't quite get my head around the fact that it was cold and dark at home. And probably raining. But I was here, in the sun, ready to marry the man I loved.

'Sorry about that,' she said. 'Gigi is overexcited about Christmas.'

'Gigi?' I'd thought that Harry's daughter was named after her grandmother. He hardly ever talked about her to me but I was sure she was Gloria too.

'My daughter,' she said. There was a slight pause. 'Harry probably calls her Gloria, but I can't possibly. I never wanted to in the first place. That name gives me the creeps.'

'Oh?'

'You must have met her,' said Karen. 'The fucking bitch from hell.'

I didn't tell her that both Gloria and Harry thought that *she* was the fucking bitch from hell.

'Oh, come on,' I said feebly. 'She's not that bad.'

'Hah!' cried Karen. 'You don't think so? Well, maybe she's changed. But quite frankly, I couldn't bear having a mother-in-law who insisted that her precious son call round every Sunday for dinner and four nights a week; take her to the movies or her bridge sessions; be at her beck and call every single moment of every single day. I couldn't bear having a mother-in-law who could afford stuff I couldn't because her son was paying her bills out of our joint income. I certainly couldn't bear her always comparing herself to me. Asking Harry if he didn't think we looked like sisters. Sisters! Christ, if that woman was my sister I'd murder her. And I mean it. I hated the bitch and she hated me and I hope it's different for you, I really do, but no woman will ever be good enough for Harry, and in her head no woman is ever going to be better-looking than her.' Karen must have run out of breath at that point because she paused. And then she said brightly, 'But, sorry, why did you call?'

'Um . . . well . . .'

'It's Gloria, isn't it?' said Karen. 'She's there.'

'How did you know?'

'How wouldn't I know?' demanded Karen. 'I remember her at our wedding. Practically pushing me out of the photos and shoving her tits at the camera. You know she says she never had them done, but I'm not so sure about that. She's far too proud of them.'

'She's had work done over the last few years,' I said. 'But not them as far as I know.'

'It'd take more than work to turn her into a decent human being,' snorted Karen.

I giggled. I couldn't help it.

'So, look – is it Gloria?'

I succumbed. I told her everything. I told her I felt terrible for thinking that my future mother-in-law was a free-loading cow who was so much more than a traditional Irish mammy who thinks the sun shines out of her son's arse. Because she made him think that the sun shone out of hers too. Only not in a comfortable, mumsy way. In her Barbie's granny kind of way.

Karen laughed. 'That woman made my life hell,' she said. 'I was never good enough for him and I never will be. And it's a shame, because he's a decent bloke and I used to give a shit about him, but when you're always playing second fiddle to a guy's mother, well then . . . I couldn't hack it any more. I thought it would be different after Gigi was born, but it wasn't. Gloria didn't actually like having a grand-child. She thought it was ageing.'

'Oh.'

'Are you having second thoughts?'

'I'm getting married in less than half an hour,' I told her. 'I can't have second thoughts.'

'Of course you can,' she said. 'Think about living close to Gloria for the rest of your life.'

I shuddered.

'Good luck,' she said.

'Yeah, thanks.' I snapped the phone closed and sat on

the bed again. Then Deirdre and Sarah knocked at the door.

They looked great in their gorgeous new dresses which they'd bought in Harvey Nicks, and with all the expertise of the spa and beauty shop behind them in making them absolutely fabulous. They'd brought a bottle of champagne with them. It was the free house champagne.

'You look fantastic!' cried Deirdre as she popped the cork. 'We've just seen all the lads making their way to the wedding bower. Harry looked particularly snappy.'

I smiled half-heartedly.

'Well,' said Sarah as she raised a glass. 'To the future Mrs O'Hara. May God bless her and all who sail in her.'

My smile was even more half-hearted.

'Hey, Jen, what's up?' She realised I wasn't quite getting into the spirit of things.

I shrugged. 'I . . . I'm not sure . . .'

They looked at me aghast.

'Not sure?' repeated Deirdre.

'I'm just . . .'

'. . . having last-minute nerves,' finished Sarah. 'Come on, Jen love. You know you're crazy about him. You know he's crazy about you. And you're in Paradise, for heaven's sake.'

'I know, I know,' I wailed. 'But . . .' And then I poured out all my reservations about Gloria and how worried I was about the future and I told them that I'd phoned Karen and what she'd said.

'But come on, sweetie, she's his ex-wife,' Sarah reminded me. 'Ex-wives never have a good word to say about anything to do with their previous husband.'

'Sometimes they do,' I told her.

They exchanged looks.

'She sounded really nice and normal,' I said. 'But he always told me she was horrible.'

'You've heard her being horrible,' Deirdre reminded me. 'What about the message on his phone?'

That was true. I felt a little better.

'And Gloria is probably just a bit nervous with you too,' she added, somewhat less helpfully.

'My arse,' I snapped. 'The woman is a self-centred lunatic.'

This time the looks they exchanged were more than stricken.

'She's a bit . . . loud, perhaps,' said Sarah finally.

'Would you like her as a mother-in-law?' I demanded.

There was total silence.

'Oh shit,' I said, and started to cry.

They clustered round and begged me to stop or I'd wreck my make-up, and then they reminded me once more of how great Harry was to me. They pointed out that I hadn't had a whole heap to do with Gloria in the entire time I'd known Harry, and that there was no reason for that to change, and that I was getting into a state over nothing. Everyone had nightmare mothers-in-law, Sarah told me. Everyone.

'Am I being a total fool?' I asked them, and they both nodded.

I nodded too. 'I'm sorry,' I said. I rubbed my eyes and streaked the so-called waterproof mascara across my face.

'Shit,' said Sarah.

'Oh God,' I wailed. 'I can't get married like this.'

'Don't worry,' Deirdre told me. 'It only takes a little repair work.'

'But I'm going to be horribly late,' I wailed. 'We agreed ten minutes late but it's past that already and . . . and . . . Harry will be wondering what's happened.'

'I'll leg it down and tell them there was a bit of a make-up hitch,' said Sarah. 'By the time I'm back again you'll be ready.'

'OK,' I said as she whirled out of the room.

I felt calm again. The crisis had passed. Yes, Gloria was overwhelming, but no, she wouldn't overwhelm my life. Harry loved me. I loved Harry. That was all that mattered.

The mobile phone rang and Deirdre was so startled that she streaked the mascara again.

I picked it up.

'Are you still there, Jennifer?' It was Karen.

'Yes.'

'Look,' she said, 'I feel bad about the things I said. You go and marry Harry and have a great life with him. Don't worry about Gloria. You can deal with her.'

'Why couldn't you?' I asked.

'You know, I was crazy about him,' she told me. 'He's a great guy. And I loved him. I still love him a bit, to tell you the truth, even though I shout at him so much. But he was weak when it came to her and I couldn't take it. He never said no to her and . . .' She started ranting again. Clearly the whole Gloria thing had been a big issue with her.

Deirdre was motioning me to get off the phone, but I was listening to Karen and thinking that she didn't sound half as horrible as Harry and Gloria insisted but that marriage to him had totally traumatised her. And I was worrying that marriage to him would totally traumatise me too.

'Everything's fine.' Sarah came back into the room. 'Harry

laughed. Said he knew you'd keep him waiting . . .' When she saw I was on the phone, she looked enquiringly at me and then at Deirdre. Deirdre shrugged her shoulders and the two of them sat on the end of the bed and waited while I listened to Karen.

'Jeez, I'm sorry,' she said eventually. 'I guess it still gets to me. And I meant to say to you that everything would be fine.'

'I know,' I said.

'When are you due to marry him?' she asked.

'Fifteen minutes ago.'

'What!' she shrieked. 'I'm stopping you marrying him.'

'Of course not,' I said. 'I was going to be late anyway.'

'Thank God.' I could hear the relief in her voice. 'I couldn't bear it if my flipping neuroses over the whole thing messed up your life too.'

'Is your life messed up?' I asked.

She sighed. 'Only because I thought it would all be different,' she replied. 'And I couldn't cope with how things turned out. But you, Jennifer, you sound like a tougher cookie than me. And I bet it all works out great for you. I do hope so. Really.'

'What about money?' I asked.

'What d'you mean?'

'Well, if me and Harry have a kid. Maybe he won't have so much for Gigi . . . for treats and stuff.'

She snorted again. 'He doesn't spend money on Gigi. He only spends it on Gloria.'

'Oh, but come on, he loves his daughter. And you get loads . . .'

'No I don't,' she said fiercely. 'I get money from him for maintenance but not that much. He only gives me the

114

bare minimum. It's Gloria he spends it on because he loves Gloria more than Gigi and more than he ever loved me. I'm telling you, the woman can do no wrong in his eyes, but of course a baby cries and poops and gets in the way.'

I thought she was losing it a bit now. But even so . . .

'Go on,' she said again. 'Everyone knows I'm a bit loopy. You're not. Marry him and be happy.'

'Yes,' I said. 'I will.'

I snapped the phone shut again.

'What was all that about?' demanded Deirdre, who'd been hopping from foot to foot in agitation, the mascara wand in her hand.

'Karen again,' I told her unnecessarily.

'Is that woman trying to nab him back?' asked Sarah. 'Is that it?'

'Oh, I really don't think so,' I said. 'She says she loves him but she hates Gloria more.'

Nobody said anything. We were all wondering whether I hated Gloria more than I loved Harry.

'Will I fix your make-up?' asked Deirdre.

'Of course.'

I sat on the chair beside the dressing table and let her loose on damage repair. I was marrying Harry, not his mother. I had to remember that.

When Deirdre had finished with the mascara and concealer I walked on to the balcony. I could see the guests clustered at the bower where the ceremony would take place. I felt bad that the men, in particular, were probably sweltering in their black tuxedos. Gloria would be OK, though, I told myself. Her little magenta number was light enough for the heat.

I could see her now, standing beside a figure which I

knew was Harry. As I watched she put her arm around him and hugged him.

Harry. Gloria. Gloria. Harry.

Oh shit, I thought. This isn't what it was supposed to be like. This was supposed to be the happiest day of my life.

'You ready?' asked Sarah.

I walked back into the room. The two of them were looking at me expectantly.

'No,' I said as I tugged at the zip of my dress.

'Jennifer!'

I continued pulling at the zip until it was down all the way and I was able to step out of the mass of satin and lace.

'Jen!' Sarah tried to stop me. 'What are you doing?'

'I've changed my mind,' I told her simply. 'I can't marry Harry *and* his mother. Would you mind awfully going down and telling them? I think Gloria would probably just kill me. Thanks very much.'

And then I went into the bathroom and scrubbed my face until none of the make-up remained.

Room 205 (Gala)

They arrived at the hotel before midday because the ship had docked early in the morning. They were the only passengers to leave – everyone else was staying aboard to complete the entire two-week cruise. But Hugo didn't like being at sea for more than a week, and so, for the third year in a row, they disembarked after six nights on board and took a local taxi to the hotel while their fellow passengers enjoyed their few hours ashore indulging in some tax-free shopping.

Hugo thought the narrow streets of jewellers and perfumeries, all proclaiming that they offered the best prices on the island, extremely vulgar. He had no objection to paying as little as possible for anything he bought (thrift had been drummed into him as a child by parents who were asset-rich and cash-poor), but he always refused to come into town to look at the shops with Bette and Gala, assuring them that whenever he bought them jewellery he drove a hard enough bargain, and that he preferred to give the business to people at home where he could be absolutely certain of the quality of what he was buying.

Gala often wanted to point out to her father that the only jewellery he had ever bought her was a plain gold disc with her name and date of birth engraved on it. And that had been for her twenty-first birthday, almost fifteen years earlier. Naturally he'd bought a good deal more for Bette – his wife insisted on a piece for her own birthday in July of each year. But Hugo's presents were always simple and never extravagant. They weren't even modern and simple, Gala thought, each time her mother opened a present. They were just plain and boring.

They suited Bette. Gala didn't consciously think of her mother as plain and boring, but she was a woman of simple, old-fashioned tastes. Bette disliked fashion. Gala sometimes thought that she deliberately ignored whatever was popular simply because it offended her to think that everyone was wearing the same outfit or perfume or type of jewellery. Gala understood her mother's feelings on the issue (if, indeed, they *were* Bette's feelings – it wasn't something they actually discussed) because she felt the same way too. But she did like nice jewellery even though she didn't own any.

When it came to clothes, though, she simply couldn't understand why hordes of women would want to wear the same dress or skirt or shoes as some undoubtedly tarty Z-list celebrity – or even most of the so-called A-list celebrities. Why would you want to look like a two-bit soap actress or a talentless but vacuously pretty pop star? she wondered. And yet magazine after magazine gave readers hints on how to copy the latest look of whoever the hell was flavour of the month. On board the ship she'd read one which had detailed the fashion style of the latest winner of some so-called talent competition. From what Gala could see, the style was to wear very little at all; in fact most of the coverage seemed to be on the woman's legs, courtesy of a pair of totteringly high patent-leather boots. But apparently everyone wanted to look like the Pop Princess, and sales of dominatrix boots had rocketed in the last month. The whole thing was a mystery to Gala, who bought all her clothes in either Debenham's or M&S and steered away from their new-season ranges in favour of whatever looked the most useful.

For their winter holiday in the Caribbean she'd bought five white blouses with candy-coloured stripes to go with the two pairs of Bermuda shorts (white and navy) and two knee-length skirts (taupe and blue) she'd acquired the previous year. Although she'd got some wear out of the skirts, she hadn't worn the shorts since then because the following English summer had lasted for about a week. Not enough time to start faffing around with shorts, and anyway, she always thought that English people looked ridiculous in them at home, their milk-white legs unattractive beneath the intermittent glare of the sun.

She was wearing them now, though and they were sticking to her because the fifteen-minute drive in the taxi (although calling the battered customised van a taxi was undoubtedly a violation of the Trades Descriptions Act) had been hot and airless. Hugo had muttered under his breath that the hotel had obviously ignored his suggestion of the previous year to acquire a decent air-conditioned car to collect visitors from the port and the airport.

They stood in the thankfully cool reception area of the White Sands Hotel while the receptionist (another new one, thought Gala; why don't they remain with the place, it would be so much nicer) booked them in. A second member of staff offered them cocktails while they waited but Hugo told her that he rather hoped they wouldn't be standing around the reception area long enough to be drinking cocktails, that he wanted to get to his room and change.

'Of course, Mr Brand,' the receptionist, whose name tag read 'June', said calmly. 'I'm just checking that your suite is ready because, of course, you are that tiny little bit early for us. But perhaps you'd like Royston to bring cocktails to your room later?'

'I don't know why you're all so damn keen to get us drinking cocktails,' said Hugo rudely. 'They're not even well made. And they're mostly fruit juice with only a sniff of alcohol.'

'Well, you'll find the mini-bar in your room is well stocked with alcohol,' said June.

'I don't drink alcohol,' said Hugo. 'Except wine.'

'There's a selection of wine too,' June told him brightly.

'I know exactly what's in the room, young lady,' Hugo said. 'This is my third year here and I suspect your first, so I rather think I'm more up to speed on things than you.'

'I'm so glad that you've returned to us.' June handed Hugo a coded key card and another one to Gala. 'I hope you enjoy your stay on this occasion too.'

Hugo and Gala took the keys while June clicked her fingers at the long, lanky porter who was loading their luggage on to a trolley. 'Sylvester will show you to your room.'

'I don't need Sylvester to show me to the room if I have the one I requested,' said Hugo. 'And if I haven't, I want to know why.'

'Room 205,' said June. 'As you did, indeed, request. A junior suite with a separate room for your daughter which has its own door.' Her eyes flickered over Hugo, Bette and Gala. 'I hope you enjoy your stay too, Miss Brand.'

'I'm sure I shall.' Gala nodded imperceptibly.

'Follow me,' said Sylvester.

'He's going the long way round,' muttered Hugo. 'You'd think he'd have more sense. I know which way is best. I'm the one with the gammy leg.' He thrust his walking stick in front of him.

'There may be a reason,' said Gala as she walked through the carefully tended tropical gardens a few paces behind Sylvester. 'Not that I can think of one myself at the moment, but perhaps there is one.'

'I'm not sure we shouldn't try a different hotel next time.' Bette was puffing slightly as they walked up the slight hill. 'I know that this is a five-star establishment and that there are advantages to having the rooms dotted around the hillside, but I do think they should take people's health into consideration.'

'We could have asked for one of the sea-front rooms,' Gala said. 'Of course we'd have had to get two of them so that I'd have somewhere to stay.'

'No.' Bette shuddered. 'People walking past you every day, looking in at you, making noise. No, if one has to have a room in a hotel, a private suite is best.'

Gala said nothing. Her mother was right. The sea-front rooms were too public, despite the fact that many people apparently requested them specifically. Room 205, further up the hill, was perfect for their needs. And the reason that they'd chosen White Sands in the first place was because it had the suites with the double room for Bette and Hugo and the single room for Gala. They'd come back because the room had more than met their expectations. It had everything they wanted and the additional benefit of being wonderfully secluded. Hugo liked seclusion. He'd also liked the suite's spacious lounge area and large balcony. Although he'd been pleased with it, he had nevertheless complained to the manager of the hotel, an Englishman named Charles Mallory (Hugo had been disgusted to learn that the owner was actually French), that it wasn't exactly like a junior suite in a London hotel.

'You can't expect it to be,' Gala had told him afterwards. 'This is simply a holiday hotel, no matter how much it tries to pretend that it's something else.'

'There's no reason it can't be of the highest standard,' said Hugo.

'Daddy, this is the most expensive hotel on the island,' Gala pointed out. 'The next step up is to hire the Villa. And we don't want to do that. That would be actually wasting money, which you know we're never going to do.'

Hugo smiled when she said that and ruffled her hair as he had when she was a little girl.

Sylvester opened the door of the junior suite with his master key and showed them inside. He began to give them a rundown of the amenities in the room but Hugo stopped him by shoving a dollar into his hand and telling him that he knew it all already. As Sylvester closed the door behind him Hugo looked at his watch and (as he had done the previous two years) remarked that by the time they'd finished unpacking and had a drink on the balcony (their own drink, a nice chilled white wine, and not some God-awful cocktail), the restaurant would be open for early lunch. He didn't want them to miss out on a meal. (Strictly speaking the all-inclusive package didn't start until dinner, but the hotel had always allowed them to have lunch too, given their arrival time. Hugo felt that it was the least the management could do, since he'd recommended the place to some of his friends. Of course none of them had actually visited yet, but if and when they did it would be because of him.

Which made the extra lunch an entitlement really.)

There were two restaurants at White Sands, but only the more casual Green Garden served lunch. It was an open-air restaurant, built out over the sea so that the gentle waves lapped beneath it and diners could see tropical fish scurrying through the water below. Hugo preferred the air-conditioned splendour of the Mariner's Reef restaurant, but the family usually only ate there once or twice during their stay. It was on the upper level of the hotel and reached by a steep set of steps which Hugo, thanks to his gammy leg, found difficult to negotiate. Bette found the steep steps difficult too. She was a heavy woman and she didn't like the effort involved in climbing stairs unnecessarily.

'I really don't know what I want to eat.' Gala looked at the menu. 'I rather think I overdid it on the cruise. Perhaps I need to cut back.'

'Don't be ridiculous.' Hugo looked at her over his half-moon glasses. 'To get the best value you should choose from the menu. But if you're not hungry you can try the buffet.'

Most of the lunchtime diners were clustered around the extensive buffet and telling each other that they were holding back (marginally) so that they could gorge themselves on the wonderful evening meal that the Green Garden provided.

'Maybe I'll just have the soup.' Gala sighed. 'Though I can't quite understand soup in this weather. Don't you think it's too warm for it, Daddy?'

'Hot meals are good in hot weather,' he told her. 'Help you sweat it out of you. I'm going to have the steak sandwich. What about you, Bette?'

His wife was studying the menu conscientiously. 'It's

exactly the same as last year,' she said. 'I remember the crab salad.'

'I do rather suppose there are a lot of crabs,' remarked Gala.

'Well I'm going to have the lobster tonight,' said Hugo. 'I love a good lobster and it's one thing that they manage to do well here. Even though it's an extra.' His gaze flickered towards the huge tank which contained a number of lobsters, elastic bands around their claws.

Gala winced. 'It's so difficult to choose one,' she said. 'Rather like you're executing it.'

'Don't be so damn silly,' said Hugo. 'You're probably putting it out of its misery. If it has the capacity to be miserable. Which I doubt.'

Gala nodded and traced a series of lines in the smooth white linen tablecloth with the tines of her fork. Her father was right. There was no such thing as a miserable lobster. Only miserable people.

Hugo did, indeed, have lobster for dinner and he said that it was delicious, well worth the time he'd spent peering into the tank before making his selection. Afterwards they sat in the lounge and listened to Cool Carlo and his Calypso Band which, Bette said, wasn't at all bad for the kind of thing that it was, if you followed her drift. A girl joined the band and sang a few suitably tropical songs in a sultry voice. She wasn't local but they couldn't tell whether she was American or European. Hugo remarked that she was an addition to the entertainment although one would think that the hotel would change everything rather than simply hire one new singer. Gala sipped bitter lemon. Bette and Hugo both had white wine. At ten o'clock they left the Palm Bar and walked back through the subtly lit tropical gardens to their room.

'Don't you find this easier than the cruise?' Gala asked her parents as they sat on the balcony and sipped a nightcap. 'Easier to get around? Should we simply spend more time here rather than on the ship – maybe not bother with the cruising part next year?'

'I have good sea legs.' Hugo stretched out his gammy leg (a hunting accident, although in his case the break in it had been caused by an anti-hunt saboteur who'd pulled him from his horse). 'Despite this.'

'There's only one tablet of soap in the bathroom.' Bette's remark came out of the blue. 'Gala, call them and get them to send up some more.'

Gala obediently left them on the balcony while she contacted housekeeping. 'And do please make sure that the soap is replenished daily,' she added. 'My parents like everything to be in order.'

Gala was at the restaurant at 7.25 the following morning. Rather annoyingly, she wasn't first in line. The queue was headed by an elderly woman who'd overdone it slightly on the blue rinse, followed by a dark-haired girl who had a laptop computer under her arm and a hunted expression on her face.

Bette and Hugo had asked Gala to get there early so that she could ensure that they would have their favourite table. They wanted her to make it plain to the supervisor that during their week at the White Sands Hotel this was to be their table, reserved for them. They knew that White Sands had a policy of not reserving specific tables because it said so in the information book in their room. It was up to Gala to make sure that they got what they wanted regardless of the hotel policy.

Fortunately, the supervisor in the restaurant, whose name was Marilee, remembered her from the previous year. She smiled her wide island smile, showing her gold front tooth, and asked her how she was doin'. Gala responded that she was doing very well thank you and that her parents would be joining her very shortly for breakfast and that she would appreciate it if they could be allocated the corner table beside the rail, overlooking the sea. And she slipped the supervisor a twenty-dollar bill.

Marilee had been offered more than twenty dollars in the past for the table. But not generally in the week before Christmas when most people who came to White Sands were taking advantage of the much cheaper rates for a very off-season time. So she pocketed the money deftly and told Gala that she would do what she could. The only time, she said, that the table might not be available was if Miss Sahndhi Jeffries asked for it. That was unlikely, she assured Gala, since Miss Jeffries was staying at Coco Villa which had its own kitchen and chef, but she had already requested that should she decide to eat in the Green Garden restaurant she would like that particular table.

'Who the hell is Sahndhi Jeffries?' demanded Gala.

'A singer,' Marilee informed her. Who'd won a prestigious competition in England beating lots of other hopeful singers. And who'd had a very successful tour. She was staying alone in the Villa, Marilee confided. She was exhausted.

Gala frowned. The name was vaguely familiar but she couldn't remember where she'd heard it before. And then suddenly she did remember – Sahndhi Jeffries was the woman in the magazine she'd read on the cruise ship. She couldn't believe that a hotel like White Sands would even consider bowing to the demands of trailer trash like Sahndhi Jeffries ahead of people like herself and her parents. It was a sad reflection on the way the world had changed, she thought, as she followed Marilee to the table.

Gala decided not to say anything to her parents about the fact that the winner of a popular talent show, who was now a possible superstar, was staying at the White Sands Hotel. Once superstars started appearing she knew that they would never come back. Which would be a shame, because she liked the White Sands Hotel. Until now, it had always been unostentatiously luxurious. The people staying in Coco Villa had been quiet about the fact that they could afford its staggeringly expensive rates. But if pop stars began staying there then the allure of White Sands would be diminished. Not, of course, that it was up to her anyway. She went wherever her parents went and didn't really have any say in their destinations. It was her duty to be with them wherever they elected to go. Her duty as a daughter and, of course, her job too.

Not that she really thought of it as a job. Not that they thought of it as a job either, otherwise they'd pay her properly for being with them and looking after them and making sure that her father didn't alienate the staff of the cruise ship or the hotel or wherever it was they were staying at any given time. She was their private secretary and she was also their nurse. She gave Bette her daily injections for her diabetes. She monitored Hugo's intake of painkillers for his leg. She looked after them. She had to look after them. She was their daughter and she didn't have any choice.

She didn't know whether or not she would have preferred Andrew's situation. Her brother had taken over the crumbling house, too small and too ugly to be a proper stately home but a bloody listed building all the same. Naturally he'd had to open it up to the public to help pay for its upkeep, and naturally he didn't really have enough money to do what needed to be done, but he had high hopes that one day, when Bette and Hugo were too old to care, he'd be able to sell it to some multimillionaire with more money than sense. A pop star, he'd told Gala once, and she suddenly thought once more of Sahndhi Jeffries in Coco Villa and wonder whether she'd be a possible candidate to take it off their hands. But honestly, thought Gala, how fair was life when a woman who'd won a stupid talent contest could probably afford to take the Hall off their hands and turn it into a monument to tackiness while (until recently) they hadn't even been able to heat the damn place properly?

The Brands had a history behind them; they had ancestors who'd fought for their country and had been rewarded with the now crumbling pile. People like them deserved what they now owned although, as Hugo had once said, a bit more pillaging and a little less raping by his forebears might have meant a better return.

The reason Bette and Hugo were able to cavort around the Caribbean now had nothing to do with their ownership of the pile, or their carefully hoarded money. Even though they sometimes talked about their wealth they were really talking about the house and the heirlooms that had been handed down through the family. Like every Brand before them, they didn't actually have very much hard cash. No, the money that they had now, that had been enough for them to hand over the house to Andrew and tell him to get on with it, had been the result of Hugo's buying a lottery scratch card in the village shop one day purely because Mrs Palmer was nagging him over it, then forgetting about it for a couple of weeks before finally scratching it and discovering that he'd won a quarter of a million quid.

And so he'd told Bette that since they were now definitely in a greater comfort zone as far as cash was concerned, they could spend two of the most miserable weeks of the English winter somewhere warm. It was the only time that Hugo actually agreed to spend money on what he would normally consider fripperies. The problem with her father, Gala thought as she sat at the table and waited for him to show up, was that he was a man who couldn't spend money at all. Who believed that it was his, in trust for the next generation. But who didn't really want the next generation to spend it either.

Hugo and Bette weren't interested in any of the excursions provided by the White Sands Hotel. They liked to spend their time reading the newspapers in the lounge (that day's English newspapers were downloaded from the internet and provided free of charge to clients staying in junior suites) or else reading novels on their balcony. Hugo liked Dick Francis and Ian Fleming. He'd read all of the books at least twice but, as he told Gala, by the time he'd worked his way through them he'd forgotten the first one again. Bette read romantic fiction – she was a subscriber to a variety of Mills & Boon imprints and had a selection of books sent to the house every month. Both Bette and Hugo read the papers in the morning and the books in the afternoon while Gala sat with them. She, too, read the papers in the morning and books in the afternoon (in her case historical biographies, although she did, occasionally, dip in to something a bit more light-hearted, but always with a guilty feeling that she should be improving her mind). Sometimes she wondered whether it would be nice to lie on the crescent-shaped white-sanded beach in the afternoons, but Bette and Hugo hated the beach and so there was no point in thinking about it. They usually spent an hour or two at the pool nearest their room. Most people didn't bother with that pool because it didn't have a view of the sea. So it meant peace and quiet for the Brands. Even though Gala herself did like the view of the sea, she followed them to the pool. She had to be there if they needed something, which usually they did. More suntan cream for Bette, whose skin was alabaster-white and would always be alabaster-white because (despite the factor 30+) she didn't actually sit in the sun; more ice for Hugo, who normally drank a couple of whiskies in the afternoon and liked ice with it; a copy of a different newspaper – Hugo might suddenly request the *Express* or the *Mail*, even though he really only wanted to read the *Telegraph*.

She sat there and brought them whatever they wanted because that was her job and she was their daughter and because she didn't actually have anything better to do.

On the third evening they didn't get their seat overlooking the sea. The Jeffries woman was there, looking pleased with herself (as well she might, given her table allocation), her long dark hair caught back from her face and rippling down her back. She was accompanied by a middle-aged man with a slightly florid complexion who was, nevertheless, impeccably dressed. He was doing most of the talking and she was listening intently. Eventually she began to speak, becoming more and more animated as the words tumbled from her lips. She seemed to be pleading with him about something, her dark eyes anxious. After a while the man shrugged and nodded his head and then she smiled at him, showing perfect white teeth. Gala wondered how people managed to have perfect white teeth. She'd brushed hers with a so-called whitening toothpaste for years but they still had a yellow tinge.

Hugo was furious about the table. 'Why should she be here at all?' he muttered as Marilee brought them to a table at the far corner of the restaurant. 'If she's staying in the damn Villa she's paying for her personal chef. She doesn't need to come here, taking up other people's tables.'

'Daddy, it's just one night.' Gala didn't want him getting upset. His blood pressure was high at the best of times although they never spoke about it. Hugo didn't like having high blood pressure. He said it made him sound tense and he wasn't.

The new table (the substitute table, Gala hoped; she couldn't bear the idea of the Jeffries girl taking their table for a second time) was closer to the lobster tank.

'Maybe it's a ploy,' said Hugo. 'To make me order lobster again. I don't see anyone else eating it.'

'I'm sure plenty of people have done.' Gala frowned. 'Wasn't there one with a black mark on his shell the first night? He's gone.'

'You're right.' Hugo looked happier. 'One likes to think that they catch them fresh. But they needn't think they're going to dupe me into another one tonight. No, the evening before we leave, that's when I'll succumb again.'

Gala had known that already. Hugo always had lobster on the night they arrived and the night before they left. He chose it each time as though it was a major decision, but of course it wasn't. It was as predictable as him demanding she find out why the internet version of the *Telegraph* hadn't arrived at seven in the morning so that he could have it at breakfast (the hotel's guest directory did say that papers would be delivered by eight, but that was irrelevant as far as Hugo was concerned since he got up at seven like a lot of the people there and that was when he wanted the paper); it was as predictable as him complaining that none of the white wines stocked by the hotel were really acceptable; it was as predictable as him telling her that he needed more attention to his gammy leg when she gave him his daily massage (she hated giving her father a massage but his doctor recommended it). It was as predictable as everything in her life, which was fine by her because she liked predictable.

She knew that not everyone would. She knew, because she read the papers and watched the TV (even sometimes Sky One, though Hugo couldn't bear the channel), that there were a whole heap of people who lived a different sort of life to her, where it was all about having a good time and getting hammered and having casual sex. Gala had once had casual sex but she hadn't liked it very much. It had been with the third son of an unimportant peer, a nobody really, even though he thought he was somebody; and to be really truthful about it, the sex hadn't so much been casual as inevitable. They'd met at a birthday party of a mutual friend, where Gala had been a little woozy thanks to an unaccustomed couple of glasses of wine and some insane cocktail dreamed up in honour of Roberta. And so, when Will had put his arm around her and told her that she was a gorgeous young thing, she hadn't been able to help herself smiling at him and allowing him to kiss her, and somehow she hadn't quite been able to stop his fingers sliding up the inside of her leg and beneath the silk and lace of her M&S knickers.

She'd been twenty-three years old and a virgin. He was shocked at that and so was she, as well as being embarrassed. She never knew whether she'd enjoyed it or not. She didn't know whether he had either; afterwards he'd zipped up his trousers and looked at her in astonishment and said wonderingly, 'A virgin,' as though she was the last of an endangered species. It couldn't have been that great, of course, or he would have asked to see her again. She didn't see him again – not by herself anyway, although they both ended up at a few of the same parties. And then, a few years later, she'd read about his marriage to Sammy-Jo Sharpton, whose father had made his fortune in the mobile phone industry and who'd bought a real stately home and had the money to do it up! A few years after that she'd read about the birth of their twin daughters. And a few years after that she'd read about their divorce. She'd smiled when she read about the divorce because she'd been pretty sure that Will had married Sammy-Jo for the money. She was as brainless and vacuous as any talent show winner.

There had been two other men in Gala's life. One of the relationships could probably be called a casual sex one too, though it hadn't been casual on her part; she'd always liked James McConnell and had been flattered when he'd finally asked her out (and thankful that she wasn't a virgin!), but after that first night together he hadn't called her again.

The other had been Simon Carmody, who'd actually taken her out to dinner three times before getting her into bed. And who'd taken her out another three times afterwards before telling her that he didn't think it was working.

She hadn't loved Simon but, sitting beside him in the Odeon one night, she'd wondered what it would be like to be married to him and away from her parents and living a different sort of life. That evening, as the images of the film they'd attended flashed across the screen, she'd run her own mental images instead. Of a house near Primrose Hill; of a couple of children who took after Simon (because he was rather attractive in a pale, English kind of way); of introducing herself as Mrs Gala Carmody. She should never have had those thoughts. That had been the night Simon told her that he didn't think it was working out. That had been the night he dumped her.

'Ring for more ice.' Hugo's voice was abrupt, and Gala frowned.

'Didn't they leave any this morning?' she asked.

They were back in their suite. Bette had complained of a headache and so they'd returned to the room directly after dinner, not staying to listen to the night's entertainment – Reggae Ray and his Righteous Band.

'We used ice on your mother's head,' said Hugo. Gala frowned again. She'd given Bette a couple of Panadol.

'When?'

'When you decided that you wanted to spend an hour standing on the balcony instead of helping out,' said Hugo acidly.

'An hour!' Gala looked incredulous. 'Ten minutes.'

'More than that,' said Hugo. 'Anyway, we need more ice. I want a drink.'

Gala nodded and picked up the phone.

'Room service is busy,' she said.

'How can room service be busy?' demanded Hugo.

'Maybe someone else is ordering ice. I'll ring again in a moment.'

Hugo snorted. Gala ignored him. A couple of minutes later she tried again.

'Still busy.'

'That's ridiculous.'

'Maybe there's something wrong with the phone.' She tried reception. That was busy too. 'It's the phone,' she concluded.

'Well don't just stand there,' said Hugo. 'Do something about it.'

'Like?'

'Like report it. And get ice.'

'I'll do it now,' she said.

It was warm outside. It was always warm outside because the night-time temperature only varied a couple of degrees from the day-time temperature. Gala thought it was blissful even though she knew that she was the sort of girl who should be more at home on a windswept moor than a Caribbean island. Her family's genes were country genes – huntin', shootin' and fishin' genes – which meant that though her brother Andrew was attractive enough in a beefy sort of way, she was what they called solid. Or plain. Or (sometimes) horsey. It was because her face was a little too long and her nose a little too prominent; and because her hair was strong and coarse and unruly. Which was why she kept it short nowadays. Keeping it short also minimised the grey that had become more and more obvious over the past few years.

How did that happen? she wondered as she walked into the bar. How did I become a person with grey hair? Grey hair is meant to be for older people and I'm still someone who lives at home with her parents!

The band was still playing and a lot of people were dancing. They all looked very glamorous. White Sands was big into glamour, just like the cruise ship had been. Gala wondered why people in a modern era enjoyed dressing up so much. Although, she conceded, as an elegant couple drifted past her, he dark and attractive while she was stunningly beautiful, if she looked like that woman she'd get dressed up too.

She looked around for a waiter. She could order the ice now and have it brought up to the room while she went to reception to enquire about the phone situation.

The nearest waiter was leaning against a stone pillar. Gala was glad that Hugo couldn't see him. She knew that his casual attitude would rile him. Funnily enough, it riled her too a little. She felt that since they were spending so much money on a five-star de luxe hotel, the least the staff could do was to be attentive at all times.

She walked over to him.

'I'd like ice sent to our suite,' she said. 'Two-oh-five. Right away.'

'Excuse me?' His enormous brown eyes stared at her.

'Ice. Room Two-oh-five. Now. Thank you.'

He laughed. Gala felt herself bristle with anger.

'I don't see what's so funny,' she said coolly.

'Asking me for ice is.'

'Why?'

'Because I don't work here.' He grinned at her. 'I'm surprised you even think I might. I don't have the figure of these guys.'

'Well why are you standing here then?' Gala didn't actually believe him.

'I'm standing here listening to the band and thinking that maybe things happen for the best even if you don't believe it at the time.'

Gala frowned.

'I'm with the would-be wedding party,' he said, as her face still wore a puzzled frown. 'And I don't want to really piss you off or anything, but don't you think it's an incredible kind of racist leap to decide that I must be working here just because I'm black and wearing a tuxedo?'

Gala felt a wave of embarrassment engulf her. She knew that her cheeks had flamed red. But she regarded him as evenly as she could. 'I'm terribly sorry,' she told him. 'But if we were in England and in a hotel and you were white and wearing a tuxedo I might think you were a barman there too.'

He grinned at her. 'I doubt it.'

She shrugged. 'You can believe me or not.'

'I'll believe you on one condition,' he said.

'Which is?'

'That you have a drink, of course.'

She stared at him. 'Why?'

'Why not?' This time his grin was even wider. 'I'm tired of talking to the same people. You're on your own. Join me.'

'I have to order ice for our room,' said Gala. 'I don't have time for a drink.'

'Don't have time!' He looked at her in astonishment. 'Girl, this is the Caribbean. There's always time. Plenty of it.'

She smiled at that but shook her head. 'My parents are waiting.'

'OK,' he said. 'Let's get them some ice.' He waved at one of the waiters, who came over to him. 'Hi, Tony, can you bring some ice to this lady's room?' he asked. 'Two-oh-five. And man, they want it right away.'

'Sure thing,' said the waiter.

'See?' he looked at her. 'Easy-peasy. Now you can have a drink.'

'My parents will be wondering where I am.'

'Excuse me?'

'My parents will be wondering where I am.'

'Well, it seems to me that you're an adult and it shouldn't matter to them where you are.'

'They'll be expecting me.'

He frowned. 'One drink won't hurt.'

'Why do you want to have a drink with me?' Gala looked around. The party was still in full swing and there were plenty of younger, prettier women for him to drink with.

'Do you want an honest answer?' he asked.

'Yes.'

'I see you every morning at breakfast. With your parents. And I don't see you for the rest of the day. You're not on the beach, you're not in the gym, you don't go on any of the trips . . . so I'm curious about you.'

'There's no need to have a drink with me simply to assuage your curiosity,' she told him. 'If there's anything you want to know about me I can just tell you.'

138

'But better fun, don't you think, to tell me while sipping a margharita or a pina colada?'

'I don't generally drink cocktails.'

'Bit of a waste being here in that case.'

'No,' she told him. 'There are plenty of other alcoholic drinks if that's what I want. They don't all have to be garish or garnished.'

He laughed.

'That wasn't meant to be funny,' she said.

'I know. Look, in the time we're talking about it you could have knocked back two of them. Come on, try something garish.'

She shrugged. 'Whatever.' And then she remembered. 'But I have to report the phone too. In our room. It's not working properly.'

'I'll order the drinks while you deal with the phone,' he said.

'OK.' She would just do the phone thing and walk right by him, she told herself. Stupid man.

She strolled to reception, where June was entering information on to the computer screen. She frowned when Gala told her about the phone and said that she'd get someone to check it out straight away. Gala thanked her and walked back through reception and out on to the patio area beyond the bar.

'Here you are.' He handed her the White Sands Special, a frothy creamy concoction which came with an umbrella, a maraschino cherry and a slice of pineapple.

She looked at him.

'You can't get away from me that easily,' he said. 'I was watching you.'

She shook her head.

'C'mon,' he said. 'It won't kill you. One drink. That's all.'

'I really don't drink this sort of thing,' she said as her mouth found the straw.

'But it's nice, isn't it?'

She sipped it cautiously. 'It's OK.'

'Alexander will be devastated.'

'Alexander?'

'The head barman. He created it.'

'Better not disappoint him then.' She slurped the drink and then flushed with embarrassment at the noise.

He nodded towards a table just inside the bar which was being vacated by a couple of men.

'Shall we?'

'Shall we what?'

'Sit down, of course.'

'Well, all right. Until I finish this drink.'

They settled into the huge wicker chairs with their brightly coloured tropical print pattern. A waitress cleaned the glass top of the table and asked if she could get them anything. He raised his eyebrow questioningly at Gala, who shook her head emphatically.

'Not for the lady,' he said. 'But I'll have a vodka martini.'

This time it was Gala who raised an eyebrow. 'Shaken or stirred?'

He smiled. 'I don't know that it makes much difference. Are you a James Bond fan?'

'Not me,' she said. 'My father is, though. I was named after a character in a Bond book.'

'Really?' His eyes widened. 'Not . . . not . . . Pussy Galore?'

Gala sighed. 'He might be a fool, but he's not that much of a fool. My name is Gala.'

'And I guess everyone asks you if it's Pussy Galore?'

'Only if the topic gets there,' she said shortly.

'Well my name's Winston,' he said. 'Which character?'

'Gala Brand. *Moonraker*.'

He looked puzzled. 'I don't remember her,' he said. 'Wasn't *Moonraker* the one with Jaws and Lois Chiles?'

'In the movie,' said Gala. 'The book was different. Naturally. And much, much better. *Moonraker* was a stupid movie. In the book, Bond worked with a detective called Gala Brand. Our family name is Brand, so it was kind of inevitable really.'

'And what was she like, this Gala Brand?'

'She was engaged to a Detective Inspector Vivian,' said Gala calmly. 'So even though James saw her naked she never truly succumbed to his somewhat obvious and slightly pathetic charms.'

'I never think of him as pathetic,' said Winston.

'Probably not,' agreed Gala. 'Men like to think that blokes with cars, guns and women have it all.'

'Hey – they do!' He laughed.

She finished her cocktail. 'Well, thank you for the drink,' she said. 'I'd better be going.'

'Oh, come on, Gala Brand,' he said. 'I'm enjoying my chat with you.'

'I don't know why.'

'Because you're different,' he said. 'Interesting. I want to know why I don't see you in the day-time and why you're here with your parents and what you do for a living and all sorts of stuff.'

'Why?'

'Innate curiosity,' he said.

'Not because you've fallen madly in love with me and can't live without me?'

'Until two minutes ago I didn't even know your name. So not exactly,' he said. 'But who knows, Gala Brand, who knows.'

She stood up. 'I'm sorry. They'll be waiting for me. I have to get back.'

'But . . .' He was talking to thin air. Gala had left.

She walked along the narrow footpath which traced its way through the lush gardens. She was a little light-headed from the cocktail and more than a little confused by her encounter with Winston. She'd liked him. Sort of. He seemed friendly and kind and . . . and not what she'd expected. The thought seared through her brain and she felt herself flush again. Not what she'd expected from someone of a different colour. It was so politically incorrect to think like this that she felt incredibly guilty, but how the hell could she help it? She'd never had a conversation with a black guy before. Why would she? There weren't any in her part of England. The multicultural country that people talked about hadn't actually reached her. Her only experience of people who weren't born and bred within a ten-mile radius of her home was through the TV.

I'm pathetic, she thought, as she began to climb the steps to Room 205. I know nothing. I lead a boring life with my boring parents. I'm thirty-six years old and I'm still a fucking child! She blushed again at the swear word. Hugo hated swearing.

She let herself in to the suite. Hugo and Bette were watching the TV.

'Where were you?' demanded Hugo.

'I had a drink at the bar after I reported the phone,' she said.

'Oh, really?'

'Yes, really,' she replied. 'And now I'm going to bed.'

Hugo and Bette exchanged puzzled glances. Gala went into the bathroom, squeezed a line of toothpaste on to her brush and began to clean her teeth.

When she'd finished, she looked at herself in the mirror. Two grey eyes stared unwaveringly at her from a square face with a pronounced jawline. Her dark hair was held back by a couple of nondescript clips. Her skin was slightly dull, with a smattering of fudge-coloured freckles. A pair of plain gold stud earrings gleamed softly in her ears. Her lips were thin.

Why am I here? she wondered. What am I doing on a goddamn island in the middle of nowhere with two people who don't give a curse about me?

She bit the inside of her lip at the thought. It wasn't true, of course. They did care about her. But they cared about her in the same kind of way as they cared about Assam, their black labrador. They didn't care about her in the same way as they cared about Andrew. The son and heir. It was practically feudal when you thought about it, she often muttered to herself, but Hugo and Bette really did believe that there was a difference between being the firstborn son (the only son) and being the hopeless daughter. She sometimes wondered if Prince Harry felt the same way as she did. Everyone told you that you were loved and wanted and that you were important. But in the end you were born second and so you weren't that important at all. And at least Harry was a bloke. She hated being a girl. She really did. In Hugo and Bette's world, being female was being irrelevant. It wasn't that they hadn't looked after her – they'd sent her to school (and how she'd hated it); they'd got her summer jobs in a friend's riding school (she'd hated that too, she was bloody allergic to horses); they'd paid for her to do the cordon bleu cooking course in Paris . . . and then she'd had to come home because Bette had taken one of her turns and they needed someone to look after her.

And from their point of view, why wouldn't that some-one be Gala? After all, it wasn't as though she had a burgeon-ing career as a chef. It wasn't as though there was anything important going on in her life. It wasn't as though – even in Paris – she'd met someone who meant something. Maybe if Paris had worked out, everything else would have been completely different. But she'd felt like a fish out of water there and hadn't managed to find the rhythm of the city in the two short months that she'd rented a chic studio apartment in Neuilly-sur-Seine and tried to make herself understood in her appalling schoolgirl French. She'd been glad to come home really, even though she'd been equally disgusted at herself for agreeing to return. She hadn't stuck it out. She never really stuck at anything on her own.

So now she was a thirty-six-year-old spinster who lived with her parents. She wasn't a thirty-six-year-old single woman. That would be different. Bridget Jones-type women had options. They might be looking for men but they also had lives of their own. She didn't. And it was all her own fault for being weak and hopeless.

The thing was, she couldn't leave Hugo and Bette now. They depended on her. She couldn't really blame them for her life.

'Gala! What are you doing in there!'

It was Bette's voice. Gala heaved a sigh.

'Getting ready for bed. I'm tired.'

'Is everything all right?'

They care about me, she told herself sternly. Bette wouldn't have asked that question if they didn't care.

'Everything's fine,' she said. 'I'm just sleepy, that's all.'

She heard them go to bed an hour later. When the suite was completely silent she got up and walked out to the balcony. She looked over the rooftops of the rooms in a less elevated position across to the velvet blackness of the sea.

She wished that she didn't feel so unsettled. After all, her life was pretty good. She didn't have to worry about anything. Andrew was responsible for the house, and despite the lack of long-term funds to keep it going he was doing OK with it. That was because, as well as the day-trippers, he'd managed to get permission from the horrible National Trust to set up conference facilities in part of the house and was now getting enough bookings to cover the costs of the bank loan. Andrew wasn't stupid. He actually deserved to be in charge of the pile. She would have been hopeless with it in the same way as Hugo had been hopeless because she wasn't good with money. She wasn't good with anything!

She leaned over the balcony. She couldn't hear any sounds coming from the bar. It was probably closed up for the night – it had surprised her the first time they came to the island that, at the White Sands Hotel at any rate, people got up incredibly early and went to bed equally early. So the band had probably finished and the wedding party were probably back in their rooms, emptying their mini-bars (free to everyone except those in standard accommodation). Winston and his friends were undoubtedly laughing and talking and being ordinary people having a good time. Which she was so singularly unable to do.

He was wrong to be curious about her. To ask questions about her. To take an interest in her. There was nothing to take an interest in. Her life wasn't interesting. There was nothing she could say to make it sound anything other than impossibly dreary. But then, she thought wryly, how many people's lives really were all that exciting? Would hers have been any more dramatic if she'd finished the cordon bleu course and stayed in Paris? Wouldn't she have been just as boring there? And wasn't it the same for everyone really? They all wanted to sound interesting, pretend they were interesting, but most people lived dull and boring lives. She knew that. It was because they led dull and boring lives that they devoured celebrity magazines, that they went on inane reality shows like Pop Whatever, that they wanted to be other people. But there was no point in wanting to be someone else, wanting to do something else. Life didn't let you.

She went back into the lounge area and opened the mini-bar. There was still plenty of alcohol on the shelves. It was a waste, she thought, for the entire family to stay at White Sands on an all-inclusive basis. They didn't eat enough or drink enough to make it worthwhile no matter how hard they tried.

She took a miniature bottle of gin from the fridge and poured it into a glass. Then she took a bottle of lemon and decanted it on top of the gin. Might as well get some value out of it, she thought. Might as well try to make spending the money worthwhile.

She drank it quickly and poured herself another. She was feeling slightly fuzzy, slightly . . . chilled, she supposed. Maybe this sense of languor, of detachment, was what they meant by chilling out. If so, she approved of it. The things that normally bothered her – Bette's real and imagined illnesses, Hugo's demanding irascibility, their belief that she was available every hour of every day to do what they wanted – all of that had somehow receded a little as she stretched out on the cushioned balcony chair.

She arched her foot and looked at her toes. Years and years ago, when she'd still been a teenager and before she realised that she'd be hopeless at everything, she'd dreamed of being a dancer. But like so many aspiring dancers, she'd grown too tall. And they'd told her that the dancing didn't matter, that nothing really mattered, because one day she'd get married and someone else would look after her and so everything else was incidental. Of course when it became obvious that nobody was going to marry her and that she wasn't going to need those cordon bleu cooking skills; when they realised that they needed someone to look after them and she was available . . . suddenly she was their nurse and their secretary and how, she asked herself viciously, how did it happen that I've spent the last twenty-odd years of my life stuck with my parents when I'd planned it all so differently? How did I let that happen? There were plenty of other options, weren't there? If I'd only bothered to take them.

The sense of fuzziness increased with the next measure of gin. The sound of her father's gentle snoring wafted out on to the balcony. It wasn't, of course, that they weren't kind to her. After all, how many other women got to travel like she did? How many other women had as easy a life?

Because it was easy, when she thought about it. Looking after Bette and Hugo was a doddle. All you needed was a thick skin so that you didn't take Hugo's insults personally and so that Bette's sudden mood swings didn't influence your own.

The walls of the suite seemed to close around her as she stood in front of the fridge again and wondered what would be a good substitute for gin. She couldn't think. She was finding it hard to even form basic thoughts. She needed to be outside. But not on the balcony. She unlocked the door to the suite and walked out into the hotel gardens once more. She followed the path down to the crescent-shaped beach. In the full moonlight the sand appeared even more silvery than under the noonday sun. It had been neatly raked so that the undulations of the day no longer existed. Three stacks of sunbeds were placed tidily beside the rocks at the far end of the beach. The wooden hut, from which a local woman sold T-shirts, shorts and sundresses during the day, was locked.

Gala closed one eye and tried to imagine what it would be like to spend a day on the beach when the hut was open and the loungers were occupied. Probably awful, she thought. Bodies lying out under the sun, perspiring gently as they roasted themselves. Not for me. Definitely not.

She walked across the sand and then up the set of carved steps, through the open-air, but now deserted, beach bar and back into the hotel area itself. As she'd suspected, everyone had gone to bed. She squinted at her watch. It was past two in the morning. They were all in bed getting a good night's sleep so that they could converge like locusts at the restaurant at 7.30 in the morning. She was the only person on the wide terracotta terrace that led from the hotel to the beach. She could sit in any of the chairs, upholstered with tropical print like those in the bar. Actually, she could sit in any of the chairs in the bar. She could sit where she liked, do what she liked.

She walked from the open-plan area through the Palm Bar and then to the Green Garden restaurant. The entire White Sands Hotel was open-plan and open to the elements. But, thought Gala, why would it be otherwise when the weather was always so damn calm? Why should they lock anything away?

It was good not to lock things away. It was good to be free. Like she was now. She giggled and then hiccoughed. Then she stretched out on the wicker sofa alongside the wall of the restaurant. She was free to do what she wanted when she wanted. She was free to wander through the restaurant at half-two in the morning and no one could stop her.

She blinked a couple of times. Half-two in the morning! She should be in bed. She'd never wake up at 6.30, which was the hour she had to wake up to make sure that Bette and Hugo were ready for the day.

Fuck them, she thought, as she gazed dizzily at the ceiling and tried to figure out whether the fan was rotating or not. Fuck them. She shivered at the use of the forbidden expression. Fuck you too, she thought. Fuck you, Gala Brand, for being so feeble as to stay with them for so long.

She sat up suddenly. She wasn't feeble. She really wasn't. She was just – she was dutiful was what it was. Good and dutiful and stuck with them for ever.

She got up from the wicker sofa and walked unsteadily

through the restaurant. It was eerily quiet. The only sound was the muted gurgling of the lobster tank. She walked up to it and pressed her nose again the glass. The lobsters did nothing, their antennae moving slightly with the bubbling of the water. They seemed bored. Resigned. Lobster-like. Waiting to be eaten. One of them would probably be Hugo's last-night dinner, thought Gala. Which one? The one in the corner? The one near the bank of shells? The one nearest the oxygen outlet? Did they know? she wondered. Had they any idea that her father would choose one of them for instant death? That he'd eat it and tell them how good it was, just as he'd done on the first night? Gala didn't eat lobsters herself. She could never bear to choose one. To say that it was the one that should be sacrificed for her dinner.

Why should any of them have to be sacrificed? she wondered. They had as much right to be out there as anyone else. Why should a lobster die just because Hugo was hungry?

She looked at the tank again. A death trap, that was what it was. Where lobsters had their claws restrained by elastic bands, where their lives were a complete misery, where they pretended that they didn't care that they were simply existing and not really living, waiting for their inevitable fate.

Oh come on, Gala Brand, she told herself. They're lobsters. They're supposed to be eaten. The image of Hugo, his napkin tucked under his chin, a streak of butter on his lips, flashed into her mind. Hugo telling her how tasty they were as he discarded the shell. And how the added expense was almost worth it.

If he hadn't won money on the scratch card he wouldn't

be eating the lobsters. He wouldn't be here at all. Life was just a series of chance events, wasn't it? And these poor lobsters had been unlucky enough to get caught. Now they couldn't do anything about their fate. It wasn't chance any more. It was inevitable.

Only it didn't have to be, did it? She could change all that. Give the lobsters another life. It'd be a kind thing to do. A nice thing to do. Change the outcome.

She hiccoughed again and looked around her. There was a large pot at the end of the buffet counter. She took off the lid and peered inside. Empty. Perfect.

She brought the pot to the tank and put it on the floor. Then she took the scoop which the waiters used to grab the chosen lobsters and began to fish them out of the tank one by one. It wasn't as easy as she'd expected and she seemed to be splashing a lot of water around the place. And the lobsters, when she dropped them into the pot, made a dreadful clanging sound. She wasn't sure what to do about the elastic around their claws. They needed their claws, didn't they? She vaguely remembered Hugo saying that their claws were bound so that they wouldn't attack each other. And if she tried to take the elastic off right now maybe they'd attack her.

Attack of the Mutant Lobsters! The thought made her giggle. She dropped the last lobster into the pot. Regardless of the possibility of an all-out lobster fight, they needed their claws. There had to be a way to get the elastic off easily. And there was, of course. She realised it after a couple of minutes of watching them scrabbling around in the pot. She shook her head at her own stupidity. There was a whole tray of knives at the other end of the buffet. She could cut the elastic off. But she'd wait until she was near the sea so that they didn't start fighting in the pot. She hoped that they could survive without being in the water for a while longer. She'd no idea really. She didn't know anything about lobsters. Other than the fact that they should be free.

She took a knife and then picked up the pot. It was heavier than she'd expected and she staggered under its weight, slipping in the puddle of water and knocking into the table nearest her. The sound reverberated around the deserted dining room. She caught her breath and waited anxiously for someone to come and investigate. She really didn't want to have to explain to the manager that she'd decided to free the lobsters. She wasn't sure that he'd understand.

But nobody came. She released the breath she'd been holding for what seemed like hours and then walked as quietly as she could towards the beach.

'Ssh,' she whispered to the lobsters as they scratched against the metal pot. 'This is a rescue mission. You've got to keep quiet.'

She was halfway down the steps to the beach when a voice asked her what the hell she was doing. The words, coming out of the inky darkness, scared her so much that she dropped the pot and it bounced down the rest of the steps, scattering lobsters as it went.

'Oh hell!' she cried. 'The lobsters!'

She stared at them as they lay motionless in the sand. One, which had landed right way up, suddenly started to move and she squealed in delight.

'Run, run!' she cried wildly. 'You can do it! It's not far.' And then she remembered that its claws were still bound and she called to it to wait.

'What on earth are you doing?'

This time she turned in the direction of the voice. Winston was standing behind her, his brown eyes staring at her in astonishment.

'I'm freeing them,' she said.

'You're killing them.'

'If they die, at least they'll die in the open air.' Gala hurried down the steps and grabbed the motionless lobsters. 'They're not dead. They just couldn't turn right way up. I'm bringing them back to the sea.'

'You're crazy.'

'No I'm not.' She picked up the nearest lobster and ran towards the rock pools with it, cutting the elastic holding its claws together with the knife. She didn't wait to see whether it moved or not but raced back to the others, piling them into the pot again.

'Gala, stop it,' said Winston. 'They'll die for sure.'

'How do you know?' she demanded. 'And better they end up dead in the sea than in my fat father's belly!'

She went back to the rock pool. The first lobster had gone. She beamed with joy and turned to Winston. 'You see. He's free.' She took another lobster and cut its elastic, placing it among the rocks. The waves broke gently over it and suddenly it was gone too.

'I can't help thinking that the hotel won't exactly see it like that,' said Winston. 'I'm quite sure that they never thought they'd have to have security on the lobster tank.'

'I don't care what they think,' said Gala defiantly. She cut the elastic from the rest of the lobsters. 'And what on earth are you doing wandering around the dining room in the middle of the night terrorising people?'

'I couldn't sleep,' said Winston. 'I'm a night person, always have been. After the whole palaver today I wanted some time to myself and no pretending that everything was fine.'

'What palaver?' asked Gala. 'What pretending?'

Winston looked at her in amazement. 'You didn't hear. I thought everyone . . .'

A shriek from the hotel interrupted him. Gala bit her lip.

'I'm surprised someone didn't hear your free-the-lobsters escapade before now,' said Winston. 'There's usually somebody on reception all night and sound carries, you know.' He shrugged. 'Maybe they simply thought it was late-night revellers.'

'Well so far I've got away with it,' said Gala. 'And the lobsters have too.'

'I didn't really peg you for a loony animal rights person.'

'I'm not,' said Gala. 'Of course I'm not. I eat meat, for heaven's sake, and I've shot pheasant. But I couldn't bear looking at the lobsters. I never can. They're like – well, I guess they're dead men walking, aren't they? And I don't know whether it's worse for them to be chosen as a meal or not.' Suddenly she started to cry. 'I wanted to give them a shot at freedom. A second chance.'

Winston looked at her gently. 'I'm sure they're grateful,' he said.

She peered at him through her tears. 'Are you being sarcastic?'

'No,' he told her. 'Absolutely not.'

She sniffed and then looked doubtfully at the empty pot. 'I suppose I'd better bring this back and face the music.' She bit her lip. 'My parents will be furious. I'm sure that'll be the end of our visits here . . . and Daddy will hate to think that I've made a spectacle of myself. And him.'

He nodded. 'I'll bring the pot back,' he said.

'No.' She looked at him anxiously. 'They'll think you were responsible.'

'So what?'

'It's not right . . .'

'Go to bed,' he said. 'I hate to think that your wonderful gesture would end up with you having to explain yourself.'

'It's not a wonderful gesture,' she said. She buried her face in her hands for a moment before looking up at him, her eyes bright. 'It was stupid and crazy and so not like me.'

'Actually, I think it's wonderful that you could suddenly decide to do something stupid and crazy and so not like you,' said Winston.

She hiccoughed. 'Only because I met you and you made me drunk and got me thinking silly thoughts.'

'What silly thoughts?'

'It doesn't really matter what they were,' she said. 'But they ended up with me believing that freeing the lobsters was a good idea. Oh God . . .' This time she ran her fingers through her hair. 'It's not me doing this. It's really not.'

'No,' he said. 'If anyone asks, it was me. Now go back to bed, Gala Brand, Bond Girl extraordinaire.'

Gala looked at him ruefully. 'The Gala Brand character was strong and determined. I'm not at all. She faced death with courage. I'm too scared to even admit that I emptied the lobster tank.'

'But *you* know that you did,' said Winston. '*You* know that you have the capacity to be a bit crazy. It's a good thing to know.'

'Maybe.' She sighed. 'Right now I just think it's plain silly.'

'Go back to bed,' he said again. 'Don't worry.'

'Thank you.' She smiled and then kissed him on the cheek. 'Thank you very much.'

She walked back up the twisting path to Room 205. She unlocked the door and let herself into the suite. Her parents were sleeping; the familiar sound of Hugo's snoring still wafted out from the bedroom. She let herself into her own room and closed the door behind her. She switched on the light and looked at herself in the mirror.

She was the same Gala Brand who'd gone downstairs almost an hour earlier. She had the same dark hair with the grey threads, the same grey eyes, the same over-long face. The face that looked older than she wanted it to be. But she felt different. She'd done something ridiculous and stupid and crazy in that hour. Freeing the lobsters. What in God's name had got into her? What sort of insanity had taken over?

But they were free. She'd done it. And what other un-expected things could she do? Just because she was with Hugo and Bette didn't mean she had to be like them, think like them. She was Gala Brand. Fearless. Sort of. She hoped Winston had managed to placate the hotel staff. It couldn't be right for him to take the rap for her moment of madness. Though he was really sweet to deal with it for her. She couldn't have coped, she knew that. She wanted to live with the excitement of what she'd done for a little longer rather than have to go into long and tedious explanations to an irate manager. She yawned widely. She'd thank Winston properly in the morning. But right now she was, quite suddenly, exhausted.

She fell into bed and closed her eyes. Her sleep was deep and dreamless. And she only woke the following morning when Bette shook her by the shoulder and told her that she'd overslept and so had they and that they were going to be late for breakfast and maybe not get their special table.

At which she shrugged and told her mother to chill out, that it didn't matter what table they got, the food was all the same. And that she'd get up in a minute. Or maybe two. As soon as she was ready.

Room 608 (Isobel)

Everyone was talking about the wedding incident. The fact that the girl chickened out at the last minute and that all the planning – the gorgeous dress, the bower of palms and brightly coloured tropical flowers, the Caribbean band, the photos on the fine white sand – all of it had come to nothing because none of it was going to take place now. It was the hot topic of conversation around the hotel and I wasn't one bit surprised. Everyone was speaking in hushed tones and saying how sorry they felt for the groom, who'd waited patiently for nearly an hour in the gazebo at the edge of the turquoise water for his bride to show up before realising that the wedding wasn't going to take place. Sympathy was very definitely on his side and I understood that, of course I did. He'd been humiliated in front of loads of people. As for her – well, everyone agreed better now than later, but there was a definite feeling that she could at least have gone ahead with it given the amount of planning that had gone on and just have it annulled afterwards.

Despite the wedding fiasco most of the guests had made the best of it. At first they'd disappeared from the bar and foyer where wedding guests normally gathered, but later that evening a group of them had arrived down to dinner and had partied afterwards to the sounds of the calypso band. The reluctant bride had apparently headed off to a different hotel with some of her closest friends, so I suppose the remaining guests felt as though they might as well get what they could out of the evening, safe in the knowledge that she wouldn't reappear looking pale and wan and devastated.

I felt sorry for her, though, no matter why she'd done it. I couldn't help it. I knew exactly how she was feeling because I'd felt that way myself.

People really don't know how to treat you when you've abandoned your fiancé with minutes to go before tying the knot. They're a little bit scared of you, tread warily around you, talking about something completely different but wanting only to ask you why on earth you did it. Maybe they feel that the kind of girl who would leave a bloke sweltering in his tux on a tropical island in front of a gaggle of interested spectators, or the kind of girl who'd leave a bloke standing at the altar in front of a packed church while fleeing down the aisle before leaping into the waiting Merc, is the kind of person who'd do anything. And they're afraid that you might do anything in front of them. That's my theory anyway. That's the reason why I didn't think that girl's life would ever be the same again. That's the reason mine wasn't either, after I dumped Tim at the altar.

I hadn't intended to dump him, of course. Right up to the moment where the priest asked 'Do you Isobel take Tim' I'd fully intended to say yes, even though I'd spent the night before with my mind in a whirl about my whole life up to that point. I wanted to be sure that I was marrying Tim for the right reasons, because I loved him, and not simply because I'd finally caught him again after he'd chickened out of our wedding the first time. And after all of my agonising I really was sure. Until the priest asked the question and then, all over again, I wasn't. You'll think that this makes me a particularly flaky person but I'm not really. I never was. I'm the most ordinary person in the world. I'm the girl who just dreamed of getting married, having a breathtaking wedding, and living happily ever after. Naturally I've changed a bit. But I don't think there was anything so terribly wrong about the dream! Don't we all want to live happily ever after? Don't we all want one day to be the most important day of our lives?

That was the nub of the problem as far as Tim was concerned. He called it off that first time (with only two weeks to go, so let's face it, he humiliated me first) because he thought I saw the wedding as being more important than him. And he had a point. I was wedding-obsessed. Menus, flowers, colour schemes, music, scattered rose petals on the tables . . . there was nothing too trivial as far as I was concerned to need my undivided attention. So every time I met Tim I talked weddings until he felt that he'd become a bit player in the biggest day of our lives.

It's funny how things turn out, isn't it? If I hadn't been so manic about the whole wedding thing in the first place then maybe Tim and I would've got married on the day that we'd chosen and none of the rest would've ever happened. And now I'd be Isobel Malone, married with a couple of kids and happy as a sandfly just like I'd always expected. People wouldn't think of me as flaky. Nor would they wonder if my whole agreeing to the second attempt at a wedding wasn't just a pretext so that I could dump Tim publicly in a much worse way than he ever dumped me.

I worried about that for ages. I worried about what people thought. I worried about what they were saying. I worried that I'd forever be defined as Isobel, the girl who'd run out of her wedding. But, you know what, even though I worried about it, I didn't really care. Because in the time between the first wedding and the second, in the time when I'd missed Tim dreadfully and felt unwanted and unloved; in the time when I'd also gone to Spain and found a new job (and a few short-term lovers to make me feel wanted), I'd managed to add a new dimension to Isobel. I'd got an interesting job and made new friends and carved out a life that didn't revolve around getting married and having kids and feeling that if I didn't do all that there was something wrong with me. So although I worried about these things I also knew that they didn't really matter in the whole fabric-of-life stuff and the most important thing was that I hadn't married Tim for the wrong reason and that I'd actually realised that in time.

But abandoning him like that did define me in people's eyes. And that wasn't something that I could deal with easily.

I'd dealt with Tim's original dumping of me by running away because I just couldn't cope with being in Ireland any more (and because most of the people I knew, my ex-boss included, couldn't cope with me either). But my new job in Madrid, with a corporate training company, had been wonderful. The people were great and my boss, Gabriella, was one of the most supportive people I know. It was the first time I'd ever truly enjoyed going to work for the work itself instead of for the gossip and meeting people and complaining and waiting for the weekend! And it was the first company in which I'd ever been promoted and given real responsibility. I'd thrived there and sometimes I think that it was because of the person I'd become then that I'd had the nerve to walk out on my wedding later.

When I'd come home from Spain to get married to Tim I'd been much more upbeat about the sort of job I could get back in Ireland and my confidence wasn't misplaced. I managed to land a position as the administrator of a private college, less frantic in some ways than with the Spanish company, but equally busy. I started there a week after the walking-out-on-the-wedding débâcle.

The thing is, a lot of other people were more upset by the wedding thing than me. My mother (poor Mum!), who'd gone through the whole trauma the first time, was absolutely gutted the second. Tim's mother was, understandably, furious with me and vented her spleen on Mum. The two of them had never really hit it off together, and as far as Denise Malone was concerned, I was nothing but a selfish cow who'd made a fool of her darling son. Apparently the dingdong battle between the two of them took place in the car park outside the church – a kind of flowery pastels-at-dawn type of confrontation. The entire congregation had – after their moment of stunned silence – rushed out after me but of course I'd nabbed the Merc and was instructing the driver to put his foot down and get me the hell out of there. So Mum and Denise had their set-to in the wake of the departing car while Dad and Mr Malone tried to keep the peace even though Mr Malone was fuming too. Meantime Tim stood there beside his best man and muttered 'bitch, bitch' over and over again. My sister Alison, who'd never really got on with him, told me afterwards that she'd barely been able to contain her glee. It was, she informed me, the very best wedding she'd ever been at.

After my mother and Denise were prised apart, Mum (with remarkable if belated sang-froid) invited anyone who wanted to come back to the hotel for the meal. After all, she told them (her voice breaking at that point), it was all paid for and there wasn't much point in letting it go to waste.

A surprising number of people, mainly from my side of the family – we're all good trenchermen when it comes to our food – headed off to the hotel, where the staff took my non-appearance in their professional stride, and it seems that a really good time was had by all. Thing is, most of my family thought that my marrying Tim was a mistake. So they were happy to celebrate my great escape even if none of them actually approved of the way I'd done things.

Oh, look, I don't approve of it myself. It was a rotten thing to do. But it would have been more rotten to have married him for all the wrong reasons and to have the whole thing unravel messily a few months later in hot tears and stinging recriminations. I did the right thing. I just should have done it earlier.

There are, of course, drawbacks to running away in a long white dress and veil. I lost the veil on Howth Hill when I let the breeze catch it and carry it out to sea, but there wasn't much I could do about the dress. When I got back to the car the chauffeur looked at me enquiringly and asked where I wanted to go next.

Home was the obvious answer, and so he dropped me back to our house in Sutton where I then realised that nobody was there and that you don't bring your house keys to your wedding. So I went around the back and sat like an idiot in my long white dress in the garden (where only a few hours earlier Dad had taken photos of me in all my finery) while I waited for someone to turn up.

Alison and Peter eventually showed. Alison hugged me and said that she'd been trying my mobile but, of course, you don't bring your mobile to your wedding either. At first they'd thought I would come to the hotel (although she had wondered whether I might make some kind of extravagant gesture like rush to the airport and go back to Spain), and then they decided that I'd probably prefer to be at home, so they'd volunteered to come looking for me. I informed her tartly that, along with not bringing your mobile phone, you also don't bring money or your passport to your wedding and so I couldn't have run away to Spain again. She laughed at me and then rang the hotel to let Mum know that I hadn't thrown myself off Butt Bridge or anything equally dramatic and informed me that (after the initial fracas) everyone was being remarkably calm about it all.

And then she let me into the house, where I took off my lovely (second) wedding dress and changed into a pair of jeans and a T-shirt.

'You are such a fool, Issy,' said Alison kindly. 'But you did a brave thing. Really.'

For the next few weeks that was pretty much what everyone said.

I got used to living with the tag of being the girl who'd run out of her wedding and with the whole flaky thing, and because my job at the college was going quite well, I was able to rise above it. Sort of. But I didn't really settle back in Dublin. I'd come back because of Tim. Now, because of Tim, I didn't really want to stay. All the same, I couldn't run away again. There's a time for running and a time for staying put, and besides, where could I run to this time?

The answer came about six months later. From Gabriella. She'd been at the non-wedding, along with some of my ex-colleagues from the Spanish training company. She hadn't been crazy about the wedding to Tim either, although that was partly because she knew I'd been seeing a guy in Spain while I was there and she didn't think I was properly over him. Gabriella believed that Nico and I had a real thing going. A part of me had thought that too, but when Tim and I got together again I decided that Nico and I were just a passing whim. (Well, passing whim isn't fair. Nico meant a lot to me. But I had no future with him. *Isabella querida*. That's what he used to say. As though he meant it. But he didn't. Not really.) Anyway, Gabriella called me up one day and asked how I was doing, listened to me wittering on about how great my life was, and then offered me a job. As always with Gabriella, she pretty much got to the point straight away. Her company, the one I'd worked for, was based in Madrid but they'd bought another smaller training firm, in Alicante. They were looking for someone to head it up. She'd thought of me.

'Oh, but Gabriella,' I protested, my heart beating faster at the thought of going back to Spain even if it was miles away from all my friends there, 'I have a job here. And I'm sure that there are plenty of people there already who would do a good job for you. Magdalena, perhaps?'

'Isobel, why is it that whenever I offer you a job you always suggest someone else?' There was a hint of amusement in her voice. She was remembering the time she'd offered me the promotion, when I'd been pleased and flattered but secretly terrified and had suggested that almost anyone else in the firm would be better at it than me. 'You are doing well in your current position, yes? It is very senior. Very responsible. I thought you might be interested in this one. I know you liked living here. But if you have set up a new life in Ireland, that is perfectly fine.'

A new life in Ireland. Well, yes, to a point. But I was still living at home, hadn't quite managed to get myself an apartment of my own yet and hadn't quite managed to get myself a new social life either. My best friend, Julie, was in the States with her husband, Andy. Alison and Peter were inseparable. There weren't many social opportunities in the new job. But in lots of ways that was what I wanted. To be busy. To keep my heart intact. To not get involved with people any more. To stay single!

'Isobel?' Gabriella's voice broke into my thoughts. 'It is up to you. But I would really like to have you here. I want someone I can depend on.'

I nearly laughed out loud at that. Of all the things that I was, I really didn't think dependable was going to be that high up on people's lists.

'Let me think about it,' I said.

'Two weeks,' she told me. 'Then I must advertise for someone else.'

I didn't need two weeks, of course. I never would have needed two weeks. I'd loved my life in Madrid even if it had been an escape and a reinvention. Maybe I could have a good life in Alicante too. I didn't know the city but, I reckoned, I'd gone somewhere before where I didn't know anyone and I'd made lots of friends and it had been good for me. So why not do it again?

My mother looked at me despairingly. My father shrugged his shoulders. Alison told me to go for it. Ian, my brother, muttered that maybe this time he'd get the chance to take

Sheila O'Flanagan

a Spanish holiday with somewhere decent to crash out, and wasn't Alicante on the coast, which would be excellent for a bit of R&R? Julie sent me an e-mail telling me that it would be good to live in a different country again for a while and asking me had I ever heard from Nico and what was the likelihood of bumping into him? I responded that I hadn't and that Madrid was at least four hundred kilometres away from Alicante, so no, bumping into people from my life there wasn't going to happen.

In the end it wasn't really a struggle at all. I took the job and I went to Alicante.

Gabriella had set me up in an apartment in a tall but ugly block in the city which had the compensating factor of having a huge balcony and a view over the marina. The office, a mere five-minute walk away, was in a truly beautiful renovated building with high ceilings, marbled floors and elaborate wrought-iron Juliet balconies outside the floor-to-ceiling windows. It was the most elegant place I'd ever worked in my life.

The job was great. I recruited new people, set up course timetables, scoured for clients and generally worked my butt off. But I loved it. My social life revolved around my work because there was a vast amount of corporate entertaining to do. I did, occasionally, meet people for dinner or for drinks but it never amounted to much. In many ways I was at my most content on my own, in the late evenings, walking along the psychedelically tiled Explanada de España, listening to the animated chatter of the people around me as they strolled arm in arm (or, in the case of some of the older townspeople, sat on the red and blue wooden chairs that lined the Explanada), and not allowing myself to feel anything other than a feeling of relief when, on the way

168

back to my apartment, I strolled along the Calle Gerona which housed some of Alicante's most luxurious designer wedding dress shops. Whenever I stopped outside the windows and looked at the extravagantly elegant dresses I wished only good things for the girls who wore them and I didn't think of a wedding for myself any more.

It was at the end of a busy November that Gabriella made an unexpected visit to the office and gave me the tickets for the Caribbean.

'You don't take holidays,' she told me. 'You go back to Ireland for a week or so. You take a day off from time to time. But you don't take proper holidays and you should, Isobel.'

I tried to protest that I wasn't a holiday kind of person. That working in a country where the sun shines and the weather is balmy (Alicante didn't suffer the same bitingly cold winters as Madrid; in a lot of ways I preferred it there in the winter when the tourist hordes had gone and the locals reclaimed the streets) was as good as being on a permanent holiday.

Gabriella was having none of it. She handed me the tickets for a week's stay in the five-star, all-inclusive, ultra-luxurious White Sands Hotel, and told me to go and have a good time.

Which was why I found myself standing on the balcony of Room 608, musing on the day's cancelled wedding, remembering my own, thinking that Spain was a beautiful country and I now regarded it as home, but that the Caribbean was probably the most idyllic place on earth. You couldn't actually live here, I thought, as I gazed at the setting sun disappearing into the silk-blue sea in a ripple of pink and gold. It was far too beautiful for everyday life!

I sat down in the plump cushioned recliner, stretched my lightly tanned legs out in front of me so that they caught the final rays of the sun and flicked through a copy of *Hola!* to catch up on the Spanish gossip.

It was because I was reading in Spanish that I didn't at first realise that the people on the balcony next to me (who I couldn't see properly but could make out as blurred images because all of the balconies were separated by walls of glass blocks) were talking in Spanish too. And it was the Spanish of Madrid – Castellano – not Latin American Spanish which might have been less unusual in this part of the world. It was strange to hear Spanish at all; most of the guests at White Sands were American or British, with one or two Germans; and so, when I heard my second language I tuned in to what they were saying.

It was a woman's voice speaking, bright and cheerful, bubbling with enthusiasm.

'We are so lucky!' she was exclaiming. 'Seems we got the right end of the deal for once.'

Her companion, a man, was obviously still in the room because I didn't catch his reply though I could hear the timbre of his voice.

'. . . and this is so great,' she continued. 'Look at the views. Much, much better than the other place.'

I caught a glimpse of movement out of the corner of my eye. She was hanging precariously out over the balcony, peering down into the colourful tropical gardens below. I could see her profile as she swept her long dark hair from her face – a perfect face, with smooth olive skin, long dark eyelashes and high cheekbones. She reminded me of Letizia Ortez, the elegant and ever more glamorous woman who'd married the Crown Prince of Spain and who was a regular cover girl for all of the gossip magazines. The woman next door caught sight of me and grinned. Her lips were rosebud pink, her mouth wide and generous and her eyes chocolate brown. Then she drew back and called to her companion again.

'Do we have time before going out, Nico?' she asked.

Nico. My heart hammered in my chest at the familiar name. Nico.

Well, obviously not my Nico. Nicolas Juan Carlos Alvarez, who had told me he loved me and that he would have married me if that was what I wanted before storming out of my apartment in Madrid and never coming back. I moistened my suddenly dry lips. Nico, who had been such a wonderful lover and who'd made me feel wanted and cherished but who wasn't really the man for me because I was still somehow in love with Tim. Or (at that point) the idea of Tim. After Nico left me, he started going out with a friend of mine, Barbara, who'd always fancied him. I'd met them once together when Tim had come to Madrid and it had been horribly embarrassing. I don't think their relationship lasted but I never heard from him again.

Nico. The name brought the memories flooding back. *Isabella querida*.

I shook my head. Nothing to get in a knot about. Wherever Nico Alvarez was these days, and whatever he was doing, it certainly wasn't hanging out in the White Sands Hotel with a Spanish beauty.

'Pilar, let's go!' Suddenly he was on the balcony too because his words carried clearly to me although his body was distorted through the glass blocks. 'We can't be late. They'll move us out of here if we are.'

My heart was beating even faster. For a moment it had

sounded just like him too, a rich, deep voice. Musical. Nico had been musical. He played the guitar with some friends and they often got bookings in hotels around the city. He also wrote jingles for advertising companies. But his real job was in the pharmaceutical industry. He came from a family of doctors. He was the only one who didn't practise medicine.

'Pilar!' He laughed. I didn't know what Pilar had done, but I could imagine it was something to do with kissing him. And maybe more than that.

I shook my head again. It didn't matter what they were doing. But I wished I could get the unexpected memory of Nicolas Juan Carlos Alvarez out of my head.

They weren't at dinner. I was shown to my usual table in the corner of the restaurant overlooking the underwater-lit sea and from which I could observe everyone else. Once or twice since I'd arrived at the hotel I'd eaten with other guests – there was another woman here on her own and I'd joined her one evening, though I hadn't been able to get a word in edgeways as she'd recounted her life story as the private secretary to an industrial magnate; and there'd been a sweet American family who wanted to take me under their wing and were horrified when I didn't join them every evening. There was a second solitary woman who (according to Dee, the private secretary) was a famous novelist who was doing some research on the island. Fancy, Dee had said, we could all end up between the pages of a book! I shuddered. I couldn't bear the thought of my life ending up between the pages of a book. In fact I liked being alone, reading my own book, eating my dinner and drinking a couple of glasses of ruby-red wine. I used to hate being by myself in public places but now I was used to it. And, as I often told people who called me solitary and worried about me, there was a world of difference between being on your own and being lonely. Sometimes you can be lonely in a crowd of people. Sometimes I'd felt lonely even with Tim beside me. I wasn't lonely now.

Tonight I nodded at the tall coloured guy who had been one of the guests at the aborted wedding the day before; smiled at an elderly lady who was also on her own but who'd made it clear that she didn't welcome company; and managed to avoid catching the eye of the talkative private secretary. But there was no sign of the Spanish beauty and her Nico.

Then the waitress came to take my order, telling me that due to circumstances beyond their control there was no fresh lobster that night, and frowning as she said so. I didn't care. I ordered the Caribbean salad followed by wahoo and steamed vegetables. Then I opened my book and lost myself in the fictional world I'd brought with me.

Night life at White Sands was fairly limited. After dinner people gravitated towards the piano bar where the conversation was general and where card games or backgammon were often played. I wished I was any good at either but I wasn't. I tucked myself into a huge bamboo chair, read a little more and then chatted briefly to a girl who I'd seen around the hotel and always in the company of her elderly parents but who, tonight, was on her own in the bar and was reading the same book as me.

We exchanged a few comments about the book (a kind

of crime caper novel) and then she told me that she had some things to do. As she left the bar I saw Pilar walk by. She was wearing a black silk bustier and a calf-length red silk skirt overlaid with a delicate pattern of flowers in black lace. She'd pulled her hair into that severe, tight bun favoured by flamenco dancers which served to highlight her wonderful cheekbones and her almost aristocratic beauty. She was tall and slender and, despite the precarious height of her heels, moved with the grace of a dancer through the crowded bar. There was no sign of her companion. I looked at my watch. Almost eleven. Things generally wound down by midnight, and although I was used to the much later nightlife of Spain I was getting used to it.

I closed my book and finished my drink.

It was starting to rain. Actually it seemed to rain every night on the island around this time; fat, hot drops of water that instantly soaked you to the skin.

I hurried along the wet path and let myself into my room. As abruptly as it had started, the rain stopped, but I knew that there would probably be one more downpour before the skies cleared again. I changed out of my wet clothes and into a casual beach dress, then opened the patio door and stepped on to my balcony.

Cigar smoke wafted from next door. I don't know much about cigars (my asthma means that I hate smoke of any description) but I knew that Nico occasionally smoked an expensive Romeo y Julieta after dinner. I had no idea what cigar was being smoked on the adjoining balcony, but once again the image of Nico imprinted itself on my mind.

This is ridiculous, I muttered to myself. Nico Alvarez is in Madrid. Thousands of miles away. And if you were ever to meet him again, how likely is it that it would be on an island in the middle of the Caribbean Sea. Get a grip, Isobel!

But I couldn't. I kept thinking of him. I'd been think-ing of him all through dinner and all through the evening in the bar, even while I buried my nose in my book and chatted to the girl called Gala. I couldn't stop thinking about him.

Isabella querida.

I'd treated him very badly. As badly as any man had ever treated me. I'd never quite got over the guilt I felt about Nico. The memories were flooding into my head now. Our first meeting near the Retiro park, where he'd paid for my café solo because I'd forgotten my purse. Going to an Irish pub with him. Listening to him playing at the Lux Hotel. Falling in love with him.

Damn it, I muttered savagely to myself, I hadn't fallen in love with him. I'd fallen in love with the idea of some-one as wonderful as him. It was completely different.

There was a sizzling sound and another waft of smoke and I realised that he'd extinguished the cigar. Then the sound of his patio door opening and closing again. He'd obviously gone to bed. With the beautiful Pilar.

He couldn't be the same Nico. But it worried me that I seemed to want him to be.

I went back into my own room and closed the door. But I couldn't let it go. I kept thinking about him and wonder-ing if by some incredible chance . . . But so what if it was him? He was with Pilar, wasn't he? And what did we have in common any more? Why would I want to talk to him? To be friendly, I reminded myself. To let him know that I'd grown up. To apologise again for not having told him about Tim. To tell him I'd once loved him.

I thumped the cushion on my chair. I most certainly

wouldn't tell him that! I hadn't loved him. I'd used him. I might have loved him if I hadn't been Tim-obsessed. But that was all in a different lifetime and with a different Isobel. I was older now. More sensible. And – despite what people thought – not flaky.

This was what I told myself as I stepped out on to my balcony again and leaned over the rail, as precariously as Pilar had done earlier that evening. I was trying to see into the room next door. My reasoning was that if by some extraordinary chance Nico Alvarez was there, I wanted to know. I didn't want to bump into him around the pool or at the beach and be taken by surprise. I wanted to be ready for him. And so I needed to know who the man in Room 607 actually was.

The light was on in the room but I couldn't hear anything. Nor could I see any movement through the heavy drapes which covered all but a sliver of the window, the sliver from which the thin slice of light gleamed. I thought about it for a moment, then swung myself out over the pastel blue and white wooden balustrades of my room and grabbed hold of the rail of the balcony next door. I swallowed hard as I glanced downwards. If I fell I'd probably break something. White Sands wasn't a single building and the rooms were dotted around the green hillside so that none was more than one storey high. It wasn't that far to fall really, but it would be directly into the succulent cactus plant below. I tightened my grip on the wooden rail. I definitely didn't want to fall into the cactus plant.

It started to rain again. I swore softly under my breath and hauled myself up on to the balcony of Room 607, and stood on the wet tiles panting slightly. I realised that what I had done was incredibly stupid and foolish and that if the occupants of the room came out on to the balcony for any reason I would have a hell of a lot of explaining to do. I also realised that there was no possible way that Pilar's companion (husband, fiancé, lover – who knew!) was the Nico I'd known. So I would basically be standing on the balcony of a complete stranger's room and he would probably call the police and God only knew what would happen to me.

The rain beat down even harder. There was no way I could get back to my own room while it fell in its relentless torrent. I slicked my wet hair back from my face and prayed that it would stop soon.

Then I heard the sound of someone at the patio door. I slithered across the wet balcony and tried to fold myself into its darkest corner while my heart fluttered like a trapped bird in my chest. The door opened. I flattened myself against the wall and told myself that everything I'd always believed about not being flaky was wrong. I was incredibly flaky. And this was my flakiest stunt yet.

The man stood in the open doorway looking out at the rain. I couldn't see him properly because the light from behind him meant that he was in silhouette. I sure as hell hoped he couldn't see me either. I think I closed my eyes, just like I used to do as a kid when Dad played hide and seek with me. I always supposed that if I couldn't see him he couldn't see me either. He usually let me win. Maybe if he hadn't I would have realised that closing your eyes isn't a great way of hiding from anyone!

There was a sudden exclamation from the man in the doorway. I allowed one eye to open slightly and then I groaned as I realised he had seen me and was walking towards me. I wondered what the jail sentence was for prowling on guest balconies at five-star hotels. And I wondered how I'd manage to explain it all to Gabriella.

'*Qué hace?* What are you doing?' he asked angrily.

I opened my eyes a little more.

'I'm sorry,' I said helplessly in Spanish. 'I got the wrong room.'

'The wrong room?' He stood in front of me. The two of us stared at each other. I couldn't believe it. I opened my mouth but I couldn't speak.

'Isobel?' He sounded as gobsmacked as me. '*Isabella?*' *Isabella querida.*

'Hi, Nico.' My voice came from miles away and sounded unaccountably bubbly and cheerful and completely insane. 'How are you?'

'Isobel,' he said again. 'I do not believe it. Why are you here?'

'Same as you, I suppose,' I said breezily. 'Holiday. Though I'm on my own and I saw your lovely Pilar earlier. She's gorgeous.'

He stared at me as though I was an alien from another planet. As though I'd materialised in front of him, a life form he didn't quite understand.

'Isobel, why are you here, and on the balcony of my room?' He frowned again. There were more lines around his eyes than I remembered, but even in the blackness of the rain-filled night, they still smouldered. There was more grey in his hair too, around the temples. It made him look distinguished.

'Isobel?' He was waiting for me to answer, and although I knew that I was supposed to be quick-witted (everyone in the Alicante office thought so), I really couldn't think of a single sensible thing to say. I cleared my throat.

'I heard a noise,' I told him unconvincingly.

'But of course you would hear a noise,' he said. 'This is my room. I am in it. There would be a noise.'

'Well, yes . . .' My heart was thudding in my chest now, in a mixture of fear and embarrassment and shock. 'So everything's all right then,' I said as brightly as I could. 'Excellent. I'll just be getting back.' I walked over to the balcony and – despite the still-teeming rain and the threat of the cactus below – threw my leg over it.

'Isobel! For heaven's sake, stop! You will fall.'

'Not at all.' I was getting good at sounding breezy.

'Please.' He bounded across the balcony after me and caught me by the wrist. His dark, dark eyes stared into mine. I blinked.

'Well, if you insist,' I said reasonably, 'you can let me out through your room.' Though what the gorgeous Pilar would have to say about a drowned rat woman walking through her bedroom was absolutely beyond me.

'Isobel, I . . .' He stared at me as I clambered back on to his balcony. 'I am sorry, but I am at a complete loss. I don't understand why you are here.'

'Like I said, a holiday,' I told him. 'And, gosh, Nico – it's lovely to see you again, and maybe we'll catch up in the bar or something, but now I'd better get back to bed.'

And with that I marched through the open patio door and across Room 607 (my eyes flicking towards the queen-sized bed, though I didn't see any sign of Pilar at all) and out of the door before he had half a chance to stop me.

Naturally I didn't sleep a wink that night. Of all the places I might have expected to meet Nicolas Alvarez again, here in this hotel had to be right at the bottom of the list. Because, and despite what I'd told Julie about Alicante being four hundred kilometres away from Madrid, I *had* often wondered what it would be like to bump into Nico there. Strolling down by the marina, for example. Or sitting on the beach. Or shopping in the Corte Inglés. I had wondered and imagined it and thought about it from time to time but I always pushed the thoughts to the very back of my mind because – well, because I didn't want to think about Nico any more.

That passing whim stuff. That 'loving him but being in love with Tim' stuff. It's only partly true. I *had* loved Nico when I lived in Madrid but I was afraid to admit it, even to myself. Nico had baggage in his past too, you see. A failed relationship with a girl called Carmen which bugged the hell out of me because he kept a photo of her on the shelf in his apartment. I didn't want to commit to Nico knowing that he was still in his heart committed to Carmen. (The fact that he'd gone out with my friend Barbara afterwards was irrelevant. As far as I was concerned Carmen was the issue when I'd been dating him.) And he was too damn nice to me. I didn't trust him. I was used to Tim, who hadn't been quite so nice. Back then, I was a bit of an emotional mess. And seeing Nico again had made all of those conflicting emotions come back.

He'd been great in bed.

I tossed and turned beneath the single sheet and remembered Nico being good in bed. I opened my eyes in the dark and listened for sounds of Nico still being good in bed. With Pilar.

'Oh for God's sake,' I said out loud as I sat up and punched the big pillow. Forget all this. Forget Nico. Forget Tim. Forget all of it. You're fine the way you are.

As is always the way when you've been awake all night, I fell asleep just before dawn. That meant that I was late for breakfast, not arriving down to the restaurant until nearly nine o'clock, when almost everyone else had finished (and despite the mountains of food that White Sands always provided, the complement of guests managed to devour most of it each day. So it was a couple of slices of watermelon and no bread for me that morning. But what the hell, I wasn't really hungry). There was, of course, no sign of Nico or Pilar. Nor was there any sign of them on the beach during the day. I wondered, my heart lurching suddenly in my chest, whether they'd come to the Caribbean to get married. It would be the sort of thing that Nico might do. Especially if he was still on uneasy terms with the rest of his family. If that was the case, I mused as I sipped on a pina colada and stared at the empty gazebo at the edge of the water, where had he met Pilar and was he totally over Carmen?

I reckoned I was right about the wedding. People who came to the island to get married usually disappeared for a day or so while they checked out the arrangements and did whatever it was they needed to do. Then they spent a couple of days on the beach acquiring the smattering of a tan (though the hotel's luxurious spa offered a comprehensive package of beauty treatments that included a spray-on gold mist which went very well with white) before tying the knot (or chickening out of the whole thing).

I wondered whether I'd still be around for Nico's wedding. I only had another couple of days left. Somehow I thought that it would be better if I wasn't still here.

* * *

The manager's cocktail party was held that night. It was a weekly event that took place in the bar area beside the pool, with champagne and canapés, where the general manager of the hotel introduced himself to the guests and hoped that we were enjoying our stay. How could we not? The weather was perfect, the food was sublime and there really wasn't anything you could possibly want that wasn't already being provided by the hotel. But the party gave everyone the chance to dress up and chat together in different surroundings to the hotel bar. And the whole thing was both jolly and sophisticated, with coloured fairy lights strung up between the palm trees and gently burning candles dotted around the edges of the pool.

I wore a dress in deep purple silk which I'd bought a couple of months earlier in a tiny boutique off the Calle Gerona (I didn't have the time to make my own clothes as I used to), along with a pair of very high-heeled but exactly matching sandals in softest leather (from one of Alicante's many shoe shops). My hair – always a problem for me because I was forever trying to grow it and then getting too impatient and lopping it off again – I allowed to fall loosely to my shoulders in its soft dark waves. I wore make-up for the first time in a week and a pair of gold earrings along with a matching necklace which I'd bought for myself the previous Christmas courtesy of my bonus. I looked at myself in the mirror before going out and knew that I looked great.

But not as great as Pilar. She and Nico were already standing side by side when I walked into the pool area. In Ireland and the UK people usually associate continental style with the French or the Italians, but honestly, the Spanish are a very, very stylish race. They have an easy elegance about them when they dress up, and Pilar was effortlessly beautiful in a sky-blue chiffon dress which accentuated every curve on her otherwise lithe body. Her shoes also matched her dress but her jewellery was silver. And once again she'd put her hair up, though this time not in the severe style of the night before, but in a gentle twist so that occasional wisps brushed her perfectly complexioned face. I forgot to mention that she was younger than me. In her mid-twenties, I thought. Whereas I, twenty-seven when I'd first met Nico, had now embraced my thirties. Suddenly my gorgeous dress made me feel as though I'd tried too hard.

I watched them as they talked easily together. Every so often Nico nodded in agreement at whatever Pilar said to him and I decided that she was the one who wore the trousers in the relationship. I wondered how Nico coped with that. He liked independent women but, like all men I guess, he also liked getting his own way. She said something else to him and he laughed heartily, then made his way over towards my side of the pool.

I walked quickly into a group of people and accepted a glass of champagne from one of the waiters. I chugged back rather too much and the bubbles went up my nose. I sneezed, then coughed. My asthma was virtually nonexistent these days, what with living in a much drier climate, but whenever anything went against my breath I still needed my inhaler. I took it out of my tiny purple clutch bag and took a puff.

'Are you all right?' Nico stood beside me. I glanced towards Pilar, who was looking into the depths of the swimming pool.

'Yes, thanks, fine.' I thought I sounded like one of those no-nonsense cinema teachers in British 1950s movies.

'It still bothers you, the asthma?'

'Not really,' I said. 'It's improved a lot since I moved back to Spain.'

His eyes flickered and I realised that he wouldn't have known that I was living in Spain again.

'Alicante,' I told him, and launched into a not-very-coherent account of the job offer from Gabriella. 'But look, you know, how are you?' I asked. 'How's the song-writing? And the band? And . . . and everything?'

'Why were you on my balcony?' he asked.

I'd kind of hoped he wasn't going to go there!

'Look, Nico, please please forgive me for that. It was so stupid of me. I . . . well, I heard your . . . I heard people speaking Spanish, you see, and the name Nico, and I wondered . . . and I guess I just thought I'd check it out and see if it was you, that's all. I didn't really think it would be. I got a tremendous shock.'

'But why didn't you simply knock at the door?'

Why hadn't I? I didn't really know. The thing was, it seemed to me that when it came to my emotions and my relationships with men, I never really knew what I was doing.

'You know, Nico, I've really no idea.' I shrugged my shoulders.

He laughed suddenly, an infectious laugh. 'You always were a bit crazy, *Isabella*.'

My mouth twitched. 'Maybe.' I took another slug of champagne.

'It's nice champagne,' he protested. 'You're knocking it back.'

'I'm still in shock,' I said shortly.

'Hey, come on, if anyone should be in shock it's me. You were the trespasser, remember?'

I nodded and glanced towards Pilar again. She was talking to a couple I'd noticed earlier, an older man and a younger woman. He looked distinguished. She looked like me when I'm having a bad hair day. But she was smiling broadly at whatever he was saying. They were holding hands. I'm always very cynical about people who hold hands in public. I gave the relationship a few more weeks at the most.

'So are you here to get married?' I asked.

He looked at me appraisingly. 'Always interested in the getting married,' he said.

'Oh, come on . . .'

'You left me to get married to someone else,' he reminded me tartly.

'But I didn't marry him.'

His damn eyes were smouldering yet again as he continued to look at me. An awkward silence was beginning to develop between us.

'I heard,' he told me eventually.

'So, I'm footloose and fancy-free,' I said. 'And loving it.'

He frowned.

'It's an English expression,' I told him. 'It means . . . it means I don't have a boyfriend.'

'That must be difficult for you,' he remarked. 'You always had a boyfriend.'

'That was then.' Suddenly I recovered the composure that I'd gained over the past few years and that had deserted me since the previous day. 'I'm a different person now. A better person.'

'Yes?'

I nodded. 'And, well, look . . . Nico . . .' I floundered a little, then shrugged dismissively. 'I'm truly sorry about how I treated you in Spain. I was a bitch to you and I have no excuse. I should have dealt with things properly and I didn't. I probably wasn't even a very nice person when we were going out either. You were lovely to me and I was a fool.'

'Why didn't you contact me?' he asked.

It was my turn to frown.

'When you left your boyfriend – in the lurch, no?'

I laughed suddenly. 'In the church, actually.'

Nico smiled slightly. 'Yes. Yes. But whenever. Wherever. You didn't contact me, Isobel.'

'I couldn't see the point,' I told him. 'You were going out with Barbara. And there was still the thing about Carmen. But more importantly, I didn't want to contact anyone. I needed to be on my own. Isobel without a boyfriend. Any boyfriend.'

He nodded in understanding. 'But after a time . . . I thought you would contact me after a time.'

'Why?' I asked. 'Why mess up our lives all over again just because I was a fool?'

'Not a fool,' he said. 'Not really, *Isabella*.'

I wished he hadn't called me Isabella. It made the hairs stand up on the back of my neck and a frisson of forgotten desire run along my spine.

'Oh, come on, Nico. I was more than a fool. I had no idea what I wanted. I messed things up. Much better that I didn't call anyone. Besides . . .' I glanced around for Pilar and spotted her again, this time talking to the novelist, chatting easily. She seemed to have the ability to get on with everyone. 'You have someone else now.'

'Why do you think that?' he asked. 'I am here and Pilar is here but that doesn't mean we are together the way you think.'

186

I grinned at him. 'Nico, *querido*, if you're not with her the way I think, then you're sadly out of touch.'

He laughed again and so did I, and suddenly I felt comfortable with him once more. Then the manager came over to us and introduced himself and said that he hoped we were enjoying the hotel and the facilities and we told him politely that we were; and when he left us the food and beverage manager took his place and said the same things and hoped we were enjoying the food and the type of menu that the hotel provided and I said that I was enjoying it far too much, and then, finally, Pilar came and joined us too.

Her dark eyes slid over me appraisingly as she told me that she was delighted to meet me. We talked of completely inconsequential things for about five minutes and then she rather pointedly looked at her watch and told Nico that the taxi was probably waiting and they'd better get going.

He looked at his watch too and agreed with her.

'Perhaps I will see you when we get back, Isobel,' he said.

'I doubt it.' I didn't want to give Pilar any reason to doubt him either. 'I'm sure I'll just go to bed with my book.'

'Oh dear.' Pilar's eyes danced with merriment. 'That sounds a little dull.'

'But safe,' I commented drily and walked away from them.

So what do you do when you suddenly fall in love with a person all over again? And when that person is with someone else?

I sat on my balcony, my book unopened on the table,

and thought about Nico Alvarez. How could I have dumped him for Tim? What had I been thinking? How could I have believed that I didn't love him when now he occupied every single moment of my thoughts?

Maybe, I muttered to myself, maybe it was because he'd found someone new himself. I remembered the flash of jealousy that had spurted through me when I'd seen him in a restaurant with Barbara Lane. Maybe, even though I didn't want Nico myself, I just didn't want any other woman to have him either. God, but I was a mean-spirited bitch, I told myself. Horrible, just horrible.

I wrapped my arms around my body. I was lying when I said that I didn't want Nico.

I did.

I'd wanted to contact him when I'd walked out on Tim. But I hadn't trusted myself then. Later, when I'd kind of got it all together, I'd wanted to contact him again. But I'd told him the truth when I said I was madly guilty about the way I'd treated him; and I'd doubted whether I could take him being nasty and horrible to me in return. Or cool and distant, which I knew he did well.

And there was another reason. Nico had pointed it out himself earlier. I always had a boyfriend. And after the whole wedding thing, I didn't want a boyfriend. I didn't want any man in my life. Even Nico. Even though I loved him.

I took a sip from the glass of wine on the table beside me. It's difficult when you're describing your thoughts at a certain time because you're describing them with hindsight and you can always justify your actions. Truth is, I was always hopeless at knowing when I was in love because I was in love with the whole idea of being in love! I read romantic novels. I cried at chick-flicks. I loved the soppy photos in *Hola!* of celebrity couples who were supposed to be in love even though I knew they'd probably split up a few weeks later. There was a core of me which was a romantic idiot and it was much, much better for me to ignore that side of me completely. That's why I hadn't bothered over the past few years. That's why I hadn't contacted Nico. I thought I was better off on my own rather than getting involved with someone all over again. And I was right. Only now, on one of the most romantic islands in the world, and having bumped into the man who had been the best lover in the world to me . . . I sighed deeply and closed my eyes.

I'd thought I'd grown to know myself. But I hadn't. At all.

No sign of them at breakfast the following morning either, although I was down early. I smiled acknowledgement at the elderly lady and got trapped by the secretary on her own. I supposed that it was a sign of my horrible bitchy self that I let her rabbit on at me about something that was probably tremendously important to her while not listening to a word she said. I wondered whether Pilar was having beauty treatments ahead of the wedding. I wondered whether Nico was nervous about the whole thing. I wondered when it was going to be, because this was my last full day on the island; I was going home the following night.

What would happen, I asked myself, if I knocked on the door of Room 607 that evening and confessed to Nico that I was still in love with him? Would it matter to him? Did I matter to him? Would he leave Pilar for me? I shivered in the silk-warm air. I couldn't mess up another wedding – one that wasn't even my own! And the hotel had already had its wedding drama. I would do nothing. I would put Nico back into that part of my mind that was now locked away and I would pack my bags and go back to Alicante where, thanks to the four hundred kilometres, I wouldn't see Nico again.

I spent the day on the beach, finishing my crime caper and thinking that at least I only had to worry about being in love and not dastardly plots against vulnerable girls by evil anti-heroes. I was a woman in command of her own future, and that was a good thing to be.

The shadow inched across the white sands, creeping over the edges of my lounger and finally leaving me in its shade. The other sun-worshippers left the beach and wandered up to the hotel pool, set higher in the grounds and the beneficiary of late-evening sunshine. I lay on my back and watched as tints of rose and orange streaked the sky.

'*Isabella.*'

He sat on the edge of my lounger.

'Nico.'

'Can we talk?'

I remained lying on my back, staring up at the sky.

'I don't want to mess things up for you Nico,' I said. 'I don't think there's really anything for us to talk about. I am truly and deeply sorry about how things went between us.'

'Me too,' said Nico. 'I should have gone after you.'

I pulled myself up so that I was sitting facing him.

'No you shouldn't.'

He made a face at me. '*Isabella querida*, I knew you were mad for this man, but it was all wrong for you. Everyone said so. Gabriella, Magdalena, Luis, Alejandro . . .'

'For heaven's sake,' I interrupted him irritably. 'Did half of Madrid spend its days talking about me?'

He grinned. 'Only your friends.'

'It's in the past, Nico,' I said tiredly. 'It's all over.'

'Not for me,' said Nico gently. 'Never for me.'

'D'you mean you've been pining away for me?' I asked. 'Because it doesn't much look like it. And it's been years!'

'I wanted to come and get you,' he said as though I hadn't spoken. 'And I would have done. But then I thought that it would be a mistake. You'd walked out on one man and I wasn't sure that you would walk into the arms of another. Even me. Especially me.' He looked at me ruefully. 'So I decided to wait for you.'

'A long wait,' I remarked.

'Yes. I thought you'd come to me, *Isabella*. I really did. And then I thought that I was a fool too, because you didn't.' He shrugged in his continental way. 'And so . . . I gave up on you.'

There was a bit of me which thought, as we sat on the lounger together with the fiery sun finally spilling into the soft blue sea, that this was the kind of romantic setting I'd read about in my novels and seen in my movies. And that in romantic settings like this true love always wins out. But not this time. Not without hurting other people. And I wasn't prepared to do that. I knew that I was a fool but I wasn't really a bitch. Besides, he'd given up on me. He'd just said so.

'Are you and Pilar getting married here?' I repeated my question of the day before.

'Why would you think that?' he asked.

I shrugged. 'Why else would you be here? She's absolutely gorgeous, Nico. And it's not an ordinary holiday, because you're never on the beach, never in the restaurant . . . in your room obviously, or getting on with wedding details.'

'Oh, Isobel.' He smiled at me. 'Still the same, even though you're different.'

'Shut up,' I said peevishly.

'Pilar and I are not going to be married,' he told me.

I stared at him. 'Not on my account,' I said. 'Please, Nico.'

'If I loved Pilar and was going to marry her, then I wouldn't abandon her for you or for anyone else,' he told me sharply.

I blushed.

'But I don't love her and we're not going to be married.'

Christ, I thought. Not another cancelled wedding. The hotel staff would do their combined nuts!

'But you're still here together,' I commented.

'We are both in this hotel. We have separate rooms.'

I didn't know what to say about that.

'We are colleagues, *querida*, not lovers.'

I looked at him, startled.

'Yes. Colleagues,' he repeated. 'We are here for the conference on drugs to treat HIV. It's being held in the Blue Skies complex.'

The Blue Skies was an impressively huge hotel and conference centre about a mile down the road.

'There was a problem with our booking at the hotel, so Pilar and I were accommodated here,' Nico told me. 'Room 607 and Room 109.'

192

'But she was in your room,' I told him.

'Of course,' he said. 'Just before we went to the evening introduction session. She called to see if I was ready. She's never stayed in my room at night.'

My damn heart was thumping in my chest again.

'There is nobody in my life, Isobel. There hasn't been since you left it.'

'Barbara,' I said flatly.

'Oh, come on.' He looked at me complicitly. 'You remember how it was. She asked me out. I agreed. I wanted to make you jealous.'

'You succeeded,' I said.

'Not jealous enough,' he said. 'You still went home to get married.'

I ran my fingers through my tangled, sea-matted hair.

'I love you, Isobel,' said Nico. 'From the moment I first went out with you to the day I blazed out of your apartment and every day in between. From the times we argued about everything and nothing. From the day you left Spain to now, I have always loved you.'

I think my jaw dropped.

'You didn't try to get in touch with me,' I said eventually.

'I wanted you to come to me.'

'Bloomin' heck, Nico, you'd have been waiting a long time.' I fiddled with the ties of my bikini top. 'I couldn't come looking for you. I told you, I made a new life.'

'I'm glad you made a new life,' said Nico calmly. 'But I would like it if you made another new life. With me.'

The energy between us, the chemistry, whatever it was, was absolutely crackling. I could feel Nico even though he wasn't touching me. I knew that he could feel me too.

'This is too weird,' I said slowly. 'We're here, so unexpectedly. It's all . . . unreal.'

He nodded.

'And I'm going home tomorrow.'

'Home to Spain?'

'Yes.'

'So I will find you there,' he said. 'In Alicante.'

'Nico . . .'

'Yes?'

'I don't want to make a mistake,' I said.

'*Isabella querida*,' he said.

And then he kissed me. And I knew that it would never be a mistake with him.

Afterwards, when I'd finally come down off cloud nine and started to think like a normal person again, I wondered at the coincidence of meeting him in such a setting at such a time. I called Gabriella when I got back to Alicante and told her that she'd clearly been under the influence of some higher force when she'd given me the tickets and made me go on holiday. I wittered on for ages about fate and karma and how true love really does find a way.

'Either that,' she agreed easily, 'or the fact that we have landed Nico's company as one of our clients in Madrid.'

'Gabriella!' I was shocked. 'Did you *know* he'd be there? Did you – did you *plan* it?'

She laughed but didn't answer the question.

'You shall be my matron of honour,' I told her grandly when I could speak again.

She chuckled. 'Only if you promise to go through with it this time.'

I smiled. 'Wild horses wouldn't stop me,' I said as I looked at the magnificent engagement ring on the finger that had been bare for so long. 'Nothing on earth can stop me. This time Isobel really is going to have a wedding.'

Room 311 (Rudy)

Rudy normally went to the poolside bar around noon. His favourite seat was beneath the straw sunshade at the very corner of the bar, overlooking the long white beach and the azure-blue sea, and after a few days people got used to seeing him there and would leave the high bamboo seat free for him. They realised that he chose the seat so that he could keep an eye on Steve, his ten-year-old son, who spent most of his time in the water, his snorkel clamped to his face, and who practically had to be hauled out for food. Steve was averagely tall but beanpole thin and Rudy, who'd found himself talking to the elderly woman who'd arrived at the same time as them a couple of days earlier, had expressed his concern that the child didn't eat enough.

'They go through phases,' the woman had told him. 'I wouldn't worry if I were you.'

But of course Rudy did worry. He couldn't help worrying. No matter how hard he tried not to.

He'd always been a worrier. At school and at college he'd worried about his grades. Then he'd worried about finding a job. Once he'd got a job, he worried about everything to do with it. Although when it came to his job, worried was maybe too strong a term for it. But he'd been concerned all the time because in his Wall Street firm, it was part of his job to be concerned all the time. He had to know stuff that other people didn't even care about. As a trader in the arcane world of municipal bonds he had to know about the borrowing requirements of the different US states. He had to know what their administrations' plans would be for the coming years. He had to know whether the governors were fiscally prudent or total spendthrifts. He had to be aware of anything that might affect the value of the bonds that he held and that might make them less valuable in the future. And of course a lot of the time he did worry about all these things because it was important that the value of his portfolio stayed strong. If he missed something and if he was left holding a rubbish municipal bond instead of a valuable financial instrument, it meant that the honchos on the thirty-third floor would furrow their brows when it came to Rudy's year-end bonus and, even worse, have a discussion on whether or not he was truly pulling his weight and making the Wall Street firm the sort of money it deserved to make.

Rudy wasn't a natural trader. That was why he'd ended up in munis instead of trading derivatives or the Nasdaq. Munis were a more comfortable place to be. But he still had to make money and he still sweated at night if he discovered that he'd somehow managed to land himself with a position that he didn't want. Real traders didn't worry. The guys who were born to it never worried. They had supreme belief in their own abilities so that no matter what happened they were always convinced that they'd come out on top. It didn't always work out that way, of course. But those guys, even if they had made a horrible loss on a shit trade, somehow always managed to convince another firm that they were worth hiring. Rudy didn't have enough belief in his own abilities for that. He'd kind of stumbled into trading munis and he liked it, but he still felt a fraud among the type of people who'd make a price on two flies crawling up a wall. Or two wasps circling a jar, just as the two behind the poolside bar were doing now, enticed by the lure of the sugary cherries inside. Royston, the barman, flapped a towel lazily in their direction, then picked up the jar and popped two cherries on top of the brightly coloured cocktail he'd just mixed for the dark-haired girl with the worried frown who'd arrived at the bar while Rudy was taking the first sip of his first beer of the day. Rudy watched as she walked cautiously across the wet terrace and plonked herself down on one of the loungers. He'd heard somebody say that she was a writer. Quite a well-known writer, in fact. Rudy felt that there was a certain irony in the fact that a well-known writer might be staying at the same hotel as him when he was here without Anna. She'd be pissed to know that. He was sure of it.

Rudy's eyes flickered away from the writer and back towards the sea where Steve was ploughing through the clear blue water, the luminous green of his snorkel just above the waves. As he watched, the boy kicked his feet and headed downwards. Rudy watched anxiously until his son's head bobbed up again. Steve looked in his direction and Rudy waved at him. The boy waved back and then disappeared underwater again. He did this a number of times before Rudy felt confident that he could look away.

He opened the newspaper and spread it out in front of him. It was the real printed edition bought from the hotel shop that morning because, unlike the Europeans, US visitors were able to get same-day copies of the newspapers.

Out of habit, and even though it shouldn't really matter to him right now, he looked at the financial pages first. He noticed that interest rates were down again, which was good for his portfolio. He exhaled slowly and stopped reading the financial pages, turning instead to the rest of the newspaper. He was still reading it closely when Steve ran up to him with a pail of water.

'Look, Dad,' he said. 'A starfish.'

'Wow.' Rudy looked into the murky depths of the pail. 'Cool.'

'Isn't it?' Steve beamed with delight. 'But I'm going to throw it back. I just wanted you to see it.'

'Thanks,' said Rudy. 'You about ready for some lunch?'

Steve made a face. 'I'm not hungry.'

'Your mom will be pretty pissed at me if I don't feed you,' Rudy told him.

'But we're going to the barbecue later, aren't we?' asked Steve anxiously. 'You promised.'

'Of course we are,' said Rudy reassuringly. 'I just thought you might want something now.'

'No thanks.' Steve's smile was relieved. 'I had lots and lots of breakfast.'

That was true. Breakfast was Steve's favourite meal. He loved the bacon and eggs and waffles with maple syrup that the hotel provided every morning. It wasn't actually that his son didn't eat, Rudy conceded, it was just that he was extremely picky about what went into his mouth. He'd never realised before what a fussy eater Steve was.

He watched his son race back down to the seashore, then signalled for another beer and continued to read the newspaper carefully, from first page to last. When he'd finished, he folded it neatly, left it on the bar counter and resumed his gaze out over the sea. Now that he'd read the paper he could relax. He supposed that he was, in a kind of way, doing what everyone had told him to do over the past few months. He was chilling out. Though it was a stupid phrase to use when he was in a place where the ambient temperature never seemed to fall below eighty. Nevertheless, he was feeling chilled right now. Well, as chilled as he could be, which probably wasn't very chilled at all.

Chill out. It wasn't an expression used on Wall Street very often. Even when people were supposed to be chilling out, that wasn't what really happened. They might indulge in leisure activities like trips to the theatre or the opera or the latest to-be-seen-in restaurant; or they might invite or be invited to houses in the Hamptons or beach-front properties in LA, but they weren't chilling out. They were showing off, which was a completely different sort of thing altogether. Rudy had never gone anywhere to chill out before. He hadn't had time. He was working too hard to chill out, even on those occasions when he too went to the Hamptons or met clients in the Beverly Hills Hotel and ordered expensive meals with company money. Rudy didn't think he was the sort of person who could chill out any more. He wondered if he ever actually had been.

However, he'd been told to give it a try. Not just by Anna (who was forever telling him to chill when he got annoyed with her) but also by his doctor, whom he'd gone to see about the persistent headaches and string of colds one after the other that he'd had since October. Dr Russell had asked him about life since the divorce, prescribed some eyedrops for his bloodshot eyes (which Rudy told her were because of the glare from the monitors on the trading desk) and told him that he needed a vacation. Rudy protested that a vacation was the last thing he needed, that actually he needed to do exactly what he had already been doing for the past nine months and lose himself in his work. There was pressure in the firm these days and he had to keep up with what was going on. Dr Russell had regarded Rudy from her clear grey eyes and told him that he'd be a long time dead and that he should cut himself a little slack. She reminded him that he earned good money and had a decent standard of living and that it was necessary sometimes to do that thing that everyone talked about and take time out to smell the roses.

He'd snorted at that. The only smell in his life at the moment, he told her, was the stench of crap, because that's how it was since Anna had moved out. Or, he'd added sarcastically, that's how it was since Anna had thrown him out of the house he was still paying for.

Dr Russell suggested that maybe Rudy might like to talk things over with someone, but he told her (as he'd told Anna before) that he was damned if he was going to allow himself and his life to be examined by some asshole who talked complete nonsense and would try to find out what event in his childhood was responsible for the fact that he hadn't been able to hold his family together now. And she'd looked at him from those grey eyes again and asked him whether he was blaming himself for the fact that his marriage had broken down.

Rudy didn't dignify that comment with a reply. There was no doubt that he'd contributed to the breakdown of his marriage – those long days at the firm obviously took their toll – but it wasn't all his fault. He hadn't any choice but to work those hours if he wanted to keep Anna in the style to which she sure hadn't been accustomed when he'd first met her. The style which she'd happily embraced after his first really good end-year bonus which had paid for the family trip to Europe. The bonuses had paid for a lot of things since then. For Steve's exclusive school. For the bigger, better house out of town. For the gleaming black SUV in the driveway. For the expensive clothes and jewellery that Anna liked to wear despite the fact that her job as an editorial assistant in a far too literary and absolutely uncommercial publishing company (which didn't have any even vaguely well-known writers on its list) wouldn't pay for just one of the diamonds in the earrings he'd bought her for Christmas last year.

So he was the one who'd hauled his ass into Wall Street at six in the morning and worked his butt off to make her happy, even though sometimes he actually hated the damn trading desk and the damn municipal bonds and the whole damn lot of it. And he resented the fact that she swanned around meeting authors who were full of their own importance and going to pretentious literary gatherings while at the same time looking down her nose at foul-mouthed traders even though they were the ones who paid for it all. And then – then she had the nerve to say that Rudy wasn't there for her, and that he didn't engage with the family, and that he was a crap husband and a crap father and that he hadn't got a clue about anything.

He ground his teeth. He didn't want to think of all this stuff again. Not now when he was starting to feel ever so slightly relaxed about everything and when everyone around him was laughing and joking and doing the whole chill-out thing. He was on a Caribbean island after all. Paradise Island, it had said at the airport. Everyone was supposed to be happy here, weren't they? People came here to relax and have fun and do all the things they didn't have time to do back home.

In his case, though, he reckoned that it was some kind of masochistic influence within him that had made him come back, nearly fifteen years after his first visit. An even more masochistic streak that had led him to return to the White Sands Hotel. Or maybe he'd simply wanted to recapture what he'd felt then – a spirit of hope and expectation which had slowly been extinguished over the following years.

As the crowded taxi had bounced merrily along the pot-holed roads bringing him and Steve from the airport on their first day here together, it seemed to Rudy that absolutely nothing had changed in the intervening period. There were, perhaps, more houses dotted around the lush green landscape than he remembered, and there was an indefinable air of greater wealth about the place; but the island itself was still an apparently tranquil emerald fingerprint in the blue sea and there was a timelessness about it that made him sit back in the taxi and stare silently out of the window while Steve chattered incessantly to their fellow passengers who were being dropped off at another hotel further down the road.

He experienced a major flashback as they drove down the narrow driveway to White Sands – the blue and white barrier at the entrance was surely the same blue and white barrier that had been there years before, although the palm tree beside it was much taller; but it wouldn't have surprised him at all to learn that the grey-haired security guard in the little hut was the same guy who'd been there fifteen years earlier either. It was as though he'd literally stepped back in time.

This is stupid, he muttered as the taxi jolted to a stop outside the hotel. Things change. People change. I've changed, for Chrissakes. I'm here with Steve for one thing. And this hotel is probably nothing like it was when it seemed the height of luxury to me and worth blowing the bonus on. Besides, I've stayed at better, more luxurious places since then. Much better. Much more luxurious. I've stayed at the Beverly Hills, for heaven's sake. In a suite.

He tipped the driver as they got out of the cab – in US dollars and more extravagantly than he'd intended, which led to the man telling him that his name was William and that he'd be happy to take Rudy on a tour of the island any time. Rudy nodded absently and stepped inside the building, Steve following and pulling his navy and red Superheros rucksack behind him.

The White Sands Hotel hadn't faded in the last fifteen years at all. In fact, Rudy realised, it had been dramatically upgraded since then. It was clean and modern and scrupulously refined in a five-star American luxury way. Rudy knew that the hotels in the Caribbean competed for US tourist dollars. White Sands was obviously extremely vigorous in its competition. Actually, he thought, as he looked around the reception area, a bit of faded dignity might not have been a bad thing. Its relentless elegance made him think of the clients he met, always in opulent surroundings, always with the trappings of wealth around them even when they weren't necessarily that wealthy at all.

The receptionist beamed her megawatt beam at him and checked him and Steve into their sea-view superior room. The rooms, scattered around the hillside, had also been upgraded (and he certainly wasn't going to complain about the well-stocked mini-bar and Aveda bathroom products), but the views were exactly the same as he remembered – the sparkling sea, the clear sky and the lush tropical gardens sloping gently towards the shore.

Steve hustled around checking everything out – the trouser press, the mini-bar and, of course, the TV. He insisted on making coffee for them both by boiling water in the small kettle provided in the room. He told Rudy that Anna always allowed him to make coffee and that he was perfectly capable of doing it without pouring boiling water all over himself. He was, he told Rudy, a competent child.

'Oh yeah?' Rudy had smiled at him.

'Yeah.' Steve made a face back.

'Who says?'

'I says.'

'Fair enough.' Rudy ruffled his hair and Steve groaned and told him that a competent child didn't need his hair ruffled like a kid.

After the coffee Rudy had opened the mini-bar and mixed himself a whisky and soda while Steve agitated to go down to the beach before it got dark. After all, Steve said, it had been snowing in New York. This place was absolutely mega. Rudy had nodded in agreement and walked down to the beach with Steve. That was when he'd first had a beer at the poolside bar.

Later that evening they'd had dinner together in the Green Garden restaurant, and afterwards Steve's head had suddenly drooped with tiredness so that he was almost asleep by the time they got back to the room. Rudy put his son to bed and sat outside on the enormous balcony, watching the shifting reflections of lights on the ink-black seawater and listening to snatches of conversation as people strolled along the pathways to and from the restaurant.

'Do you want to join me?' The man's voice suddenly carried clearly to him on a waft of air. Rudy could hear the underlying stress in the question. And then he heard a muffled sob. He could see the outline of the speaker, standing between two tall coconut trees off to the right of his room. And as his eyes adjusted to the dimmer light from that area, he realised that he was talking to a girl who'd been lying in the hammock strung between them. He'd seen them in the restaurant earlier but hadn't taken much notice of them then.

Trouble in Paradise, he thought sourly, as he watched the man hand her a hanky. But then there's always trouble in Paradise.

He took his phone from his pocket and looked at it warily. It was switched off so there was no way anyone could ring him. But he still looked at it as though it might bite. He shoved it back into his pocket and resolved not to think about it. He was here now and there was no point in caring about who might or might not be trying to call him.

He couldn't help wondering, in the following two days, as he shuttled between the beach and the poolside bar, always watching Steve (and glad to see that his son had made friends with an English girl of around the same age), how many of the couples stretched out under the clear blue sky, cheerfully accepting the brightly coloured cocktails brought to them on their sun-loungers by the army of waiters that patrolled the beach area, were really happy. They all *looked* happy. They all smiled as they took their drinks or strolled along the water's edge. They seemed content enough. But then he probably did too, as far as other people were concerned. So he wondered whether the other guests had come to the island to prove to themselves that everything in their lives was all right. Or did they come because they already knew it was? You couldn't tell, he mused, by looking at anyone that they were anything but blissfully happy. Even the pair he'd seen quarrelling the first night now seemed to be totally loved-up. He didn't know what made a good couple. He didn't know how the whole relationship thing worked. He didn't know what he was meant to say and when he was meant to say it.

Was it because he'd refused to go to counselling like Anna wanted?

He snorted under his breath. Bloody counsellors and their bloody counselling. It was nothing but a racket really. Take your money and tell you that you had issues with your parents. Christ, everyone had issues with their damn parents. Surely you weren't normal unless you had fucking issues with your parents?

He didn't want Steve to have issues with him, though. He wanted, when his son remembered back, to think that Steve's memories of him were good ones, that he thought of him as a decent bloke who didn't unduly nag him or berate him and who didn't embarrass him in public. Rudy's own father (also Steve) had made a career out of embarrassing him in public – picking on him in front of his friends, or treating him like a kid when they were out together by telling him not to slouch or to pick up his heels, or generally making him feel small and inadequate in the company of a man who was built like a brick shithouse and had the personality to match. He'd been afraid of his father, although he never really knew why. Steve Senior had never actually beaten him or mistreated him physically. Anna had told him that the mistreatment could just as easily be classified as mental torture, but Rudy had been annoyed by that and snapped at her that she was being seduced by watching too many psychobabble programmes on the TV and that she knew nothing about his life and would she kindly stop analysing it. Thank you.

Anna went to a therapist on her own. She said that she needed to see someone because she was unhappy with her life. Rudy had felt himself tense up at the implication that it was because of him that she was unhappy. Hadn't he given her everything she'd ever wanted? Hadn't he worked his ass off for her? Hadn't he? Hadn't he?

That kind of attitude was the problem, she'd replied. Instead of simply accepting that there were things that made her unhappy, he had to get aggressive about it all. He treated everything like one big trade. Something to be done and sorted and treated well if it was making you a profit, but disposed of if it wasn't.

When she said that he felt the first ice-cold band of fear tighten around him. He'd no intention of disposing of anyone in his family. But he certainly wasn't going to follow her suggestion of relationship counselling or her second choice of personal counselling. If they had problems, they'd work them out themselves. And to keep her happy he'd try to get home a bit earlier in the evenings.

In the end, though, they hadn't sorted anything out themselves and her damn therapist hadn't helped any. Anna told him that she was going to file for divorce because of his mental cruelty and his refusal to do anything about it. He'd been astonished at that, demanding to know what the mental cruelty could possibly be. He didn't, he told her, go round calling her names or saying nasty things about her. He always treated her with the utmost respect. There was no question in his mind of any mental cruelty whatsoever.

She'd laughed at that and asked him what he thought all of those times when he promised to be home but wasn't constituted? The times he'd promised her that he would definitely make it by a certain time so that she arranged her schedule to fit his and then he wouldn't turn up and she'd call him only to find that he'd gone to a bar with some of the guys. The times, she'd added cuttingly, that he'd promised Steve he'd go watch him playing football or baseball or at the swimming gala, only he hadn't been able to come and had left terse messages on the phone saying that he was too busy.

Rudy had snorted at that. It was his job, he'd explained, he couldn't do anything about it. The job, he reminded her, which paid for her to ponce around with her pretend career that realistically wasn't going anywhere, that had never gone anywhere. The career which was just an excuse for being able to say that she'd once met Tom Wolfe and Maya Angelou.

Anna had looked at him scornfully and told him that he was a case of arrested development and that she wasn't having her son turn out like him – already he had what she considered to be a very unhealthy attitude towards women. He thought they were there to pick up after him and ensure that he was looked after – he didn't seem to realise that he had responsibilities towards them too.

Feminist bullshit, Rudy had yelled. Get a lawyer, had been her retort.

Royston refilled his beer glass and Rudy's gaze flickered along the beach, past Steve and the English girl, towards the promontory where the weddings took place. There was another one scheduled for this afternoon – in fact one every day this week as far as he could tell; the place was a wedding factory, for God's sake. He hadn't realised that when he and Anna had married here. As far as he could remember, there had only been one other wedding that week. And his memory of their own day was that it had been absolutely one of the happiest of his life.

He'd met her in a bar, which was horribly mundane. They'd struck up a conversation and he'd been charmed by her laid-back manner and sparkling green eyes. She'd been impressed by the Wall Street job then, even though he told her that he was at the start of his career really, only just through the graduate training programme and earning good, but not spectacular, money. It'd be a few more years, he said, before the big bucks would start to roll in, but she'd told him that money really wasn't the most important thing in her life – even though later on in their relationship he'd heard her bragging to her friends about her Wall Street banker boyfriend (despite the fact that he'd told her on more than one occasion that he wasn't actually a banker).

She'd been a bit miffed in the mid-nineties when he wasn't making the pots of money that everyone on the Street claimed to be making, even though he'd explained the whole muni bond thing to her and told her that it had nothing to do with the dotcom business. But she'd complained that all her friends – even people who hadn't a clue about finance – were cleaning up on dotcom IPOs and why weren't they? And when he'd said that it was because the world had gone crazy and that he didn't think most of those deals were worth the price of a postage stamp, she'd grown angry with him and asked him why it was that he was such a wimp when Wall Street bankers were meant to be ruthless money-makers.

When he reminded her that money wasn't the most important thing in her life she'd thrown a cup at him and told him that it might not be important to her but it sure as hell was going to be important to their child and could he for once think of the future? But that was the point, he always had thought of the future, which was why he'd kept his savings in safe but unspectacular investments. Right up to the time that she'd told him that if he wasn't going to do something about it she would and he'd liquidated some of the bonds and put it all into Money–Down–The–Drain.com instead.

It wasn't the worst thing that could have happened, although it had been pretty bad. But despite losing a chunk of their investment money it wasn't an absolute disaster because he hadn't put everything in the smoke and mirrors that had been the industry. All the same, it had changed things between them for ever. There had been the gut-wrenching knowledge that money he'd worked hard for had simply evaporated before his very eyes. The horrible realisation that he wouldn't be able to retire as early as he'd hoped. That there'd have to be a bit of cutting-back, at least in the short term. And, worst of all, he'd lost Anna's respect. Not because of losing the money, he thought, but because he hadn't been strong enough to say no to her when she'd ranted and raved about the killings to be made and how they were the only people she knew who weren't making them. The fact that they were still better off than most of her friends was irrelevant. It seemed crazy to him that she was the one with the crap-paying job who wanted more and more whereas he was the one who was earning money but somehow didn't care.

He pushed his glass towards Royston. The barman nodded at him and filled it while he waited for his cocktail mixer to crunch ice for the four pina coladas ordered by the curly-haired girl with the dark, dancing eyes who reminded Rudy a little of Anna when she'd been younger. Rudy had seen the girl a few times already; she was here with her boyfriend and another couple and he thought, but he wasn't certain, that she was attached to one of the wedding groups. She grinned at him as she caught his gaze and flicked her black hair behind her ears. For a nanosecond Rudy thought that she might actually be flirting with him, but he quickly dismissed that idea. She was too young and too pretty to give a shit about a man like him. And besides, she was definitely here with a guy. His gaze followed her back to the beach where she sat down amid a group of friends who laughed raucously at her return. Rudy nodded to himself. Definitely a wedding party. He took a long draught of the ice-cold beer. When he'd married Anna here, they hadn't brought anyone else with them. Two witnesses from the hotel was all. But it hadn't been like now, when people arrived for their get-away-from-it-all wedding with all of it actually in tow. He thought that his way had been better. Certainly it had been more romantic. Of course now whenever he remembered it he actually hated Anna for how things had changed. He'd loved her on the day he'd married her here and he'd loved the attention from the people on the beach who'd shouted congratulations at them as they'd had their photos taken beneath the picture-postcard palm tree which overhung the water. He'd felt part of something really important that day. Proud of himself. Proud of her. Confident about the future. They'd had such a great time that evening too, dancing on the terrace to the sound of the house band, Anna looking tanned and gorgeous in the magnificent white dress which she'd only bought when they'd arrived on the island. He'd been shocked at her casual approach to the dress, but then she'd told him that there was a well-known dressmaker in the town who ran up copies of designer wedding dresses in a couple of days and that she had a specific kind of dress in mind which she knew the woman would be able to do. Rudy had been astonished that Anna could find out about dress designers two thousand miles from home, but her wedding dress had been truly beautiful and he'd almost burst with pride when he'd first seen her looking so stunning.

Now, even photographs of her managed to enrage him. He swatted at one of the wasps which had been attracted to a drip of beer on the bar counter. Why am I getting so uptight about this? he asked himself. Marriages fail. Lots of marriages fail. We stuck with it for a long time. It was nobody's fault.

But it was the fallout that was making him uptight, he knew that really. It was the way Anna had become vindictive, using Steve as a negotiating ploy between them, telling Rudy that it shouldn't really matter what his access to his son was like because he hadn't been around for most of his life anyway. When she'd said that (left the message on the phone in his rental apartment), he'd almost driven back home and hit her. The fact that he'd wanted to do that frightened him. He'd never been a violent man. But she was making him feel that way. Angry and violent and useless.

His lawyer had told him that it was just a ploy. That she was attacking him because her case wasn't all that great – he was a decent man who'd done his best for his family, but Anna wanted everything. And she was using Steve to get it. Rudy's pals commiserated and shared their own divorce hell stories. But all of them had eventually worked out better access to their children than Rudy had with Steve.

Anna had pleaded that he was unreliable as a father. She'd actually produced a calendar of times when he wasn't home and it had been quite shocking. But he'd always called, that's what he told them. He'd always called and said that he'd be back.

He drained the glass. Four beers. But only two pints. Not too much. That had been another of Anna's stinging accusations. That he was an alcohol abuser. Rudy had laughed at the term. He said it made him sound as though he took bottles of beer from the fridge and beat them up or something, when the truth was that he normally had a couple after work and that was it. He rarely touched spirits and only drank wine with meals. But she made two drinks every day sound like the descent on the slippery slope to alcoholism. It was astonishing, thought Rudy, how people could take facts and twist them into something totally different.

He got up from the bar stool and walked down to the beach. The boat would be pulling in soon, the boat that was taking them to the little deserted island a couple of miles offshore where they were going on a snorkelling expedition followed by a beach barbecue. That was why he hadn't been as worried as usual when Steve didn't want lunch. He knew that his son was excited about the expedition and he'd make sure that Steve ate well at the barbecue. He wondered whether he should worry so much about his son's eating habits, but it seemed to him that food was something parents always worried about. His father used to hit him on the back of the head (although not hard, just in a kind of threatening way) if he didn't finish everything on his plate.

The boat arrived as he was standing ankle-deep in water

while Steve pointed out the transparent fish which swam in the shallow depths. The fish were immediately abandoned as Steve rushed to climb on board the boat. Rudy felt a sense of liberation as he sat on deck beside his son and they left the island behind. It was beginning to feel like a Disney movie, he thought. Father and son together on a boat. (Although in the movies it was usually just the two of them alone, having a bonding experience. The reality today was that there were about a dozen other people along for the ride. But still, it was something!) He leaned back on the wooden deck and closed his eyes.

The boat anchored a little way off shore and the crew carried the barbecue equipment on to the beach while the guests jumped into the clear water. Steve loved snorkelling. He loved the brightly coloured parrot fish and the exotic corals; he was delighted when he saw a turtle and thrilled to spot a manta ray. Rudy thought that he looked like a fish himself as his thin white body in its shocking-green swim shorts cut through the water. He wished he was as good a swimmer as Steve but he was a plodder in the sea – he churned up lots of wash without getting anywhere fast.

The barbecue was spectacular. The crew of the boat built a real fire and Steve snuggled up close to Rudy as they sat around it and watched them grill swordfish and bake potatoes.

'This is the best time ever, Dad,' whispered Steve as (much to Rudy's satisfaction) he wolfed down the food. '*You're* the best.'

I am, thought Rudy, as they got on the boat afterwards. I may be only an average muni dealer. I may have been a crap husband. But I know that I'm a good father despite what Anna and her damn lawyer tried to say and despite what the judge ruled. I'm a decent man and a good father and my son had a good time with me today.

Steve fell asleep on the return journey, so Rudy had to carry him off the boat. He was pleased that Steve was sleeping so well on the island. One of Anna's complaints was that Steve didn't sleep enough. She blamed that on Rudy too. Claimed that it was because the boy was stressed out. Rudy was pretty sure that it was Anna who was stressing out their son. And he was going to do something about it.

Despite his slender frame, Steve's sleeping weight was heavy. The sun was sinking below the horizon, and the water, as Rudy waded through it, was a swirl of pink and gold light.

The policeman was standing at the edge, a female colleague on one side of him, a male on the other. Behind them, a gathering of people on the beach watched either covertly or with undisguised interest while the other passengers on the boat stood in the water and stared.

'Rudy Baker?' he asked.

'Yes.' Somehow Rudy had known they'd be here today. He'd sensed it.

'Is that your son? Steven Dillon Baker?'

'Yes,' said Rudy.

'Mr Baker, you know that you are wanted in the US for the abduction of Steven Dillon Baker?'

'I didn't abduct him.' Rudy held the sleeping body close to him. 'I took him on vacation.'

'You didn't have the right to take him on vacation,' said the policeman.

'Yeah, I know.'

'Your wife has been frantic with worry,' said the policeman.

'Only since last night,' said Rudy. 'Only since she got home from her damn literary conference and discovered that I'd brought him with me.'

'Mr Baker, you've committed a serious offence.'

'You know, I don't see what's so damn wrong about it.' Rudy looked at them despairingly. 'I don't get to see my boy very often. This was the first time she let him stay over with me in more than six months. I'm his dad, for Chrissakes. I'm not a child molester, I'm not a criminal, I've never done anything wrong in my life. I'm Steve's dad and that bitch wouldn't let him stay with me. And the only reason she did this time was because her folks were away for the holiday season too.'

'You took your child out of school, Mr Baker.'

'So what?' Rudy snorted. 'He's learned loads while he's been here.'

'Your wife is on her way,' said the female colleague of the policeman who had done all the talking until now.

'We had a good time,' said Rudy. 'Steve and me. We had fun together. You ask him when he wakes up.'

The woman's eyes were sympathetic.

'The good times don't last for ever,' she said. 'You shouldn't have taken the boy.'

'I know,' said Rudy. 'I know.'

Still holding Steve over his shoulder, he took his phone from his pocket and powered it on. He listened to the messages that Anna had left him. There were more than a dozen since she'd arrived back in New York the night before. Even with the phone off, he'd known that she'd eventually find him.

The messages were all the same. Asking where he was. Demanding he get back right now with the boy. Begging him. And then crying. He felt bad when he heard her cry.

'Maybe you need to talk to her again,' said the policewoman. 'Sort things out between you.'

'Nah.' Rudy shrugged. 'She's going to have me prosecuted. She hates me. I don't know why, but she does. And if she doesn't prosecute me, someone else will. I violated a court order. I brought him here.'

'Why?' asked the policewoman.

'It used to be Paradise,' said Rudy. 'I wanted him to experience it. With me. And I'm glad that he did.'

Steve stirred in his arms and woke up. 'What's going on?' he asked.

'Nothing, buddy,' said Rudy. 'Everything's cool. Don't worry. No sense in worrying about anything on Paradise Island.'

Room 316 (Tara)

Tom hadn't wanted to come with Tara to Suze and Kevin's wedding, but when he heard that it would take place in the Caribbean and that there was only a small group of people going along, he relented (although he'd strung it out a bit, no point in being too quick to give in, he thought. He liked Tara a lot, but when a girl asks a bloke along to a wedding, especially one on the other side of the world, he has to think long and hard before agreeing. At the best of times, in Tom's opinion, girls and weddings were an explosive mix, and he couldn't help thinking that blue skies and balmy weather would only add fuel to the romantic fire).

Tara was very relieved that he'd said yes to coming along – she was Suze's best friend and it would have been unthinkable for her to allow Suze to get married seven thousand miles away without her being there. Well, that wouldn't have happened, of course, because Tara would have been there with or without Tom anyway. It was just nicer to think that he wanted to be with her too. As a single woman, Tara believed that it was much, much better to go to a wedding with a bloke in tow than to arrive by yourself. People had a horrible habit of asking you about your own love-life at weddings, even when it was patently obvious that you didn't have anyone worth talking about. They were less likely to make condescending comments once you had someone by your side.

Anyway, this wedding would be different in every respect. For starters, Tara was the bridesmaid. She had been both pleased and relieved that Suze had asked her because, obviously, with Suze and Kevin heading off to the Caribbean to tie the knot she might have decided on no bridesmaid at all. But Tara and Suze had agreed on being each other's bridesmaids years earlier, when they were at school together; sealing the promise by pricking their index fingers with a pin and daubing a bloody fingerprint on a piece of paper with the solemn pledge written on it with Suze's best calligraphy pen. It had been a childish thing to do, but they'd been kids at the time. And Tara honestly would have understood if Suze had backed out of it all. Because (leaving aside the whole thing about having the ceremony overseas) by marrying Kevin Carlisle, Suze was marrying into a good deal more money than either her family or Tara's had ever known before. So it wouldn't have surprised her if Suze had tried to casually tell her that she couldn't be a bridesmaid because one of Kevin's gorgeous-looking sisters wanted to have the honour for herself. But Suze had stuck to their pledge (in fact nobody from either Kevin or Suze's families was coming along because they'd decided that they didn't want a big fuss; Kevin was afraid that his and Suze's big day would be hijacked by his somewhat overbearing family). Tara was pleased about that. It proved that Kevin was a decent bloke and that Suze was determined to be true to her roots. (Well, her family roots anyway. Her other roots – caramel blonde – were done on a regular basis at Harmony Hair & Nails by Tara's elder sister Jo.)

But although Tara wouldn't have missed Suze's big day for all the world, and although she was ecstatic to be staying in a fabulous hotel on probably the most fabulous island in the whole of the Caribbean, she was afraid it mightn't be as wonderful as it could be.

Because of Ian.

Ian Sugrue was the best man and he'd known Suze's fiancé, Kevin, for almost as long as Tara and Suze had been mates. Tara liked Kevin (though she found his habit of always wanting to have the last word on everything pretty irritating) but she couldn't stand his best friend. At one time, when Tara was going through a particularly bleak phase in her love-life, both Kevin and Suze had suggested to her that she might like to come out on a double date with them and Ian. She'd agreed because she reckoned that any mate of Kevin's could be worth getting to know, and at first she thought that she'd hit the jackpot too. Ian was attractive and chatty, although he had wandering hands and Tara had spent a lot of the latter part of the evening removing one or the other of them from her thigh or her shoulders (where he would drape his arm around her and allow the tips of his fingers to brush against her breast).

When he'd brought her home that night Ian had asked Tara whether she was going to invite him in for a nightcap. He winked lasciviously as he said this and she'd snapped at him that she wasn't interested in that sort of nightcap thanks very much and she didn't sleep with blokes on first dates. She wasn't, she said firmly, that sort of girl.

Ian had been very apologetic and had insisted that she was misinterpreting him and that he wouldn't dream of trying to have sex with her on a first date. And he'd asked her out again. Tara hadn't been sure whether to accept. He was all right, she supposed, but he really did seem more interested in her body than anything else. (Tara was never quite sure what to make of her own body. She'd been told by a former boyfriend that it was 'generous', which she took to mean fat; but all of her friends insisted that fat was the wrong word for her. Curvy, they told her. Well-proportioned was another phrase they used. Great tits had been Suze's contribution. Tara still felt as though fat was the most appropriate term.) But Ian Sugrue didn't seem to think she was fat. Ian agreed that she had great tits and told her (on their second date) that she was absolutely perfect. And he'd squeezed one of her great tits as he said so.

Tara didn't know whether it was because Ian seemed to want to get her into bed so desperately, or whether it was simply that she didn't like him enough to want to sleep with him, but she found herself always finding reasons not to let him into her bed. In the end Ian had fumed at her that she was clearly frigid, that everyone knew it, that it was common knowledge that she was useless in the sack. And then he'd walked out on her.

Tara hadn't told Suze exactly why she'd stopped seeing Ian (she had a horrible feeling that he might be right about her being hopeless in bed, even though he hadn't had the opportunity to find out himself, and besides, she didn't want to cause any sort of hassle between Kevin and his best friend). Instead, she just told Suze that they weren't compatible and left it at that. She didn't know what, if anything, Ian might say to Kevin, but she decided not to get too upset about it. After all, she'd obviously deny everything!

Suze had been disappointed that her best friend and her fiancé's best friend hadn't hit it off, but she'd also agreed with Tara that Ian was a bit too full of himself for his own good and so she'd understood when Tara said that he just wasn't her type. But she fretted about her friend's lack of a decent boyfriend when she herself had been so lucky to nab Kevin.

Although Tara and Suze continued to socialise together (after all, they both agreed that you didn't give up your mates for anyone), Tara tried to steer clear of events at which she might bump into Ian again. After a few months, though, they'd met by chance at a nightclub and he'd asked her whether she'd learned how to loosen up a bit. Fortified by a few vodkas and Red Bulls she'd told him that it wasn't her, it was him. He was a smarmy git with wandering hands and she wouldn't touch him with a bargepole. At which he'd laughed loudly and said that one day she'd realise what she was missing.

Only that day didn't come, because she met Tom instead. The thing was, as Tara confided to Suze a few days before they set off for the Caribbean, Ian was an OK kind of guy even if he was too in love with himself for his own good. But she'd turned him down and now she was going to be stuck on an island with him for the best part of a week and it would be a bit uncomfortable even though Tom would be there.

'Oh, Ian won't give a stuff now,' Suze assured her. 'He's bringing his own girlfriend. Her name's Elmarie.'

Tara looked at Suze in surprise. She hadn't heard anything about anyone called Elmarie.

'Well I don't talk about Ian very much in front of you,' retorted Suze when Tara said this to her. 'You always make faces and give out to me for having introduced you to him in the first place.'

Tara had shrugged at that and said nothing. But she still

worried about Ian and what he might say to her. She didn't want him making horrible comments to her in front of Tom. Not when she was pretty much coming to the conclusion that Tom Parrish was the man for her and when she was hoping that the romance of Kevin and Suze's wedding might just rub off on him a little.

As it turned out, though, she needn't have worried at all. She and Tom arrived a day later than everyone else, and when they met Ian and Elmarie for the first time at the poolside bar which also overlooked the beach, things weren't as awkward as Tara had feared. Ian didn't make any smart-ass remarks to her (though she certainly would have understood him gloating over his new girlfriend, because Elmarie was stunning, with long, long legs which were already a smooth pale latte brown and a figure that curved in all the right places but which certainly couldn't be considered in the slightest bit fat. In the looks department Elmarie definitely outpointed Tara every time). Tom, Kevin and Ian had a shared interest in Arsenal football club, which kept their conversation firmly rooted in soccer and very little else. And despite being so absolutely gorgeous that it was positively demoralising to sit beside her, Elmarie was chatty and friendly and even complimented Tara on her Dior beach bag. (Which, in fact, Tara had got as a free gift with three products from their range during the summer.) As she talked, Elmarie lathered her lightly tanned skin with total sunblock because, she told Tara, she fried up just like a crisp.

'But you have a fabulous colour,' Tara protested as Elmarie adjusted her coolie-style sun hat to protect her face. 'It's so even and golden.'

'It's from the beauty centre,' Elmarie told her. 'Got it done yesterday. Why bake it when you can fake it?'

And Tara nodded in agreement as she pulled her lounger underneath the huge canvas parasol, even though her own olive skin rarely burned once she put on any kind of sun cream.

'The idea is that we all do our own thing,' Kevin told them. 'I mean, we wouldn't choose to come on holiday together . . .' He held up his hands. 'Well, who knows! Maybe in the future. But nobody should feel that they're tied to each other. Suze and I have a few things to do about the wedding arrangements. Maybe occasionally we'll nab Ian and Tara for a rehearsal or whatever. But otherwise just chill out and get ready to celebrate our big day.'

Although they all nodded in agreement, it wasn't all that easy to avoid each other in the days that followed. The beach at White Sands was long and curving but it was generally only inhabited by the residents of the hotel. And despite having two restaurants to choose from, the six of them usually met up at one meal of the day or in the bar afterwards. There was only one bar at White Sands after all, and it was the focus of the hotel's limited night-life. It was also where the girls could assess the wedding dresses of each day's bride.

'There is something of a conveyor belt about it,' murmured Elmarie to Tara one evening as they watched a pretty girl being whirled around the floor by her new husband. 'I'm really not sure that I'd like it very much for myself. Though at least I'd go through with it.'

They'd all heard about the wedding where the bride had apparently left her husband-to-be standing like an idiot in the wedding bower while she eloped with the best man. Or maybe it was the bridesmaid! She'd done something weird anyway. They weren't clear on the details.

'Suze said that December is their most popular wedding month,' responded Tara. 'Though I'm not sure whether she realised there would be so many other weddings either. All the same, it's kind of nice, isn't it? I think I'd love a wedding here.'

'You want to get married to Tom?' Elmarie arched an eyebrow at her, and Tara blushed.

'Oh, I don't know,' she said self-consciously. 'I mean, how do you know you've met the right person?'

'You don't think Tom is?'

'Maybe,' admitted Tara. 'We haven't actually being going out together for all that long. A few months, that's all.'

'I've known Ian for years,' said Elmarie idly. 'But he's not exactly the settling-down sort.'

'Really?' Tara looked at her uneasily and wondered whether Ian had been going out with Elmarie when he'd also been going out with her. And then she stopped caring because Tom came back with some more exotic cocktails and she busied herself with eating the maraschino cherries instead.

Suze and Kevin's wedding was absolutely perfect. Even though they'd seen three other weddings on the island and Tara believed that she was totally immune to the romance of it now, she still felt her eyes prickle with tears as she walked along the promontory with Suze, the tropical breeze lifting her friend's veil and blowing it gently behind her. There was no doubt that the setting was absolutely wonderful, and afterwards, as they'd sat on the veranda of the bar, Tara had daydreamed about getting married here too. She smiled at Tom and squeezed his hand, and he'd squeezed it back, which she found very promising indeed.

That evening they all ate together in the hotel's air-conditioned Mariner's Reef restaurant, and Tara found herself getting more and more relaxed as they drank the plentiful supply of champagne as well as the specially prepared cocktails. Despite the easy availability of alcohol, she hadn't actually got drunk before now, but tonight her head was slightly fuzzy from champagne and excitement. After the meal they went to the bar, where they danced to the calypso band and then listened to the tiny singer with the amazing voice who accompanied them.

'Pity we didn't know that Sahndhi Jeffries was staying here,' said Suze. 'We might have got her to sing for us.'

'She's crap,' said Tom. 'All tits and no talent.'

Tara felt herself blush as she noticed Ian looking at her chest.

'I bet she can only sing one song,' said Elmarie. 'You know what these *Pop Princess* people are like. Anyway, she's probably the last of them. Aren't they getting rid of that show?'

'That'd be a shame,' said Suze. 'I enjoy it. I always vote. And I think that Sahndhi is quite good. I love the way she sings.'

'The new song is rubbish,' said Ian.

'Haven't heard it,' Suze admitted.

'Shit lyrics,' Ian told her. 'All about doing it on your own or something.'

'Sounds like a good sentiment to me,' said Elmarie.

'Maybe she could get the writer girl to do some new lyrics,' suggested Tom.

'Writer girl?' Suze looked at him enquiringly.

'Corinne Doherty.' He nodded across the room to where the author was sitting, her nose in a book. 'That's her. She does the Jennifer Jones books.'

Suze shrugged. 'Never heard of her. What sort are they?'

'Crime,' said Tom.

'That's why I've never heard of her,' said Suze. 'I don't like crime. So what's she doing here? Researching murder at a wedding?'

'My feet are killing me,' said Elmarie as she slipped off her high-heeled shoes and rubbed her soles. 'I shouldn't have worn these. I'm covered in blisters.'

'Since my girlfriend is crippled, would you like to dance?' Ian looked at Tara challengingly. She was going to say no, but then shrugged. What difference did it make, after all? She was here with Tom and Ian was here with Elmarie. And it was silly to feel uncomfortable with him, because even if he wasn't her favourite person he was Kevin's best friend.

As they stood up, the music slowed down and the girl began singing. 'Unchained Melody'. Tara would really have preferred to dance with Tom to the slow tune but Ian's hand was already on her back, holding her to him.

'I have to apologise to you,' he said.

'Oh?'

'When we went out together. I behaved badly.'

She looked at him in surprise.

'Only because you were so gorgeous and delectable and so very obviously not interested in me. And I pressured you, which was totally wrong. So I apologise.'

'Oh,' said Tara again, only this time in some confusion. She hadn't expected that Ian would even consider apologising to her. And she was both surprised and pleased by it.

'I guess I was just at a bad point in my life,' he said.

'Elmarie?' suggested Tara.

'How did you know?' He looked at her ruefully. 'She'd

broken up with me and I was feeling down and . . . anyway,
I acted out of character and I'm sorry.'

'Apology accepted,' said Tara. 'And thank you.'

'You're welcome,' he told her. 'And that bloke of yours
doesn't appreciate you.'

'Tom?' She looked at him, trying to keep his face in focus
and wishing that she hadn't loaded up with so many glasses
of champagne followed by tequila sunrises.

'Yes. Tom.'

'He's OK,' said Tara. 'He cares about me.'

Ian snorted. 'Yeah. Right.'

'He does,' protested Tara.

'That's why he's been sniffing around my girlfriend, I
suppose,' said Ian.

'Huh?' Tara looked at him in surprise.

'Oh, come on, Tara. I'm surprised I need to point it out
to you!'

'I don't know what you're talking about,' said Tara.

'God, woman, but you're an innocent abroad, aren't you?'
said Ian. 'What about all those times we've had to head off
to do something wedding-related and the two of them have
been left together?'

'What about them?'

'You don't think they've been having conversations about
the weather, do you?'

Tara leaned back from him so that she could look at his
face.

'What have they been doing then?' she asked.

'Oh, Tara, Tara . . . I honestly don't believe you haven't
noticed the thing going on between them.'

'I haven't!' Her voice was tearful.

'Look, I know you've never been crazy about me, and

maybe I was a bit of a prat with you, but I am . . . was . . . am crazy about Elmarie. Trouble is, she's so difficult to keep. She likes lots of men in her life. Always has. That's why our relationship is so on-off. When I met you I'd just been dumped by her for the third time and I guess I was a bit all over the place.'

'Oh,' said Tara blankly.

'Like a fool, though, I came back to her. Couldn't help myself. I thought that this little trip would be good for us. I didn't count on her falling for your boyfriend.'

'Falling for my . . . falling for Tom?' Tara stared at him, not wanting to believe him. But suddenly little incidents were falling into place. Like Tom and Elmarie going scuba-diving the day that she'd had to go into town with Suze to have her dress altered slightly. Or the fact that both of them always ordered the same drink. Or the morning she'd come down late to the beach and seen Tom rubbing cream on to Elmarie's shoulders when Ian was nowhere to be seen. She felt her stomach turn over and staggered slightly on the tiled floor.

'Hey, hey – are you all right?' Ian steadied her, concern in his eyes.

'I'm fine,' she said shortly. 'I'm just . . . I don't like being made a fool of.'

'Hmm. Well neither do I,' said Ian ruefully. 'But I keep letting it happen to me.'

Tara glanced across the open area towards the bar and narrowed her eyes. She'd thought it was different with Tom. She'd thought that maybe there was something more between them. But it looked like she'd got it wrong again. She felt a wave of hurt and humiliation wash over her.

'Where are they now?' she asked.

'Didn't Tom say something about bringing down that wedding cake from the restaurant?' said Ian. 'Maybe that's what they're doing.'

'Maybe.' Tara's voice was shaky but grim. 'Or maybe they've gone back to our room.' She broke away from Ian's grasp. 'I've got to go and check it out.'

'Oh, come on, Tara . . .'

But she'd already started to walk back through the gardens towards Room 316.

Ian shrugged, then followed her along the narrow pathways. As she arrived at the room, though, she stopped abruptly.

'I don't have the key,' she said flatly. 'Tom does.' She rubbed her forehead and stared at the closed door. 'How could he do this to me?'

Ian said nothing. Tara pressed her ear to the door of the room. 'I don't hear anything,' she said. 'No groans of passion. Is Elmarie a screamer or not?'

'Look, Tara, this is silly,' said Ian. 'You don't want to know if they're in there.'

'Of course I want to know,' she snapped. 'I have a right to know if I'm being cheated on.'

'All right.' Ian took a key card from his own pocket. 'Let's go into my room. You can lean across the balcony and see if there's anyone next door.'

Tara brushed a tear from her eyes. 'OK.'

She followed him into Room 315, inhaling the scent of Allure which Elmarie habitually wore, and feeling suddenly uncomfortable about being here. But then Ian opened the patio doors and they both stepped outside. Room 316 was in darkness.

'Might have jumped the gun a bit,' she said, a note of relief in her voice.

'Hopefully.' Ian didn't sound convinced.

'What?'

'They don't have to be in a room,' he said. 'Elmarie likes doing it outdoors.'

Tara bit her lip and began to cry. It wasn't fair, she thought. It just wasn't fair. Tom was a nice guy. She liked him. So why was it that the nice guys always wanted someone else? What was it about her? Wasn't she good enough for him? Either in bed or out of it?

'Hey, come on.' Ian put his arm around her shoulders. 'Don't get upset. They're not worth it.'

'You obviously think Elmarie is.' She sniffed. 'You keep going back to her.'

'I can't help myself,' he admitted. 'But maybe the time has come for me to make a break once and for all.'

He smiled at her and touched her gently on the nose with the tip of his finger. Tara didn't exactly know when it was that her dislike of Ian suddenly disappeared. Maybe it was when he kissed her gently on the lips. Maybe it was when he slowly unzipped her pink silk dress and eased it over her shoulders. Maybe it was when she kissed him in return.

All Tara knew was that quite suddenly she wanted to make love to Ian, and she wanted to do it here and now. So she let him push her gently on to the enormous queen-sized bed and pulled him close to her, thinking she'd been wrong about him all those months ago and wishing that she'd had more sense than to chose Tom Parrish instead.

But afterwards, as Ian rolled off her and went into the bathroom, she felt sadly deflated about the whole thing. Regardless of how angry she was over being duped by Tom, she now felt angry – though this time with herself – for making love with Ian. Making love! She snorted. They hadn't made love. They'd had sex. Good sex, it was true. Angry sex, maybe. But just sex all the same.

She slid her pretty pink bridesmaid's dress over her head again and let herself out of the room before Ian emerged from the bathroom. She heard his voice call after her as she closed the door but she ignored him and hurried along the dimly lit footpaths back towards the bar. She blinked in the stronger light as she approached it but she couldn't see any of the wedding guests, although her pink clutch bag was still where she'd left it on the glass-topped table. She glanced at her watch. They'd only been gone twenty-five minutes. She grabbed the bag and hurried towards the Ladies', where she pulled a brush through her dark curly hair, touched up her make-up and sprayed herself with copious amounts of Glow to mask the scent of sex which she knew was around her.

As she came out of the Ladies', she walked straight into Tom.

'There you are!' he exclaimed. 'I was looking everywhere for you.'

'Oh really.' Her voice was unusually sharp. 'I didn't think you cared.'

'Huh?'

Tara walked ahead of him towards the bar again.

'What on earth are you talking about?' Tom grabbed her by the arm.

'You and Elmarie,' she said. 'That's what.'

'What about me and Elmarie?' he asked.

'Don't think I haven't noticed,' she said tightly. 'You and her together whenever me and Ian had to do stuff with Suze and Kevin. You rubbing suntan cream on to her fake tan! I don't care about it, Tom, but I wish you'd had the decency to tell me.'

Tom stared at her. 'You're off your trolley, woman,' he said. 'All that sun and champagne has fried your brain. I admit that Elmarie and I have been thrown together a bit because, like you said, you and Ian have had to do a few wedding things. But that's it. She's an attractive girl but she's a terrible flirt and she's got a vicious tongue in her head. She keeps trying to imply that you and Ian had a bit of a thing going, but I know how much you dislike him so I didn't take any notice of her. I think that pissed her off to be honest. So if it's her that's putting ideas into your head, maybe that's why.'

This time it was Tara who stared at Tom.

'Oh, look,' he said easily. 'Let's forget about the pair of them. I have to tell you that I really, really enjoyed myself today. In fact I've enjoyed the whole holiday. And you know what, I think it was because I was here with you.'

Tara thought she was going to faint as Tom led her back to the dance floor and put his arm around her. As he held her close to him, the only image in her mind was of Ian straddling her body, telling her how sexy she was and how much he'd always wanted her. Telling her, too, that Tom and Elmarie deserved nothing back from them. That Elmarie had always betrayed him and that Tom had betrayed her. But that now they'd be sorry. And she saw herself pulling him closer to her, wanting to get back at Tom for betraying her.

Only he hadn't.

And she knew that she was the one who'd be sorry.

Reception (June)

Her last hotel had been very different. It had been in the heart of London, a very expensive hotel frequented mainly by businessmen and the occasional businesswoman. She'd had to be businesslike when she worked there too, always polite and always friendly but never too warm and gushing, never overstepping the mark. She'd had to treat them as though they were weighed down with responsibilities and make them feel that she would sort anything out for them. Some of them were horrible – brusque and rude and treating her as though she was a nobody – but most of them were nice enough, lonely a lot of the time, fed up with having to stay away from home even if it was at a swanky hotel where a bottle of water cost almost as much as a supermarket wine, and so they were grateful for her apparent solicitousness.

Leaving hadn't been in her game plan. She'd expected to get promoted at some point, move up the chain of command. Maybe become the guest services executive, which was a coveted position. She'd worked hard enough to be taken notice of, making sure that the junior receptionists dealt with the guests politely and efficiently, helping the non-nationals with their English so that they weren't thrown by colloquialisms and so that they always appeared completely in control of what was going on, and always trying to improve her own performance so that she was the best she could possibly be. She knew that behind her back some of them called her a control freak, but she didn't care. It was better to cover every eventuality than none, and that was what she tried to do.

June liked her job and she knew that she was good at it. She liked dealing with people. She liked solving their problems. The hotel management told her that she was an excellent employee and that she had a bright future with them. June liked the idea of having a bright future. Even if it wasn't the future that had been mapped out for her.

She hadn't, of course, realised that there was a future mapped out for her. Not at first anyway, although she was acutely aware that her parents constantly told her how important it was to work hard and get good results in her exams and pretty much stressed that the rest of her life depended on it. June had never been so sure about that. Colin and Elizabeth were competitive people. She wasn't. She was hard-working, but that was entirely different to someone who walked into a classroom and made a decision that they were always going to be top of it.

Despite the fact that she was a plodder rather than an instinctively good student like her parents, June got enough points to study medicine at college. She realised then that had always been the plan. Colin and Elizabeth had studied medicine too and, after graduating, had set up their own practice together. Their hope was that when June qualified she would come and join them. They hadn't spoken about it before because, they told her, they didn't want to pressurise her. But hearing it now was pressure enough. Especially as, even though she'd got the points for medicine, she didn't know whether she really wanted to study it. Besides, although she loved her parents, the idea of working with them was entirely style-cramping.

Not that she had a particular style to be cramped. That was part of the problem as far as June was concerned. She wanted to have a style. She felt as though she should have a style. But she had no idea on earth of what that style should be.

Other people projected a style on to her. She didn't realise that at first because in her own mind her life was perfectly normal, but not everyone saw it exactly the same way. Other people looked at her with preconceptions, and those preconceptions bore very little relation to how she saw herself.

Literally, very literally (like when she looked in the mirror), she saw herself as beautiful. She wasn't being arrogant when she made this judgement because, from the moment she was born, people had called her beautiful. Why wouldn't they when they saw her huge dark eyes and her generous mouth and her creamy café-au-lait skin which was smooth and blemish-free? Elizabeth had entered her into a bonny baby competition when she was a year old and she'd knocked all the other competitors into a cocked hat with the mischievous glint in her eyes and her engaging smile and her lovely skin. (It was, she thought, entirely predictable that Colin and Elizabeth had been competitive about her status as a bonny baby too.)

Even when she was a little older people told her she was very pretty, although she could hear a slight qualification in their tone by then, as though her beauty had happened in spite of herself. And then, one day, when she was about six, as she'd waited to pay for her weekly comic at the newsagent at the end of the road, a girl she didn't know looked at her curiously and asked her whether she was black.

'No,' replied June. 'I'm Irish.'

'You look black,' observed the other girl.

When she went home June tackled the subject with Colin and Elizabeth. It hadn't occurred to her before (and afterwards she wondered why on earth not) that Colin was a completely different colour to Elizabeth. His dark skin gleamed beneath the kitchen light while Elizabeth was undoubtedly fairer, even though she too had dark hair and eyes. June knew that Elizabeth had been born in Carlow because she regularly visited her Granny Ellen there. June also knew that Colin's mother lived in England. She'd been brought to visit Granny Cyn last summer but she couldn't remember much about it other than that her grandmother had been a smiling woman the same colour as Colin and that her house had smelled of exotic spices.

'You're lucky,' Elizabeth told her firmly. 'You're a mixture of your dad and me. You're extra special.'

June had felt good about being extra special, although she found that as she grew older it didn't cut a whole lot of ice with some people. She never quite knew whether she cared or not. Most of the time she didn't, because she thought that her friends were her friends and generally it didn't matter what other people thought. But sometimes it did. Maybe it would've been different if she'd been brought up in a multi-racial town. But she hadn't. June couldn't remember when she started to feel a little isolated at school, but she knew that she did. It wasn't anyone's fault. They were all extremely nice to her. But every so often she got the feeling that somehow she didn't quite belong. The thing was, she wasn't sure what exactly she wanted to belong to.

In the end she decided to go to England to do her degree. Colin and Elizabeth frowned when she told them, but she explained that she needed to see more of life than Carlow and its surrounding areas had to offer. They suggested Dublin as an alternative, but at that time Dublin hadn't turned into the vibrant city that later attracted students from all over the world, and June had no interest in living in a squalid bed-sit in a run-down town that pretended it was a city. So she went to London instead.

It was very different. The streets heaved with people, and as she stood in Trafalgar Square, she realised that not one of them was actually speaking English. She recognised French and Portuguese and identified an unknown Arabic language. But no English.

College was different too. But it was in college that they first tried to make her choose. When she was initially asked about her ethnic background, she told them she was Irish, just as she had when she'd talked to the little girl in the newsagent. But that wasn't enough for the more radical cabal, who stressed roots and origin and who later told her that she was a traitor to her people for playing on the ladies' soccer team. June hadn't quite understood how she was a traitor to anyone by being the person to score the deciding goal in the final and win the cup for the college, but apparently she was. Trying to be white, one of the cabal had told her tartly. Trying to ingratiate herself. June had pointed out that the ethnic origins of the entire team were fairly mixed, so she was probably also, in that case, trying to be Thai, American and Brazilian – a female Pelé, she'd suggested wryly – but Alicia, the most vocal of them all, was having none of it. Alicia said that black football players in

England were exploited by the system. June told her to cop on to herself. But at night she wondered why it was that Alicia and her friends thought it so important that she behave like a black person when she wasn't actually black.

She wasn't actually white either. She was a mixture. She'd never minded being a mixture before, but now she couldn't help wondering sometimes whether it wouldn't have been easier to have been just black or just white, because then she wouldn't fall between the two. As it was, she was becoming more and more conflicted inside whenever there were programmes on the TV about racial issues, and she'd get into a moral dilemma about whether she should agree with the newscasters who said that black boys achieved much less than their potential at school, or whether she should feel that white people had a point when they said that they were becoming an ethnic minority in their own country. If she'd been one or the other she wouldn't have to worry either about calling herself mixed-race, a term her parents used easily, or multi-racial, which the cabal said more accurately reflected her status. Mixed was a term applied to mongrels, they told her. Multi-racial was a true definition of her heritage.

June thought that multi-racial made her sound like an even worse mix. And then she suffered feelings of guilt because she'd used the word 'worse', which implied that there was something bad about being a mixture at all. It was easier for Colin and Elizabeth, she sometimes thought. They had unique identities. Hers was blurred, and people didn't like blurring of boundaries. They liked things to be clear and precise. They liked to be able to choose. And they wanted her to choose too. They wanted her to pick a colour. But with her fudge skin and brown eyes, she didn't know what colour to pick.

Besides, if she chose to be white she was insulting her father. If she chose to be black she was insulting her mother. She did, however, find it interesting that more people considered her to be black than white simply because she wasn't very obviously fair-skinned. When people she didn't know spoke to her she felt as though they expected her to say things like 'you go girl' and 'right on bro' even though she'd never used either expression in her life before.

She visited Granny Cyn in Chelmsford. Her grandmother was old but full of vitality and she cracked jokes and peppered her conversation with expressions like 'everythin' cook and curry' which made June look at her in total mystification. When she asked for explanations her grandmother told her to go look it up, and eventually June learned that it meant that everything was fine. She rather liked the expression and she tried to use it herself a couple of times but it sounded as ridiculous as 'you go girl' in her Irish accent and she soon gave up on it. Which made her decide that yes, she was Irish and nothing else. Of course, the Irish part of her was another issue in London. Nobody was up front and rude about that, but occasionally she was affectionately called a Paddy and asked about leprechauns, and whenever there was anything on the news about the IRA she would try to melt into the background and not draw attention to herself. People in college asked her questions about the IRA as though she actually knew the answers, as though she had some kind of inner understanding of their thought processes. June would shrug and say that there wasn't much IRA activity around her home and that she didn't know any rebel songs. When she said this she realised that along with the island expressions and the black expressions she wasn't any good at rebel expressions either.

And then they called her Paddy-Black, which was also supposed to be a term of endearment but which drove her nuts.

Henry didn't call her Paddy-Black. Henry called her 'sweetheart' and told her that he loved her. And then they broke up on the night before her exams, causing her to fail spectacularly and finally decide that medicine wasn't for her after all.

They broke up because she wouldn't come to Jamaica with him during the summer.

'I'm heading to Europe for the summer,' she told him. 'I want to brush up on my languages.' She was better at languages than medicine.

'I want to explore my island,' he told her. 'I want you to be with me when I do.'

'It's not *your* island,' she replied. 'It's *an* island. And you don't want me to explore it. You want me along so's you can lecture me about my roots.' She looked at him defiantly as she said this. Henry was big into roots.

'You've no sense of history, girl,' he told her.

'I have a great sense of history,' she responded tartly. 'I grew up in Ireland. Haven't you heard about our eight hundred years of oppression?'

'It's not the same,' he said.

'It's exactly the same.'

'You're not English and you're not Irish,' he told her. 'And there's no point in pretending. They'll never accept you as one of their own because you have African blood.'

'Oh, give me a break,' she spat. 'Besides, I'm not Jamaican either. That's not where my father comes from.'

'Where then?' demanded Henry.

'Chelmsford,' she retorted and walked away.

But it had upset her, the row with Henry. She hadn't been able to concentrate on her exams because she couldn't help hearing his voice telling her that she'd never be accepted by her own country. Which was nonsense really. She got on well with everyone in her home town. More or less.

Colin and Elizabeth had been horrified when she failed her exams and talked about coaching her for her repeats. She told them that she was chucking in the whole medicine thing. It wasn't her. Her real skill was languages.

Her parents were even more horrified. What about the practice? they asked her. She shook her head. It was their business, not hers. And then Elizabeth had asked whether it was all about this Henry bloke and June had said of course not but that he'd opened her eyes to a few things.

He hadn't opened her eyes to her roots, of course. But he had made her think that she was trying to be someone she wasn't when it came down to medicine. And that was why she chucked it in and went on her trip through Europe.

There were good people and bad people in Europe, just as there had been good people and bad people in Ireland and England. And some of them thought she was white while others talked to her as though she were black. It was an interesting distinction, June thought. It said a lot about people. But she didn't know what it said about her that she was still unable to choose.

She went to the island for a holiday afterwards. She walked along the silver-white beaches and looked at the clear blue sky and swam in the tepid blue water and she thought that it was Paradise. For holiday-makers, obviously, because people still left in search of a better standard of living somewhere else. When she ventured away from the luxury confines of the hotel she could see that there was poverty on the island too and that many people struggled to make a living. She noticed that the hotel staff seemed happy, though, and the part of her that felt guilty at being a tourist was relieved that she wasn't exploiting the local residents. Although she wondered if they resented the apparent riches of those who could spend a full day lying on the beach doing nothing but sip garish cocktails. She wondered, too, what they would have said if she told them that her grandmother's house was a mere ten-minute walk away and that her father's cousin, Jamelia, lived there now. She never found out because she never told them.

It was the hurricane that made her go back. She'd watched the news and seen the pictures of palm trees being ripped from the ground and hotels being flattened and she'd been shocked in a visceral way that had surprised her. And then her mother had told her that Jamelia's house had just escaped total destruction, that the house next door had been lifted by the winds and shredded into matchsticks.

Jamelia had phoned Colin after the hurricane. The telephone lines were down but her son had a mobile and that was what she used to tell him that he didn't have to worry about them, that they were all OK. June had phoned home when she saw the pictures of the hurricane and her father had sounded equally shocked at the extent of the destruction.

'Perhaps I should go,' he said uncertainly. 'Maybe there's something I can do.'

But he didn't go because he had a surgery every day and a patient list which was as long as his arm.

June went. Because of her job in the London hotel she was able to get a good rate in one close to Jamelia's house. She turned up one evening and a small girl with her hair in a fat bunch behind her head shouted that there was a white girl on the doorstep.

Jamelia was tall and slender and even more beautiful than June. She wore her hair straight and her nails long and she looked at her for a moment before laughing and saying that she must be Colin's girl and she was very welcome and wasn't it a blessing that none of them had been killed but there was no reason for her to have come. And then she ushered her into the green-painted wooden house and told her to sit down and take the weight off her feet and have a cup of tea.

The house was small but modern. June hadn't realised that it would be modern. Somehow she'd imagined decor and fittings from the sixties, but the living room was bright and cheery with a tiled floor and pastel-coloured walls on which two vibrant abstract paintings hung. And through the arch that led to the kitchen she could see wooden units and a fitted cooker and hob as well as a huge American-style fridge.

Jamelia returned with the tea and handed the cup to June. She was like Colin, June realised. That was the big shock. Her smile was like his and so was her frown.

'So what are you doing here?' she asked. 'Why did you come?'

'I don't know.' June sipped the tea while the little girl, who Jamelia had introduced as her granddaughter, Butterfly, sat on the floor and looked at her enquiringly. 'It was the hurricane,' she added. 'We all wanted to come.'

Jamelia laughed. 'Well, we sure as hell wanted to run

when it hit. But like I told Colin, we were lucky. Still, Mariah next door really got it bad; her son and daughter are helping her to rebuild. We'll be OK.' She looked at June curiously. 'Did you think you were riding to the rescue of your poor Caribbean cousins?'

Butterfly giggled and June blushed.

'I don't know what I thought,' she admitted. 'I came here once before, just to see it, and it was so beautiful.'

'You didn't come see us then.'

June shook her head. 'I was a tourist.'

'Never a tourist.' Jamelia grinned. 'You got family on the island. How can you be a tourist?'

'I'm Irish.' June grinned in return. 'I'm white.'

'Yes,' said Butterfly. 'You are.'

'And that's always a problem?' Jamelia looked at her with understanding.

'Always will be,' said June.

'White here, black there?'

'Oh, both there,' said June. 'And I can live with it, but . . . sometimes not.'

'You'll be white for sure here,' said Jamelia. 'Nobody's going to think you're from the island. It was always a possibility when Colin went to England. That he'd find someone and they'd have a child and she'd be neither one thing nor the other.'

'I only want to feel Irish,' said June.

'Why?'

June frowned. 'Because that's where I was born. That's where I grew up.'

Jamelia nodded. 'You don't feel anything for here?'

'Well, it's gorgeous!' June laughed. 'But I can't imagine living here. It's too nice.'

'No it's not,' said Jamelia. 'It wasn't too nice when the hurricane came. And they do come.'

'I suppose.'

'Where are you staying?' asked Jamelia.

'The Coconut Hills,' said June.

'You can stay here,' Jamelia told her. 'I have a spare room.'

June didn't know whether it would be rude to accept or decline her relative's invitation.

'Well, how long are you staying?' asked Jamelia when she realised June's dilemma.

'A week,' said June. 'And I got a good deal with the hotel. I work in a hotel myself, that's why.'

'Don't fret,' said Jamelia. 'Go back there. It's OK.'

Later, June met Jamelia's daughter, Melissa, and her husband, James, and their other children, Chloe and Jimi. They sat on the veranda of the house and drank fruit punch and talked about the family and their lives. Melissa worked in one of the jewellery stores in town. Jimi worked in a marine biology research unit.

'This isn't some backward paradise,' said Melissa as June's eyes widened. 'We have TV and the internet, you know. The world is smaller than it was.'

'I know. I guess I just think of life here in a kind of holiday way,' said June. 'I can't imagine living here.'

'Why not?' asked Jamelia. 'People retire here, you know. We see them all the time, tourists looking for an authentic Caribbean home. Wanting the best views of the sea and then picking a spot that's exposed to the wind.' She chuckled. 'We tell them that now, though. We tell them what's best for them.'

'I have a life and a job back in England,' said June as

she felt the warm breeze tickle the backs of her shoulders. 'I can't chuck that in to come here.'

'Of course you can if you feel like it,' said Melissa. 'Besides, you can always go back.'

But she didn't go back. Not because she'd discovered her roots, although she enjoyed going to Sunday lunch at Jamelia's and meeting her extended Caribbean family. But because the job she'd got in the White Sands Hotel was the most enjoyable job she'd ever had. There were picky guests and rude guests and occasional disasters (like the other night when she'd discovered that someone had robbed the lobsters out of the tank in the restaurant and when a really nice English guy had handed over a hundred dollars to keep it all quiet), but overall she liked the life. One day, she thought, she might go back. But she couldn't be sure about that. June thought that when it came down to it her whole life was about not being sure.

She was Irish but she had an English father. He was English but with island blood. So she had island blood too. She was white with a trace of black. Or sometimes black with a trace of white. She would never fit in properly. She would never be able to choose.

She knew that people still expected her to. She hoped she would never need to.

Room 522 (Gráinne)

This wasn't where I'd intended to be the week before Christmas. It certainly wasn't where I'd intended to be on my wedding anniversary. I'd already made plans for that, and it knocked me back when they were thrown into complete disarray by the twins. I'd guessed that there was something going on, but to be honest, I'd thought it was Christmas-related. The twins like Christmas, they always have. Maybe it was something to do with the two of them ratcheting up each other's excitement over the thoughts of Santa Claus and a tree piled with presents and the whole thing. Or maybe they were just particularly sweet-natured and gullible children who turned into sweet-natured if not (fortunately) particularly gullible adults. But for them, Christmas was always a wondrous time.

For me . . . well, I reckon when you've seen forty-four Christmases, you've seen them all. There is, I guess, a certain feeling of nostalgia that comes over you when you take the decorations out of the attic where they've gathered dust for all of the previous year; you probably can't help but experience flashbacks of other Christmases where you've hung the same bauble on the tree and where something magical happened (in my case nothing magical ever really happened – the closest was when Aidan came home one year with a voucher for a turkey which he'd won in the golf club nearest-the-pin competition. Unfortunately it was a whole turkey, not boned and rolled like I preferred – and straight from the farm, so that the entire episode of having to clean it out and pluck half of its feathers rather put me off eating it). Anyway, that's not important. What's important is that the twins arrived at the house at the beginning of December with the envelope in their hands and wide, beaming smiles on their faces and I discovered that they had booked us into the White Sands Hotel all-inclusive stretching from a few days before our anniversary until the twenty-seventh of December.

I was gobsmacked. Firstly that they remembered our anniversary. Coming as it did just before Christmas, it normally got overlooked in the great scheme of things. Secondly that they were able to afford what I knew had to be a breathtaking amount of money to send us away. White Sands was an expensive hotel. I knew that because a couple of years earlier Madge, one of my best friends, had gone there with her second husband (her fairly rich second husband) and had regaled me with stories of the expense! So I found it hard to believe that Carina and Callum (both hedonistic twenty-five-year-olds) had managed to save up enough money to send Aidan and me to the Caribbean.

'Would you not worry about how we managed to pay for it?' demanded Carina when I couldn't help but murmur that it was surely way outside their earning power (both of them worked in the media – Carina as a researcher for an independent TV company; Callum in radio). 'It's something that we wanted to do for you and Dad. You've always been great to us and I know we forget your anniversary all the time. So this is a kind of accumulation of all of them. Besides,' her dark eyes twinkled at me, 'it's your silver wedding anniversary. You deserve a great break.'

'Actually,' added Callum, 'we wanted to send you somewhere called Silver Sands. But we couldn't find anywhere.'

I smiled as widely as I could. 'It's very good of you,' I told them. 'Both your dad and I appreciate it very much.'

Well, I'd no idea how Aidan would feel about it. But he'd have to appreciate the gesture if nothing else.

When I told him he frowned slightly (as I'd expected) and murmured that it wasn't a hugely convenient time to go away. And I nodded in agreement and said that he was right but that the children had gone to a lot of trouble to organise it and so the least we could do was to be totally appreciative and accept such a wonderful present as gracefully as possible.

Sometimes I still have the power to make Aidan do what I want. This was one of those times. He nodded thoughtfully and then phoned Callum to say that it was a wonderful gift and we were delighted with it.

Which is why, despite the fact that I'd made other plans, I was sitting in the sea-front restaurant of the hotel at 7.30 on the evening of our wedding anniversary and looking out over the inky blackness of the Caribbean Sea. It wasn't completely black, of course. The underwater lights illuminated the area closest to the restaurant while, further out, the reflections bobbed on the surface of the gently lapping water, occasionally breaking into glittering shards of colour thanks to a stronger than usual wave before settling back into beads of light again. Meanwhile, in the restaurant, the impeccably trained waiters and waitresses moved swiftly and unobtrusively between the tables, making sure that every whim of every guest was catered for.

At our table, the wine waiter, DeVere, was discussing the merits of the cabernet sauvignon over the shiraz with my husband. Aidan is a bit of a wine buff and so I didn't take part in the conversation but allowed my eyes to wander over the rest of the diners. When you're at an all-inclusive hotel, particularly a relatively small and certainly exclusive one like White Sands, you tend to get to know your fellow guests fairly quickly. At least you get to recognise them enough to nod at them every morning, every lunchtime and every evening in a kind of complicit 'Look, I know that there are probably loads of brilliant local restaurants out there but I'm spending a fortune to stay here and, well, what the hell!' kind of way. I'd already spoken to the older woman, Esther, who was here on her own and who reminded me very much of those Miss Marple TV programmes. The ones starring Joan Hickson, not the more recent ones. Esther looked like Joan Hickson in the role and acted like her too – slightly dippy but not really, if you get my drift. I felt as though she was altogether stronger than she let on. I'd also spoken to the guy on his own with his son who'd arrived the previous day. He seemed really nice but terribly jumpy and I guessed that it was probably the first time he'd ever been on his own with the kid, even though the boy was about nine or ten years old.

I wondered how Aidan would have been had he ever gone on holiday on his own with the kids. Funny, I wasn't even able to imagine that, because Aidan just wasn't the sort of guy who thought that taking the kids away on his own was something a bloke should ever do. Sounds crazy now (at least I think it does, because more and more men talk about wanting to be proper fathers to their kids and wanting to spend time with them), but back when Aidan and I had the twins, the concept of a New Man was one who poked the fire while you fed, bathed and changed the baby before washing the dishes from the meal you'd just cooked. And having done that, he felt as though his work was done. Maybe I'm being unfair on loads of guys in their forties and fifties. But I'm talking about my experience and the experience of most of my friends. Things did change over the next twenty years or so. But not as dramatically as many women would have us believe.

Thing was, of course, I didn't mind what Aidan's contribution was. The fact that he was there at all was enough for me. My life without Aidan would surely have been a whole heap worse.

I met him at work. Back in the late 1970s lots of girls met their future husbands at work. Work was one of the biggest social events that existed in our calendars because there wasn't an awful lot else to do. A few tawdry night-clubs, maybe. Getting chatted up in a dingy bar (and most of them were dingy even if they'd stippled the walls, painted them white and hung red lampshades from the ceiling in an effort to make it look faintly exotic). Meeting a guy at night class – honestly, that's what the magazines of the day recommended. The only night class I ever went to (car maintenance for beginners) was crammed with women hoping to meet men. Work, if you worked in a big organisation, was the best option by a mile. And I worked in a big organisation. I worked in a bank.

Getting a job in the bank was like winning the jackpot. The pay was good and so were the conditions. People treated you with a level of respect. You dealt with money at a time when nobody had very much. It's changed now, of course. You probably get more respect at a supermarket checkout than as a bank teller. (And fewer supermarket checkout workers have been replaced by machines too.) But I was thrilled when I turned up for my first day's work. Doubly thrilled because I was in head office, and that had a certain cachet about it too. I wasn't working in some poky little branch. I was in the modern new glass and steel building which housed a couple of hundred people all feeling slightly proud of themselves for having got a job here in the first place.

I met Aidan Rourke at my very first Christmas party. I'd been with the bank six months and was loving it. Not because of the work (although I was already studying for the banking exams because you got paid extra if you got the qualification), but because for the first time I was surrounded by people whose main aim in life was to earn enough money to have fun. Fun hadn't been a big part of my home life. That wasn't anyone's fault. But, you see, I lived on my own with my widowed mother, and she wasn't the kind of person who believed that life should be fun. She'd got religion when Dad had his first heart attack. And she stuck with it after he died. (Even after I told her that she was wearing out her knees in the church and what was the point of going to Mass every day when her prayers about Dad recovering hadn't actually been answered?) Anyway, me and Mam didn't see eye to eye about religion. Or illness. Or having fun.

So having fun at work was a big eye-opener. And apparently the most fun event in the entire calendar was the Christmas party. We started talking about it in October.

It was in the Burlington Hotel, a popular spot for office functions because of its vast ballroom and its ability to chuck a couple of hundred turkey and ham dinners at hungry revellers in no time. I don't actually remember the food, but I do remember dancing to Abba and Rod Stewart and Slade and kicking up my heels in my party frock.

My party frock was the talk of the evening. I hadn't intended it to be, of course. But when I'd gone in to town, expecting to buy something cheap and cheerful in Dunnes, I'd seen the perfect dress in the window of Richard Alan. It was the darkest blue with tiny silver stars on a chiffon skirt over a silk body. It had shoestring straps and a slit up the side. It was absolutely gorgeous. Naturally it was far, far more expensive than I could afford. But I'd got my first credit card that day and . . . well . . . The dress put me close to my limit. I had to have it, though. I knew it was absolutely perfect for me. So I went in and bought it and then spent the rest of my money on a pair of silver sandals that (quite honestly) were a bit tacky but which I thought were good with the dress.

At the party, where almost everyone else had bought chain-store dresses and tarted them up with glittery jewellery, I stood out. I know I did. There were a few snide remarks about the slit in the side from some of the girls, but most of them simply gasped at the gorgeousness of my dress and made me feel like a million dollars.

Which is why I danced with loads of guys that night. Including Aidan Rourke.

I guess he'd have been seen as a good catch. He was already a few steps up the promotional ladder. He was working in the international department. And he wasn't at all bad-looking. Nothing tremendous. Nothing heart-stopping. But good enough for me, all the same.

I'd arrived at the party with a gang of my girlfriends but

most of them left before me. That's because I was still sitting talking to Aidan Rourke when Juliet Shanahan came over and said that they were clubbing together for a taxi and if I wanted to come I'd better come now. But I was actually sitting on Aidan's lap at the time and I muttered to her to go on without me, that I'd manage fine on my own.

Ten minutes later I went off to get my coat and walked back into the now almost deserted ballroom. There was no sign of Aidan. There was no sign of anyone I knew very well. I cursed myself for thinking that he'd hang around for me.

It was freezing outside. I wished I'd worn tights with my silver sandals, but of course I hadn't because the toe-seam would have looked horrible and ruined the effect. Now my toes were almost as blue as the dress with the cold. I pulled my tweed coat further around me and shivered.

'Which way are you going?' asked Aidan Rourke.

I hadn't heard him come up behind me.

'Terenure,' I said.

'Excellent.' He waved at a taxi, which slid to a halt beside us. 'We can share. I live in Templeogue.'

I grimaced. I'd been fudging things a little when I'd said Terenure. I lived in Kimmage. In the same area, certainly. But Terenure was a lot more desirable than Kimmage as an address. I directed the taxi-driver as far as the Kimmage Cross Roads, where the districts of Terenure, Templeogue and Kimmage intersected, and then I told him to let me out.

'Hey, we'll go as far as your house,' said Aidan.

I shook my head and told him that I wanted to walk. I needed some fresh air, I said. I wanted to clear my head. Before I knew what had happened, Aidan was out of the cab too and walking alongside me. I debated whether or not to walk up Fortfield Road but I knew that I would only be making things worse. So I turned down the Lower Kimmage Road and shrugged slightly. I waited for him to say something, but he didn't. He kept his arm around my shoulder as we turned into the side road which led to our red-brick terraced house. And he nodded in agreement when I asked him in for a cup of tea. (I should, of course, have said coffee. But we didn't have any.)

Funny thing is that house prices in Kimmage soared in the intervening years. It still doesn't have the cachet of Terenure or Templeogue, but it's not a cheap place to live any more. When Mam died and I sold the house at auction, I couldn't believe the bidding for it. All of my life I'd felt a bit let down by my address when so many people I met lived in more affluent suburbs, but things had changed dramatically. And it still took a bit of getting used to.

But that night, the night when Aidan Rourke walked me home and then came into the house for a cup of tea, I felt inadequate. My sparkly dress couldn't take away from the shabbiness of our house, from the fact that the carpet had threadbare patches near the sofa and that our cupboards were Formica rather than real wood. It's amazing how many stupid and irrelevant things rush into your mind when you bring someone new into your home territory. I was measuring number three Davitt Villas up to whatever Aidan's Terenure address was and it couldn't match up. I didn't need to see Aidan's house to know that mine fell far short of his. I knew it instinctively.

And so, when he kissed me, in our small and neat but painfully inadequate living room, I felt honoured. So honoured that I didn't stop him as his fingers slid upwards along the slit in my dress to the top of my legs. So honoured that I was happy to let him ease the zip slowly downwards and shrug my dress from my shoulders. And I know it sounds stupid to feel honoured that I lost my virginity to him on our brown cord sofa, but I did.

Afterwards I just felt lucky that Mam had taken a sleeping tablet to help her drop off that night. The doctor had prescribed them for her but she rarely took them, always fearing that she'd become addicted even though her only addiction was to daily Mass. But the night of the party I'd told her to damn well take one because I'd be late home and I knew she didn't really like being in the house on her own at night. For once she'd listened to me. And I felt very, very lucky.

I didn't, of course, feel lucky eight weeks later when I realised I was pregnant. I hadn't even considered the notion of getting pregnant, which I know sounds incredibly naïve but was actually the case. It was my first time. How many people get pregnant their first time? It's an unfair trick of our bodies, this desire to procreate. And it's totally unfair that in the midst of doing something great like making love to Aidan, I really should have been thinking about what else was going on.

I didn't know what to do. I couldn't tell my mother. It would kill her. I couldn't confide in Madge, even though by then she was my best friend. I couldn't tell anyone. But of course I had to. I had to tell Aidan. After all, he was the father of my child and we were actually going out together. He'd called me the day after the party and asked to meet me for a drink. And that was how he became my boyfriend.

But even now I can't believe that he married me. I'm quite sure he didn't want to. He was only twenty, after all.

I was nineteen. Yet when I told him about the baby, there was no question in his mind.

My mother, when I eventually told her, wanted things done as quickly as possible because she was overwhelmed by the shame of it all. (It was still definitely shameful twenty-five years ago to be pregnant and unmarried, no matter how confident you tried to be about it.) But I didn't want to rush up the aisle. I wanted to give Aidan options. I told him that I'd rather wait until after the baby was born. Besides, I said, I was already feeling fat and bloated, already loading on weight. I'd feel a total fraud getting married when I was bursting out of the dress. Why not wait? I suggested. He wasn't keen on that idea. He felt that asking me to marry him before having the baby made it all right. I didn't know what to do. I was afraid if I argued with him that he'd change his mind, and I didn't want him to change his mind. After all, I was in love with him.

So we compromised. We got married in a registry office. A quiet, unimportant day with only our parents there. (Despite her shame, my mother was being as supportive as she could. Aidan's parents were more furious than ashamed, but they felt it was their duty to attend. Later, I grew to like them and I became more friendly with Colleen Rourke than with Mam. I hate saying that. But it's true.)

The registry office ceremony was awful, and I didn't actually feel married afterwards. But I was and so our baby wouldn't be born with the illegitimate stigma that still surrounded single mothers and their children. At the time of our marriage I still thought I was having one baby. It wasn't until a few weeks later that I discovered I was having two.

In December that year, after the twins had been born,

we combined a christening event for them and a church wedding for ourselves. The priest was young and understanding. I guess that he'd realised that times were changing and that the established churches needed to do whatever they could to hang on to their flocks. And if that meant christening the babies and marrying their parents on the same day, he was going to do it.

The church wedding became, in the eyes of everyone who knew us, the real wedding day. And it was the December date that we celebrated every year afterwards, so that we almost forgot that another date even existed. On the times that we did celebrate, of course. Aidan wasn't much for marking birthdays and anniversaries. And it became less important to me too, over the years. More important was the twins and how they were getting on with life, which was, in fact, pretty well. Because (in some ways to our surprise) Aidan and I were good parents. Sure, he wasn't exactly the world's best around the house, but he was great with the kids. A natural. He liked being with them. He had more patience with them than me and enjoyed bringing them to the park or to places like the Natural History Museum or art galleries where they were well behaved and appreciative. They were always well behaved with Aidan. They played up more with me.

Staring out over the gently lapping water, I simply could not believe that twenty-five years had gone by since I married Aidan. I really couldn't. They'd gone in a blur of having the twins and then looking after them; of Aidan getting promoted; of moving house (three times!); of my mother's final illness; of Aidan's father's stroke; of Colleen Rourke's recovery from a mystery ailment after his death (which everyone knew was depression but which led to her living with us for over a year, which, to be honest, was a bit of a strain no matter how much I liked her); of all the things that go on in your life when you're not really paying attention.

I didn't pay attention to my life. I didn't have time. There was always something else to be doing. And now here I was thinking about it again, as I had for the past few months, realising that huge swathes of it had simply passed me by when I was concentrating on something else entirely.

Aidan's hadn't passed him by. Aidan had done really well – he'd moved job twice but had been headhunted back to the original bank again. He had an office on the fifth floor. The prestigious floor. The one that everyone wanted to have an office on. He was paid well and he spent the money on our home and our children. And on me too, I guess, because he regularly bought me gifts of jewellery or perfume. He was a good husband.

And we'd been together for twenty-five years.

I saw him nod at DeVere and the waiter closed the wine list.

'Shiraz,' said Aidan.

I nodded as he took a warm roll from the basket on the table and broke it in half, scattering crumbs across his plate and on to the green linen tablecloth. He frowned and dabbed at those crumbs with the tips of his fingers. I'd always liked Aidan's fingers because they were long and sensitive and did wonderful things to my body. Less and less in the last few years, though.

He glanced up and caught me watching him.

'What?' he asked.

I shook my head.

'I should have booked the Mariner's Reef tonight,' said Aidan.

'Why?' I asked.

'Twenty-five years. More appropriate to have the classier restaurant, don't you think?'

I shook my head. 'I'm not a classy woman.'

He laughed. 'Of course you are.'

'Not really.'

'You know, it still bothers you, doesn't it?' He looked at me curiously. 'Your so-called humble beginnings.'

'Not that humble after all,' I said. 'And no, Aidan, it doesn't bother me in the slightest.'

'What then?' He frowned. 'You've been behaving oddly ever since we got here. As though you're not really enjoying yourself.'

Our starters (both of us had chosen crab) were placed in front of us. I squeezed fresh lemon over mine.

'The children went to a lot of trouble,' said Aidan. 'The least you can do is enjoy yourself.'

'I didn't ask them to.' My words were sharper than I intended and I saw a flash of surprise in Aidan's eyes.

'I think it shows that we reared two wonderful kids,' he said after a moment's hesitation.

'Yes,' I said. 'I'm glad we did that.'

'Lots of people said it wouldn't work,' said Aidan. 'They thought that we were too young and that the strain of the twins would be too much for us. But they were wrong.'

I nodded.

'What they forget is that you can make things work if you try hard enough.'

'Depends on what outcome you want, I guess,' I said.

'What more could we want?' He smiled at me and then slid his hand into his jacket pocket. He took out a small red box which he pushed across the table towards me. 'Just something,' he said, 'to let you know how much I appreciate you and everything you've done.'

I took the box and opened it. A pair of diamond earrings in a silver setting sparkled under the light of the table's candle. I touched one of them and the colours seemed to crackle beneath my fingers.

'They're beautiful,' I said.

'I got them yesterday,' he told me. 'When you were talking to that old dear. I went into town and bought them.'

I'd noticed he'd gone missing for a while but it hadn't bothered me. Aidan was never very good at sitting on a beach anyway.

'Happy anniversary,' he said, raising the glass of shiraz.

I bit my lip. I didn't know what to do. To ruin everything or not? I hadn't intended to, not on this trip, but it was as though my emotions were in a mental washing machine, tumbling this way and that, getting caught up in each other until I didn't know how I was supposed to feel.

He was looking at me with a puzzled expression on his face.

This wasn't where I'd intended to be. For today, for my wedding anniversary, I'd planned to go to a beauty salon and have a million different things done to me so that I'd look ten years younger. For Christmas . . . I hadn't known what I was going to do about Christmas. Everyone wants the perfect family Christmas. But the twins were both scheduled to work on Christmas Day. We wouldn't have had a perfect family Christmas anyway. And what was the point in pretending any more?

We were never really going to be the perfect family. We looked it, of course. But then lots of families look perfect when you know, deep down, that they can't possibly be.

We weren't perfect because Aidan didn't really love me and I didn't really love him. We respected each other, more or less. And we cared about each other. There were times when we had great sex together. But love . . . we'd never fallen in love.

I lifted my own glass slowly.

There had been other women. I knew that. Over twenty-five years is three a lot? I'd found receipts in his jacket. I'd overheard snatches of hurried phone calls. I'd seen a gift-wrapped box at the back of a drawer that had never been given to me. Three women. That I knew of.

And one man. I swirled the red wine in the glass in front of me. My man. Brett. I'd known him for six months and it was a mad passion. Even now, thinking about him made my stomach contract. It was for Brett that I wanted to look ten years younger. Brett, the yoga instructor at the gym who could bend his body into innumerable poses and who knew my body better than I knew it myself. Brett with the long dark hair and the soft dark eyes. Brett, whose touch sent me into a frenzy of desire. Brett who told me he loved me.

Brett who'd asked me to live with him.

Brett who loved me.

Wasn't I entitled to something for myself after all these years? After giving up my job to take care of the twins? After always putting Aidan and Aidan's career first because, let's face it, he'd married me. He hadn't left me to fend for myself. He'd done the decent thing and so I had to do the decent thing too and look after him. Be the perfect wife to his perfect husband. I was obliged to do that. I had no choice.

And now the kids had grown up and, OK, they hadn't

exactly moved away yet but they would soon, and I wanted some time to myself. I wanted to do my own thing. Resume my life. The life I'd wanted to have before the dark blue dress and the chiffon skirt with the sparkly stars. I wanted to get a job. I wanted to have sex in unusual places. (With Brett I already had. We'd made love in the open air; in the gym's private sauna; on the train to Belfast. . . it had been exciting. Not like with Aidan. Not the chore that our love-making had become.)

I didn't know why Brett loved me. But I knew that I loved him. And I wanted to be with him. It wouldn't matter to Aidan. He could cope on his own. He was always better at coping than me.

'Gráinne?' His voice was gentle.

My fingers closed over the jewellery box with the diamond earrings.

'Twenty-five years,' he said. 'Ups and downs in those twenty-five years. Good times and bad times. But we made it this far.'

But I could have a different twenty-five years. With Brett. Twenty-five years of someone loving me because of me, not because I was the mother of their children. Not because I knew not to buy the brand of washing powder that brought them out in a rash. Not because I was always there for them, even when they'd betrayed me with another woman.

Would Brett betray me?

Probably.

Would I betray him?

I hadn't thought I'd betray Aidan. But what did he expect with his late nights and his other women? What did he think would happen? That I'd sit at home and forgive him every single time?

'We got a message earlier,' said Aidan. 'From the twins. Wishing us a happy anniversary.'

I swirled the wine in my glass again. I could smell the black fruit and pepper aromas of the shiraz.

'They'll be in debt for the rest of their lives.' I didn't look up from the glass.

'They wanted us to remember this trip,' he said. 'It was good of them.'

'We should have told them to keep their money,' I said.

He put his own glass back on the table.

'This isn't what you wanted, is it?' He sounded sad.

'It's lovely,' I said, 'but no.'

'It wasn't what I wanted either.'

We never talked, Aidan and me. Not about ourselves. Not about what we wanted or what we felt. We talked about the children. We talked about his job. We talked about the house. But not about each other.

He was balding. I'd noticed it over the last few years but it was only now I realised how high his forehead had become. How it had actually merged into the crown of his head. And how grey his hair was. So was mine, of course, but I camouflaged it with a salon dye every five weeks.

He'd had three women. I'd only ever had him. Until Brett.

'The grass is always greener,' he said.

I looked up at him, startled.

'You think that something will be better, more exciting, will give you what you've always looked for. But it doesn't.'

'No?'

'We did good with the kids. Both of us.'

I nodded.

'We didn't do so well with each other.'

There was a lump in my throat.

'I wasn't always the best husband.'

I said nothing.

'And maybe it's not to my credit that I never left. Maybe it would have been a fairer thing to do.'

Still I said nothing.

'I didn't stay because of the kids, though. I stayed because of you.'

A bit late, I thought, to throw that one at me. I'd been devastated each time I'd found out about another woman.

'I made excuses for myself,' said Aidan. 'I told myself that I'd been trapped into a marriage that I didn't want. That I'd been too young. That life had played a dirty trick on me.'

'I didn't have that luxury.' I regained my voice. 'I was too busy to find someone to make excuses about.'

He nodded. 'But no matter what,' he said, 'it was a good twenty-five years.'

'You think so?'

He nodded again. 'I loved you. I didn't think I did at first. But later . . . I loved you.'

But sometimes it isn't enough. I was going to say that to him but I didn't, because if I said it about Aidan I should also say it about Brett.

'Do what you have to do, in the end,' he told me. 'But enjoy this holiday now.'

'How do you know I'm thinking of doing anything at all?' I asked.

'We've been married for twenty-five years,' he said. 'More than that, really, when you count the registry office. Of course I know things.'

I smiled faintly.

'So consider this a little time out,' he told me. 'From whatever.'

'You're being very calm.'

'I always am,' he said. 'Doesn't mean I don't feel things.'

'What do you want from me?' I asked.

'I want you to pretend that we've only just met,' he said. 'That it's the first time all over again.'

'I can't do that,' I said.

'I want you to make love to me in a boat.'

I looked at him in surprise.

'There's one tied up to the jetty.'

'I know. But . . .'

'Or in the hammock near the beach.'

'Aidan . . .'

'I want you to believe me when I tell you that there's never been anyone else.'

'Don't lie to me,' I said.

'Never anyone else who mattered.'

He'd never talked to me like this before. Brett talked to me like this all the time.

'Can we save it?' he said.

'I don't know,' I told him.

'I want to try.'

I never thought I'd hear him say that. And I thought of my friend Madge whose first husband had broken her heart. She'd married the second one for his money. 'Love is for fools,' she'd said.

I know why love is for fools. Because it makes us do foolish things. And sometimes we don't know what we really want.

'The thing is,' said Aidan, 'we're here on this island. We

might as well enjoy it. Regardless of what happens when we get home.'

'You think so?'

'Why not?' he said. 'What's the point in being miserable?'

I smiled a little.

'So . . . we pretend?'

'If that's what it takes.'

'OK,' I said.

We should never have got married. And yet it hadn't been the worst mistake of my life. Maybe I hadn't actually made the worst mistake of my life yet. Maybe I'd never make it. I really didn't know.

'So – happy anniversary,' he said, raising his glass again.

And I clinked my glass against his as I wished him a happy anniversary too. Even though I still didn't know whether I'd try the greener grass or not.

Room 505 (Dee)

I talk too much. I know I do but I just can't help myself. I chatter endlessly on and I can see people's eyes glaze over but I still keep talking. I talk about work, mostly, because that's the most important thing in my life right now. It's been the most important thing in my life since I left school, actually, and I suppose that now you're thinking I'm some hotshot businesswoman with her picture on the front of *Business Week* or something but I'm not. I'm the PA to Richard Brewer, who's a multi-millionaire entrepreneur. I quite like telling people that I'm the PA to a multi-millionaire entrepreneur because I can see them looking at me with a new respect. Everyone's heard of Richard Brewer (well, maybe not everyone, but he *has* had his picture on the front of *Business Week*) and they know, don't they, that multi-millionaire entrepreneurs don't employ idiots to be their PAs. And so they know that, despite the fact that I'm here on my own, I can't be an idiot.

Ron called me an idiot once. Not to my face, though. I overheard him talking to my mother – arguing with my mother, actually – and what he said was 'I've had just about enough of you and that idiot child.' I'd been sitting on the roof of the garden shed, out of sight, when he said it. I froze, not knowing what he might say next, but what happened was that Mum spoke to him in the soft voice she uses when she wants to defuse a difficult situation and suddenly Ron laughed and I knew that everything was OK.

Anyway, that's not important. It's really not. It's just me talking too much again, rambling off into different directions. It's just as well I have the job. It keeps me focused.

I like working with Richard Brewer. He's a fantastic boss and I've been with him for nearly ten years. The company is called Global Investments and it's a financial services group. When I got the job first my mother asked me what exactly they did and, you know, I found it really hard to explain because there are times when I'm not entirely sure myself. Richard trades on the world's money markets. He buys and sells currencies and interest rate futures (don't ask!) and precious metals. He makes money doing this although he once told me that it was a zero-sum game, which means that for every winner there's a loser. He said that the key is to win more times than you lose. He seems to be good at that, because I see the profit and loss figures every day and they show profits more often than losses. With the money he makes from trading he does what he calls 'strategic' investments. He buys shareholdings in public companies. Or he invests money into start-up firms. Or he finances companies that are trying to break through to a new level of business. Sometimes he says that his investments are philanthropic, but I've never really known him to do anything without thinking that he could make money out of it afterwards.

Except maybe sending me on holiday every year, and even that's not entirely philanthropic. After all, he sends me away at the least busy time for him, the time when he goes skiing in Canada with his gorgeous wife Genevieve and their two children Carlotta and Jack. When I come back, I work harder than ever.

Richard has a wonderful family. Genevieve is a power-lady-who-lunches. She's tall and graceful, with honey-blonde hair and perfectly buffed and moisturised skin. Although we're basically the same age, she always makes me feel dowdy by comparison. But then she has regular appointments with the kind of beauticians who come to your home and turn you into a gorgeous creature. I pretty much make do with occasional visits to Glow, which is the salon nearest to where I live. It's run by two great women called Anika and Tanya, who are forever trying to talk me into changing my hair colour or getting the latest facial treatment. Anika, the beautician, tells me that I have wonderful bone structure and that my skin has the elasticity of someone ten years younger. And she says that my broken nose makes my face look interesting instead of beautiful, even though she did give me the name of a cosmetic surgeon who could fix it.

I don't want my nose fixed. It's part of me the way it is.

Tanya wants me to cut my hair and have it coloured. She's suggested highlights and lowlights and a selection of tints. She's given me books to study with each season's new look. Personally I think that every look is more or less the same. Tanya thinks that my appearance would be improved immeasurably by lopping a few feet off my hair.

She exaggerates, of course. My hair is shoulder-length but it's thick and wiry and I do honestly understand when she says that it hides my face. But I'm comfortable with it the way it is. I take her point about the colour, though.

My natural hair colour is a kind of dirty blonde and so you don't really see the greys that much. But they're starting to multiply and I do think that one day I'll have to make a decision on the colour. If I do that, though, I'll have to make a decision on the cut too and I don't want to.

Sometimes Richard and Genevieve's children come into the office with him – I'll see them again at Easter when Global Investments does an Easter egg treasure hunt for the kids of the employees. Everyone loves it. The eggs are hidden in the staff restaurant (it's not really a restaurant because we bring in our own food, but there's an oven, a microwave and a fridge freezer) and the kids go wild. They totally trash the place but that's OK because we deliberately put extra cupboards and desks and plastic plants in there the day before to hide the stuff and we clear it all up afterwards. Each child is allowed to find three eggs. It's good fun. I'm in charge of organising it and I love to see them running wild and emerging triumphant with their eggs.

Am I talking too much again? I think I must be. It's because I live alone.

I bought the apartment nine years ago, after I started working for Richard. He put me in touch with a bank that gave me a hundred per cent mortgage because at that time I wasn't exactly well off. I am now, though. Not rolling in it, of course. Nothing like Richard and Genevieve's wealth, but I have a fair amount in my bank account because he's a generous employer and he pays me well.

It's not that I'm mean, but I don't spend a lot of money. I buy nice things for the apartment – I have the latest in technological gadgets (because Richard invests a lot in companies that produce them and I like to keep up with what's going on; besides, I love cool technology!); I also spend a lot of money on good furniture and nice things for my home. But I'm really not into clothes and make-up and girly things. (Which is, I guess, why Anika and Tanya despair of me.)

I know that they think I'm a bit of an old bat in Global. There are a lot of young employees, all mad keen to get on in the thrusting, pulsating world of high finance. There are guys that come in fresh-faced from their Masters degrees in some kind of business studies. They wear expensive suits that they can't yet afford and crisp shirts with cufflinks. Their hair is short and their expressions are serious. The girls (women, I suppose, I never know what to call females in their twenties and thirties; girl sounds young and silly and woman sounds middle-aged!) are equally serious and they wear conservative suits by names like Donna Karan. Chocolate brown was last season's big look and Global Investments was a sea of men walking around in navy and women swathed in chocolate brown.

They might think I'm a bit of a bat but they respect me because I'm Richard's PA and I control access to him. Nobody can contact him without speaking to me first. That makes it sound as though Richard runs an autocratic organisation but he doesn't. It's just that if he took every phone call that came in for him he'd be on the phone every second of the day and he wouldn't have time to do his investing thing. I am the guardian of his business life. And, to a large extent, his personal life too. I remind him of things like birthdays and anniversaries and occasions when he has to be home at a certain time. I placate Genevieve when he's working late and I know she's going to be annoyed. He rings her himself, of course (he's a good husband – not a great husband, but a good one), but sometimes I ring her too to reassure her that he does, absolutely, need to stay in the office. I want their relationship to work because I like both of them so much, but I know that it can be difficult being married to a successful man. It's one thing getting a Maserati as a birthday present, but you like to think that the man who gave it to you will be home for dinner that night too.

I am not in love with my boss.

I have never had an affair with him.

I admire him and respect him and he respects me too.

I think that's a good way to have it.

I panic a bit when the holiday season comes around. Not for them, of course, because they love their visit to Lake Louise and their follow-on trip to Vancouver, which is where Genevieve comes from. I went to Vancouver with Richard once and I do sometimes wonder how she could bear to leave it. I love the way the mountains sweep down to the sea and I love the big-city small-town atmosphere of the place. After that trip I bought an apartment there as an investment. I was five years into my employment with Richard at the time and I was able to borrow the money. I rent it out and it's a nice, steady income for me. I think maybe that when I retire I might move to Vancouver. It's a safe place.

I could, I suppose, retire here to the island, which is also a safe place. But although I like the sun at this time of the year I couldn't put up with it all the time. What makes the island so wonderful is that my stay here is always a perfect moment in time. A warm, indolent moment when it's cold back home and when I don't have to think about anything more taxing than what I'm going to have for dinner.

Because I'm on my own, people talk to me. And that's

when I talk too much in return. They invite me to join them for dinner or for cocktails and I don't want to appear to be rude and horrible so I agree. Then they ask me questions about myself and I start to talk about Richard and Global Investments and how I met the President of the United States at a G8 conference and how I once had to take notes for Richard at a meeting held on board a yacht anchored off St Tropez, and I know that people are stunned by what they think is my glittering life.

They probably also wonder why Richard Brewer, who could have the most glamorous PA in the world, actually has me. But the thing is, you see, I'm not a threat. Genevieve is a lovely, lovely person but I bet she'd feel uneasy if the woman who accompanied her husband around the world was drop-dead gorgeous.

I tried to explain this to Anika and Tanya once but they looked at me in disbelief.

'Global Investments isn't your life,' Anika told me. 'You can't choose how you look based on worrying about whether the boss's wife would find you too attractive! Get sense, Dee.'

'Are you insane?' demanded Tanya. 'What happens when you stop working for them? You want to look your best now, woman.'

I don't. I'm quite happy with how I look. Broken nose and all.

Ron broke it. He didn't mean to. I know that. But he pushed me away in anger one evening and I stumbled and fell, cracking my face against the arm of the chair. That's what broke my nose. Ron looked at me in horror and said he'd take me to the doctor. But I didn't want to go. Ron told me that I'd be disfigured if I didn't get my nose seen to and I said that it didn't matter. He was about to say something else when my mother walked into the room. She worked in a call centre and her shift was over.

'She fell,' said Ron.

My mother looked at the blood running from my broken nose and dripping on to the carpet.

'She's clumsy,' he told her. 'You'd think that by now she'd be better able to look after herself.'

My mother said nothing.

'I want to take her to the hospital,' said Ron. 'But she won't let me.'

'I'll take her,' said my mother.

'No,' said Ron. 'She comes with me.'

'I'll be fine,' I said through my stuffed nose. 'I'm going to bed.'

He didn't come to my room that night. I lay there and waited for him but he didn't come. I think it was because I wasn't beautiful any more. When I looked at myself in the mirror the next day I could *see* that I wasn't beautiful any more. My nose was misshapen and ugly. There were two bruises under my eyes. My blonde hair hung limply around my face. It was weird, I thought, but I liked the way I looked now. The day before I'd been perfect. Everyone thought so. Perfectly beautiful. Everyone looked at me and told me that I was stunning, even at eleven years old.

Ron especially.

We left him, my mother and me, after that. I don't blame her for what happened. At the time she met him she'd been down and he'd seemed so great. He hadn't minded the fact that she was a single mother with a child. He'd told her that he loved children. She believed him.

I don't talk about that to people at the White Sands

Hotel. I talk about Richard and Genevieve and how great my life is now. I don't want to think about the past. I don't want to think about a time when I was beautiful. Beauty didn't work for me.

I talk too much. But only about the things I want to talk about in the first place.

Coco Villa (Sahndhi)

Sahndhi sat on the rocky outcrop and stared vacantly at the horizon. She didn't see the swoop of the big-billed pelican as it claimed its fish supper for the evening, nor did she notice the stately journey of the enormous cruise ship across the azure-blue sea. She didn't see the sparkle of the sunlight as it glittered furiously across the undulating water or the pink-hued edges of the cirrus clouds etched high in the sky. The only image Sahndhi could see was in her mind and it was the choreography of the dance steps on the video which she would be performing live the following month, on stage, in London. And all that she could hear – instead of the gentle lapping of the water against the rocks or the occasional peal of laughter from the nearby beach – was the track of the new single, playing over and over again in her head.

As she thought of the performance her stomach turned over and she wanted to be sick. Along with the dance steps she could see the huge posters which she knew were on billboards around the country, in train stations and tube stations and supermarket car parks: Sahndhi Jeffries – Runaway Winner *Pop Princess* – Spectacular UK Tour . . . She cringed every time she thought about it. She didn't know what was terrifying her more: the idea of the tour itself or the fact that she was now known as Sahndhi Jeffries, Pop Princess.

She shivered. She wasn't a pop princess. It didn't matter that she'd been voted one in the last cut-throat series of TV programmes to find another chart-topper. When she looked back at the videos of the programme, and the way she'd done everything they asked of her – image make-over, a whole new wardrobe, singing songs she hated, being nice and normal when she knew the cameras were on her (worrying about the spot on her chin or the fact that she was beset by nerves just before she sang so that she wanted to be sick); then just occasionally saying something a little biting or bitchy about a fellow contestant so that viewers wouldn't think she was totally saccharine sweet – when she looked at all of it she didn't recognise herself at all. The girl on the TV with the long dark hair coaxed into a corkscrew of gleaming curls (all her own, no extensions, but normally worn in a straight mane falling down her back) was a million miles away from Sandy Jeffries, twenty-year-old daughter of Barbara and Mark, elder sister to Janet and Robert. The girl on screen, her body sprayed with gold mist tan, her startlingly blue eyes dramatically outlined in kohl and tiny diamante stones applied artfully to her cheeks, was another creature altogether. Exotic, mysterious and just a little bit dangerous. The real Sandy was nothing like that. *She* was nothing like that. But next month she had to do the main performance as well as a series of concerts and be the exotic Sahndhi all over again, and she really wasn't sure that she could do it.

Her agent was pissed off with her.

'Don't be fucking ridiculous,' he'd said when she'd expressed reservations about the tour. 'This year you're hot. Next year, unless you manage to carve out a niche for yourself, unless you keep yourself way up there in the public consciousness, you'll be nothing. There'll be another hopeful who'll work harder and wear skimpier clothes and have bigger tits and you'll be old news. Cologram have paid a good deal of money for a pop-tart and you've got to earn it.'

She'd wanted to yell at him that she wasn't a pop-tart, that she was, in fact, a serious professional singer. But she knew she'd be wasting her time.

'Listen,' he'd continued very seriously. 'You've a shelf life of about eighteen months max unless you do the reinvention thing over and over again. And nobody, except maybe Madonna and Kylie, has managed that. So be fucking realistic, Sandy. You've got yourself a window of opportunity and you've got to go for it.'

She totally understood. She really did. But what she'd hoped for when she'd entered *Pop Princess* was to make people realise that you could win a competition like that and it could be based on the fact that you were a great singer, not that you looked good in a mini-skirt that was nothing more than a bandage around the top of your legs and half the world's self-tanning product sprayed all over your body.

She had been the best singer. By a huge margin. Everyone had known it the moment she opened her mouth. But the producers had told her that if she didn't wear something a bit more exciting she'd be voted off early on. They didn't want her voted off early on because she was easy on the eye as well as having the voice. But she'd have to be more than easy on the eye. She'd have to hook the viewers and reel them in.

And so she'd ditched the pretty, but unremarkable, dress she'd worn on the first night (when the truly terrible singer had been voted off, no big surprise there) and for her next performance she'd worn the bandage skirt and a top that was barely there at all and she'd given an upbeat performance of the Abba hit 'The Winner Takes It All', singing it defiantly instead of plaintively, giving it a whole new meaning. Apparently, so they told her afterwards, it had been a defining moment in *Pop Princess* history. Overnight she became a symbol of a new kind of girl-power. Break-Up Girl. Stand-Alone Girl. Survivor Girl. She was a role model for millions of other girls. Don't-Fuck-With-Me Girl.

She leaned forward and rested her head on her knees. Her new trademark long curls tumbled over her shoulders and formed a screen around her. Survivor Girl. If only they bloody knew. If only they could bloody see her now. Survivor Girl my arse! Hopeless Girl, maybe. Sad-Git Girl probably. Messed-Up Girl – definitely.

Her mum and dad were elated with her success.

'I always knew it,' Barbara told her enthusiastically after she'd won and as they celebrated with a bottle of Cristal. 'You've a great talent, Sandy. Now you've been given a wonderful opportunity.'

It was frightening how much they all talked about this wonderful opportunity. At home, afterwards, she'd expressed her reservations to her parents, wondering if all that had happened was that she'd become a C-list celebrity who'd be asked to a whole range of parties but who wouldn't actually get any singing work.

'If you let it happen,' agreed her father, as though he knew anything at all about the industry. 'But don't you worry. Ken Carter is a great agent. He'll look after you.

And besides, so what if they do a bit of publicity stuff having you going to parties and stuff like that. It's all about profile.'

'It's all about the singing,' said Sandy.

'Of course,' said Mark Jeffries as he smiled at his daughter. 'In an ideal world. But honey, you know how it is these days. It's packaging as much as anything else, so get out there and strut your stuff.'

She did know really. She wasn't stupid. She'd got her three A levels and had taken her offered place in college. She'd chosen economics over the soft media studies option – Diva Don Girl (the *Star*); Smart Sahndhi Girl (the *Sun*); Clever Clogs Girl (the *Mirror*) – because she thought she knew how the fame game worked. It was just . . . she didn't actually want to be famous. She just wanted to be a singer.

Nobody believed her when she said that she'd prefer not to be recognised. All her friends told her that it was a bit of a laugh really. And they reminded her, just like Ken Carter reminded her, that her shelf life was short. She didn't mind her celebrity shelf life being short. But she wanted a singing career for the rest of her life. She wished some of them understood. She especially wished her parents understood. But all she knew now was that her dad had appointed himself her manager and was talking about moving to a bigger house and buying a new car. He wanted them to live somewhere more appropriate. He wanted Sahndhi to move out of her rented studio flat and in with the family again – so that he could keep an eye on her. But she didn't want him keeping an eye on her. And what if the tour was a flop? What if she didn't earn enough money to pay for the bigger house? What would happen then?

You won't get me down
I'm not your clown

Three steps to the right, make a fist, spin, three steps to the left

I'll make my choice
And it won't be you
No no no baby, no way, not you!!!!

Stamp feet, point finger, look defiantly at camera

It was a crap song, thought Sahndhi despairingly. Written specially for her by a couple of composers who churned out top-ten jingles at the drop of a hat. It was meant to capitalise on her Survivor Girl image. But the lyrics were terrible and the tune was irritating and Sahndhi was very, very worried about the fact that her career could go down the toilet before it had even started because everyone at the record company kept stressing how important it was that she consolidate her wonderful success with 'The Winner Takes It All' with a follow-up number one. But she wouldn't buy this crap record herself. Why the hell should she expect anyone else to?

Her stomach heaved again. She was glad she hadn't had breakfast otherwise she would have puked it back up and into the crystal-clear rock pool beside her.

She lifted her head and looked around. The record company had allowed her this week-long break at the White Sands Hotel, where she was staying in the exclusive Coco Villa, the expensive two-bedroomed property set in the hotel grounds but with its own private entrance, which included mooring for the occupant's speedboat. Speedboat, she thought, as if!

It wasn't really a break, of course. It was a photo opportunity and it was all being staged with the help of a celebrity magazine. The first few days had been taken up with photo shoots by the magazine on the beautiful white beach, where she stretched out on the fine sand or cavorted in the sparkling blue sea or looked pensive as she walked along the shoreline. The shoot of the exclusive photos had finished up the previous day and now she had two days on her own. Neither her agent nor the record company had wanted her to spend two days on her own, but, surprising herself, Sahndhi had insisted. She'd be spending the next four weeks in rehearsals, she told them. They could give her two days by herself now. She needed it creatively, she told them. They'd looked at her like she had two heads.

Of course her family had gone ballistic when she said that she was going to the island for the frolicking opportunity without them. Janet had pointed out that most stars took their families with them. Robert had complained that it was autumn in England and cold and that he could do with a bit of fresh air and sunshine. Her dad had told her that it wasn't right that she should be on her own with only the magazine and her agent for company, and her mum had backed him up.

She was sick of her dad and her mum banging on and on about what was good for her. She was twenty years old, for God's sake. Until *Pop Princess* they hadn't cared that she was in the studio flat a mere five minutes' walk away from college or that her part-time job was at the local Sainsbury's. They hadn't needed to know what she was doing every second of every day. It wasn't as though she'd been under their wing. She'd had a fucking life of her own! But now everyone wanted a part of it. Everyone thought they knew better than she did about where she should live and what she should wear and how she should behave. But she'd done it all on her own before now. Why couldn't they let her be?

Now Mark, Barbara, Janet and Robert weren't speaking to her. Ken, her agent, had muttered about moving her out of the exclusive cottage since she was on her own and he wasn't sure that the record company would be prepared to spend the extra couple of grand it cost to keep her there instead of an ordinary room. (This sudden streak of meanness on the part of both Ken and the record company had totally freaked Sahndhi out. A couple of grand was nothing in the great scheme of things, surely. As it turned out, the hotel told her that she was welcome to complete her stay in the cottage at no extra cost, although she told Ken that she was perfectly prepared to pay for it herself. And then the thought struck her that she sounded like a damn diva pop-tart person making her demands, and she'd burst into tears.)

It wasn't supposed to be like this. Winning the competition was supposed to be an achievement. She was supposed to feel proud. But all she felt was trapped.

The sound of the shutter snapped through her consciousness. Her head jerked up and she looked around.

He was standing about ten feet away, his camera – a professional camera – hanging around his neck.

'What the fuck are you doing!' she shrieked. 'Can't you guys leave me alone for a fucking instant! You've had all your damn photos!'

He stared at her.

She scrambled up from the rock and made her way briskly towards him. She lunged at the camera but missed. Her foot slipped on the damp rocks and she slithered towards the water. She grabbed at the stones as she fell, crying out as they scraped her palms.

He reacted quickly, moving towards her, grasping her by

the wrist and yanking her back on to the rocky outcrop.

'Are you all right?' he asked.

Tears stung her eyes. She blinked them away.

'Fine,' she said shortly.

'Thought you were going to end up in the drink,' he told her.

'I wouldn't have fallen in.' She rubbed her stinging hands on the tiny shorts she was wearing.

'Painful?'

'No.' She stared defiantly at him. 'Is it digital?' she asked.

'Sorry?'

'The camera. Is it digital?'

He nodded.

'Delete them.'

'What?'

'The photos you took of me. Delete them.'

'I don't know what you're talking about.' He brushed his fingers through his sun-bleached hair and regarded her with steady grey eyes. 'I didn't take photographs of you.'

'I heard you,' she said.

'I took photos,' he agreed. 'Not of you, though. Of the pelican.'

She looked at him uneasily, trying to weigh up the truth of his statement.

'I'll show you.' He took the camera from around his neck and pressed a button on the back. 'See?'

The photographs were all of the pelican. Poised on the post at the end of the wooden jetty. Taking to the air. Swooping towards the water. Emerging with the fish. And the last photograph was of her, head resting on her knees, hidden by her mass of curls.

'One of you,' he admitted. 'I couldn't help it.'

'Delete it,' she said.

'Why?' He grinned at her. 'I like it. Not the usual sort of Caribbean girly photo.'

'I didn't ask you to take it.'

He sighed. 'Oh, if you're that insistent.' He pressed the delete button and the image dissolved in front of Sahndhi's eyes. She swallowed the lump in her throat.

'Thank you.'

'You're welcome.' He smiled at her. It was a nice smile. Boyish, even though Sahndhi reckoned that he was in his late twenties. Wide. Honest.

'Look, I'm sorry,' she said. 'You must think me a bit cracked. But I hate having my photo taken.'

'Hey, no problem.' He shrugged. 'The ones of the pelican are better.'

She laughed suddenly, and after a moment he laughed too.

'Are you staying here?' she asked.

'The hotel?' His eyes widened incredulously. 'Are you insane? At the prices they charge?' He shook his head vehemently. 'I'm staying in a cute family-run place a mile or so down the road. It's actually great. Everyone's really nice and it's not too expensive. But it's not on the beach like this. And it doesn't have a resident pelican.'

'Why were you taking photos of it?' she asked.

'I do that,' he said. 'I'm a photographer.'

She bristled.

'Nature shots mainly,' he told her.

She looked at him warily. 'Newspapers?'

'Not usually.'

She exhaled slowly.

'Are you?' he asked.

'What?'

'Staying in Millionaire's Paradise?'

'It's none of your business.'

'Sorry,' he said. 'Makes me sound like some kind of last-bastion socialist. If you can afford it, why not?'

'Actually I've no idea whether I can.' She laughed shortly. 'I think I can but I can't be sure.'

'Why?'

'Oh . . .' She stopped. She'd never been one for unburdening herself to strangers, and she wasn't going to start now. No matter that he was the kind of guy who stayed in cheap hotels and took pictures of pelicans. No matter that he was someone as far removed from the whole *Pop Princess* culture as it was probably possible to be.

He watched her curiously and then shrugged. 'None of my business,' he agreed.

The pelican swooped behind them again and immediately he swung the camera in front of him, snapping as it made a dive for the sea once more. When he'd finished he pointed it at Sahndhi. But he didn't press the shutter.

'You look lovely,' he said. 'With the blue sky and the green hills and the sea behind you. And you're all dressed in white. It's striking.'

'I don't care,' she said.

'Are you a model?' he asked.

'Models *like* getting their photos taken.'

'Maybe not, if they're on holiday.' He made a face at her. 'Are you a famous person in seclusion from the rest of the world?'

'Do you always ask so many questions?'

'Sorry,' he said. 'Can't help myself.'

She shrugged.

'No,' he replied as she remained silent. 'I only ask loads of questions about some people. Can I ask you just one more?'

She shrugged.

'Will you have dinner with me tonight?'

It would be nice, she thought. Really nice. To sit and talk to someone who didn't know a single thing about her or *Pop Princess* or any of that bullshit. To talk to a person about ordinary things instead of UK Spectacular Tours and Image and Profile. To talk to someone who looked at her as though she was a person instead of a product.

'There's a great little restaurant past my hotel,' he told her. 'Very cheap and cheerful. But best lobsters on the island. Great conch chowder too.'

She smiled suddenly. 'It won't make me go to bed with you.'

He laughed. 'I wasn't angling for that. And I bet conch chowder isn't really an aphrodisiac, they probably just say that to make you order it.'

'Well then . . .' She hesitated but smiled again. 'I'd love to go to dinner with you.'

'Great,' he said. 'D'you want me to pick you up?'

'Guess so,' she said. 'I'll wait in the lobby of the hotel for you.'

'Fine.' He nodded in agreement. 'One other thing?'

'Yes?'

'What's your name?'

It was ages since anyone had asked her her name! She was used to them walking up to her, instantly knowing who she was. She was used to screaming kids shouting, 'Sahndhi! Sahndhi!' at her. She was used to being recognised.

'Sandy,' she said.

'Excellent.' He held out his hand and she shook it. 'I'm John.'

'OK, John.' His palm was smooth and dry. 'See you in the lobby later.'

'Seven?'

She nodded. 'Perfect.'

He'd said that the restaurant was cheap and cheerful so she didn't dress up for their date. She wore an old denim skirt which she'd brought for her time off (even though this was the first day that had happened) and an equally old pale blue Nike T-shirt. She scraped her curls back off her face and tied them into the tightest ponytail she could. She didn't bother with make-up but she did spray herself with Chanel's Chance, her current favourite perfume. She slid her feet into the brown leather flip-flops with the coral detail that she'd bought (Sahndhi buys a pair of casual footwear for the beach, the celebrity magazine had announced breathlessly) in the hotel boutique on the first day. She'd wanted something to remind her of her holiday in the sun, even if it really wasn't a holiday at all.

He was already in the lobby waiting for her. She glanced at her watch. She was exactly on time. He was early. She smiled to herself. Her last boyfriend, Shaun, had never been on time . . . and as for early! Shaun hadn't known the meaning of the word.

He'd contacted her after the *Pop Princess* win, of course. To remind her that he'd always thought she had a great singing voice and to tell her that he'd voted for her over and over again. He'd spent a fortune voting for her, he said. She'd thanked him politely. Then he'd asked whether they couldn't get together for a drink. For old times' sake. She'd gripped the phone very tightly and reminded him that they'd split up because he'd started dating her ex-flatmate. He'd laughed and told her that it hadn't meant anything and that he'd always wanted to get back with her but hadn't been able to call. She'd told him to get stuffed. He'd called her a stuck-up cow.

She felt herself grow hot and cold at the memory of Shaun. And then John spotted her and waved and she forgot all about her former boyfriend.

They took one of the island's six-seater taxi vans to the restaurant. Although, Sahndhi pointed out, it was close enough to have walked.

'Couldn't take the chance,' he told her.

'What chance?'

'That you'd be wearing high heels. It's uphill.'

She glanced down at the coral flip-flops and smiled.

The restaurant, as he'd told her, was very cheap and extremely cheerful, with fat candles stuck into coloured vases and unsteady wooden tables tucked close together. At the time they arrived it was only half full but John had reserved a table anyway.

'This way, Mr Reynolds.' The waitress led them to a secluded table in the corner.

There were no written menus, but the waitress reeled off a list of dishes from which Sahndhi chose prawns and mahu fish in a spicy sauce.

'No lobster?' John looked disappointed.

'I've had enough lobster already this week,' Sahndhi told him. 'I want something that I don't have to excavate to eat.'

He laughed and ordered it for himself, along with a bottle of red wine.

'So,' he said, when the wine had been brought, along with some freshly baked warm bread rolls, 'tell me about yourself, Sandy.'

She looked at him uneasily. She'd done nothing but tell people about herself for the past few months. She hadn't been able to pick up a newspaper without learning (as though she needed to be told) that she'd attended a local comprehensive school but that she'd been regarded as one of the brightest in her form; that she'd gone to college; that she'd sung the lead role for three years in their end-of-year musical (the last year being *Mary Poppins*); that her parents had paid for extra tuition for her because they thought she had a wonderful voice; that she'd always wanted to sing; that she had a scar on the top of her left thigh from the time that she'd fallen out of a tree, and, of course, that she'd broken her arm in the same incident. It was all fairly innocuous stuff. But she didn't want to talk about it any more.

She asked John to talk about himself instead, and so he did. His parents had split up when he was four and, unusually, he'd been brought up by his dad, who'd been fantastic. He'd always wanted to study photography and so that's what he'd done, although he sometimes dreamed of being a novelist. (Did Sahndhi know that there was supposed to be a famous novelist staying at White Sands? He'd heard something about it on local radio but hadn't really listened at the time. But then, he grinned, he might have got it wrong. Lots of famous people stayed at White Sands!) He'd gone to Thailand for his gap year.

'Why are you here?' she asked suddenly.

'Huh?'

'On the island? What are you doing here?'

He shrugged dismissively. 'Short break,' he told her.

'It must pay well, this photography.'

'Working break,' he amended. 'I can sell the pelican pictures to a natural history magazine.'

He refilled her glass. She sipped the wine, conscious of a sense of relaxation and well-being rippling slowly through her body. As though, for the first time in months, she really was Sandy Jeffries again. As though she was rediscovering herself. Unwinding was a true physical sensation, she realised. And she knew that she'd been coiled tight as an overwound watch.

When they got back to the hotel she invited him to the villa. She hadn't told him, of course, that she was staying in it but she'd suggested a drink at the hotel and then, when they arrived, said not in the bar but not in her bedroom either. She knew that she'd slurred her words a little as she'd said it, but she hoped her meaning was clear. And he'd nodded and said that he'd love to have a drink with her and not in her bedroom.

The pathway to Coco Villa was lit by tiny solar lights each side of the paving slabs. The entrance to the villa itself was guarded by an iron gate.

'This is a bit unusual, surely?' he said as she slid a plastic access card into the electronic slot at the side of the gate.

'Not really.'

The gate swung open and she walked through. John followed her, along the remainder of the paved pathway and up the three steps to the villa door. She used her key card again to open it.

'You're staying here?' he asked incredulously. 'In the private house?'

She explained that it was part of the hotel and that it was rented out to visitors. She took him on a tour of it, indicating the two bedrooms but bringing him directly to the living room, where she slid open the huge patio doors and stepped out on to the private terrace with its open-air Jacuzzi and plunge pool.

'This is amazing,' he said as he stood on the wooden decking. 'Utterly amazing.' He turned to her. 'And you can stay here? Is anyone with you?'

'Not now,' she told him.

'Rich husband? Divorce?' he hazarded.

She shook her head and moved closer to him. He put his arm around her and kissed her.

God, she thought, she'd waited and waited for someone like him. Someone to kiss her and make her forget everything except the pleasure of being with him. She returned his kisses with the hunger of someone who hasn't been kissed for a very long time. In the end, it was John who pulled away from her.

'Who are you?' he asked.

She sat on one of the wicker sun-loungers and told him.

'I've heard of *Pop Princess*,' he told her. 'But I've never watched it.'

'Yes, well, probably nobody in their right mind would,' she said acidly. 'It's horrible really. Some people are great singers and they deserve to do well, and then they pick some who are terrible but they know the public will like, and to be honest the whole format is tired and boring but somehow people still watch it. But I never really wanted to be a Pop Princess, I only wanted to be a singer.'

'So why did you enter?'

'My dad did it for me. A kind of joke.' Her jaw tightened.

'Is he a pushy dad?' John grinned at her. 'You know, like

those tennis dads who make their kids practise a million hours a day?'

'He doesn't . . .' She shrugged. 'He just wants what's best for me.'

'And your mum the same?'

'All of them just want what's best for me.'

'And you don't think that this is best for you?' His tone was astonished as his outstretched arm encompassed all of Coco Villa.

'I'm such a stupid cow,' she said. 'I have what loads of people dream about and I'm complaining about it. It's crazy really.'

'Be careful what you wish for,' he said, smiling. 'You might get it.'

'Oh, I know.' She smiled faintly. 'The problem is that I feel other people are getting more out of it than me. And I don't mean money, although that does come into it.' She looked at him hesitantly and then continued. 'I think my dad's hoping I do really well because, well, his business isn't going so great at the moment. That's why he entered my name. He told me that even if I didn't win the publicity might help.'

'And do you resent that?'

'A bit,' she admitted. 'I can't help it. He made me sign photos for him to give to his clients. We argued about it. I *am* a cow really. It wasn't any big deal.'

'You're not a cow.'

'Everyone wants a piece of me now,' she said. 'More than the last *Pop Princess* girl. I don't know why. All my old friends keep popping up out of the woodwork, people I haven't heard from in ages. Everyone seems to want something and I don't know if I can give it to them.'

'So walk away,' said John.

'I can't.' She told him about the tour and how important it was and how much money everyone stood to lose if she made a mess of things. She told him about the new house and the car and how much her mum enjoyed being recognised on the street.

'But if you're not happy . . .'

'D'you know, I'd love to walk away,' she said. 'I hate the idea of singing that crappy song to a crowd of ten-year-olds. I hate everything about what's happened to me. And yet I'm afraid because if I do . . . well, then my career is over before it's even started.'

'So did you hate everyone on *Pop Princess*?' he asked.

She shrugged. 'By the end, I probably did. You know all that stuff where you're hugging each other and pretending you're horrified when someone is voted off? It's all so fucking phoney.' She shivered in the warm evening air. 'Let's not talk about it any more. You want to share the Jacuzzi?'

He grinned at her as she slid her dress over her shoulders and stepped into the water wearing only her bra and pants. He stripped off his own shirt and trousers and joined her. She leaned back, letting the warm water bubble around her shoulders as she stared up at the night sky. The lights from the decking were too bright for her to see all but the biggest stars.

'I'll turn them off.' John got out of the Jacuzzi and padded into the villa. Suddenly the sky was filled with the sparkling of the stars. And then another flash lit the area around her and she whirled round in the water.

'Sorry.' He was holding an ordinary digital camera. 'You looked so lovely, I couldn't help myself. And this doesn't count, it's only a baby Nikon.' He looked at the photo he'd just taken. 'Excellent one of you. Why don't you sit at the edge and let me take another.'

'D'you have to?'

'I don't have to. But I'd like to.'

'Oh, all right.' She laughed suddenly and he walked around the decking snapping her as she stood at the edge of the plunge pool and then jumped in, slicking her hair back over her head in a shower of silver water droplets. He took pictures of her standing at the wooden rail that led down to the velvet sea, and one of her at the door to the bedroom.

'Now you,' she said. And so she snapped him lying on a sun-lounger in the dark and dipping his toe into the plunge pool.

'I'll e-mail them to you,' he promised.

'How long are you staying?' she asked.

'I leave tomorrow morning.'

She bit her lip. 'Pity.'

'Shame for me all right. But you'll still be here.'

'One more day. On my own.'

'You don't have to be,' he said. 'There are loads of people around.'

'Yeah, but they've all seen me being photographed on the beach and acting like a fool for a magazine that everyone knows is a gossipy rag.'

'The crowd that stay here?' he laughed. 'I bet half them don't know who you are and the other half don't care.'

She considered that for a moment. She hadn't spoken to anyone while she was here. She hadn't had the time at first, and now . . . well, she hadn't assumed that she *could* talk to anyone. But she was talking to John, wasn't she?

'I wish neither of us were going home,' she said. 'I'm only just beginning to enjoy myself.'

'I'll call you when we're back in England,' he said.

'You guys always say things like that.'

'But I mean them.'

He kissed her then, gently, the way she'd always wanted to be kissed when she'd fantasised her ideal lover in her ideal location.

'I'd better get back,' he said. 'I think they lock the doors in my hotel.'

'There aren't any doors on this one,' she said.

'We don't have twenty-four-hour reception and security guards.' John grinned at her and kissed her again, this time on the forehead.

'Why don't you stay?' She blurted out the words.

'Are you allowed to have freebie visitors in your villa?' he asked.

'I don't see why not.'

He considered for a moment, then shook his head. 'Another time, another place, perhaps,' he said. 'I've taken advantage of you enough already.'

'No you haven't. You're probably the only person in the world who hasn't!'

'Well . . .' His voice trailed off.

'D'you think I should chuck it all in?' she asked into the silence that had suddenly developed between them.

He shook his head. 'I think you should go out there and wow them on your tour, make millions and become even more famous. Shake your booty at the world, Sahndhi. Milk it for every opportunity you can and show that gorgeous body off to the press, because right now you're public property. And whatever you do, whatever happens, whatever you see in the papers, don't take it personally.'

She laughed ruefully. 'You seem to know a lot about it.'

'In this world, fame is everything,' he said. 'Everyone knows that. But talent does shine through in the end.'

'Maybe.'

'You'll be OK. You're Survivor Girl, aren't you?' He smiled at her, put on his shirt and trousers again, kissed her one more time and left.

She watched him go. She sat there for quarter of an hour, gazing at the Jacuzzi bubbles, before getting dressed and walking along the pathway to the hotel. Given that it was past midnight, she'd expected the bar to be closed, but there were still a number of people sitting at the glass-topped tables with bottles of wine in front of them. Sitting between two attractive men was the writer woman, Corinne Doherty. Sahndhi recognised her from the picture on the jacket of the book she'd bought in the airport on the way out. She'd thought it was really cool that a famous person was staying at the same place as her and had said so to Ken, who had looked at her in complete astonishment and told her that she was a million times more famous than some obscure author. Sahndhi was startled to realise that he was right. Although she'd enjoyed her copy of *Jennifer Jones and the Jellybean Jackpot*.

She walked through the bar to the reception area, where she sat down at the computer reserved for guests. She hesitated for a moment, then opened the web browser and googled John Reynolds.

It took some time, but eventually she found what she'd half expected and half dreaded. His name beneath a photograph of Madonna. An unflattering photograph, taken with a long lens. And his name under a photograph of a TV soap star along with a story about her alleged cocaine habit.

'Fuck it,' she said out loud. 'Fuck it, fuck it, fuck it.'

'Can I help?'

Sahndhi jumped at the sound of the voice behind her. She whirled around and saw Corinne Doherty standing behind her.

'Only you sounded as though something's gone badly wrong,' said Corinne, who'd been on her way to collect her room key when she'd seen and heard Sahndhi. 'Is it the computer? Maybe I can sort it for you.'

'No,' said Sahndhi through clenched teeth. 'It's not the damn computer.'

'Well then . . .' Corinne smiled at her. 'If there's nothing I can do, I'll get out of your way.'

'It's not . . .' Sahndhi sighed deeply and a tear trickled down her cheek.

'Oh look, whatever it is it can't be that bad,' cried Corinne. She pulled up a chair and sat down beside her.

'I'm sorry.' Sahndhi sniffed. 'I was stupid. It was my own stupid fault, and now . . .' She bit her lip and then exhaled sharply. She never confided in people. But she was furious with herself and with that lying, cheating bastard John Reynolds. How could she have let down her guard like that? How could she have trusted him? She was never going to trust anyone ever again. Ever.

'Tell me,' said Corinne gently. 'It can't hurt.'

Oh it can, thought Sahndhi despairingly. It can hurt terribly. But Corinne was looking at her sympathetically and suddenly, despite all her misgivings, the story came tumbling out.

'But how on earth did you figure out he was some kind of paparazzi guy?' asked Corinne.

'Because he called me Survivor Girl,' explained Sahndhi. 'He said he'd never seen the show. He said he'd no idea who I was. But he knew that I was Survivor Girl. I didn't tell him that.'

'Good deductive reasoning,' said Corinne approvingly. 'What a shit.'

'And now I guess he's going to print all these exclusive shots of me,' said Sahndhi. 'I was practically naked, for heaven's sake!'

'Might be a good career move,' mused Corinne.

'No,' said Sahndhi fiercely. 'It wouldn't be. I don't want to be the Near-Naked Girl in a hot-tub. Besides,' she bit her lip, 'a celebrity magazine is supposed to have exclusive photos of me on the beach and in the resort. God knows what'll happen if they get scooped by his shots. And you know what they're like, the papers, they'll print some kind of rubbish to go with them.' She rubbed the back of her neck. 'So far they've all been really positive about me, even though half of it is complete nonsense. But these pictures . . .'

'You didn't sleep with him, did you?' asked Corinne.

Sahndhi shook her head. 'Though that might've been better,' she said glumly. 'He couldn't have taken a photograph of that and I could've denied everything!'

'Has he sent them to the paper yet?' asked Corinne.

'I don't know.'

'I don't think he can have,' said Corinne thoughtfully. 'After all, he'd probably have to compress them to attach them to an e-mail and then the quality suffers, doesn't it? Presumably if he has great shots of you he won't want the quality to let him down.'

'Yes, but . . .'

'Y'see, if he hasn't sent them . . .'

'There might not be e-mail at his hotel anyway,' interrupted

Sahndhi, suddenly hopeful. 'He said it was cheap and cheerful and you know that there isn't a great service here yet. I think this is the only hotel with an internet connection on this side of the island.'

'So maybe the pix are still in his camera?'

'Maybe. But even so, there isn't anything I can do about it, is there? The bastard!' Sahndhi's sudden spurt of hope receded.

'Where's he staying?' asked Corinne.

Sahndhi told her. 'But he's leaving in the morning.'

'We'll just have to get the camera tonight then, won't we?'

Sahndhi stared at her.

'Well for heaven's sake,' said Corinne. 'You've said that you don't want those photos all over the place. You want to be in control of your image, don't you?'

Sahndhi continued to stare at her.

'Well, don't you?' asked Corinne energetically. 'You've got loads invested in yourself. You don't want it to be messed up by a lying shit like that.'

'But what can I do?' asked Sahndhi 'He had two cameras. He's got loads of shots.'

'OK, so you two were having a bit of a thing, right?' asked Corinne.

'Well, not really. It was just . . .'

'Yeah, but he thinks you fancy him, doesn't he?'

Sahndhi nodded. 'I did!'

'OK, so look.' Corinne was firm. 'You go to his hotel and tell him you had to say one last goodbye or something – he'll be sooooo flattered thinking that you can't stay away from him – and while you're there I'll nip up to his room and delete the pix off his camera.'

'You're joking.'

'No, I'm not.'

'But ... but ... will you be able to do that?' asked Sahndhi. 'What if his room is locked? What if ...'

'Don't worry about it. I'll think of something. And if I can't delete them, or find the memory cards, I'll just rob the cameras,' said Corinne.

'You can't! He'll report them missing.'

Corinne thought about it for a moment.

'Got any memorabilia with you?' she asked.

'What sort of memorabilia?'

'Photos – publicity ones. Posters. You know the sort of thing.'

Sahndhi nodded slowly. 'I have some stock shots.'

'Right,' said Corinne. 'Get one and sign it. And I'll leave it on his bed so that he knows it was you. He wouldn't dare report it. You'll have made him look like a fool.'

Sahndhi started to laugh. 'This will never work,' she said. 'He probably won't even get up out of bed ...'

'Girl, haven't you looked at yourself in the mirror lately?' demanded Corinne. 'Of course he'll get out of bed for you.'

'I think we might be making a whole heap of trouble for ourselves,' said Sahndhi doubtfully.

'Nope,' said Corinne. 'We're going to make a whole heap of trouble for him.'

Sahndhi didn't expect everything to go to plan. In fact, as they approached John's hotel she nearly called the whole thing off, and if it hadn't been for Corinne's unyielding insistence that it would work, she would have fled back to White Sands and resigned herself to being trashed in the papers. But Corinne had alternative suggestions for every problem that Sahndhi came up with.

'You said you'd only had three novels published,' muttered Sahndhi as they stood at the hotel entrance. 'I'm astonished. You seem to have the plot lines for about a million in your head.'

Corinne grinned at her. 'They were stuck there for a while,' she told her. 'But they've started to come back to me. Now off you go and do your thing!'

Sahndhi went into the hotel, rang John's room and cried crocodile tears in front of him, begging him not to go back to London. Then she made him have a drink in the tiny bar with her before telling him she'd been a fool and she was sorry, she had to go but she'd always remember him.

'Sahndhi . . . .' His voice had followed her as she'd run out of the hotel without looking back and met up with Corinne further down the street.

'Bingo.' Corinne held up two digital memory cards. 'Got them. And I didn't bother leaving the signed picture because he'll never work out what's happened to the cards. He can't say it has anything to do with you. You were with him the whole time.'

'You're a genius, you know that? How can I ever thank you?'

'We did it together, Survivor Girl.' Corinne grinned at her. 'And tonight has given me a great idea for an escapade to include in *Jennifer Jones and the Jamaican Jerk*. Now, let's get back to the hotel. It might be late, but you've got a luxury lifestyle to lead and I want to write Chapter Seven before I lose the plot completely.'

Now you can buy any of these other bestselling books by Sheila O'Flanagan from your bookshop or *direct from her publisher*.

FREE P&P AND UK DELIVERY
(Overseas and Ireland £3.50 per book)

Suddenly Single	£7.99
Far From Over	£7.99
My Favourite Goodbye	£7.99
Isobel's Wedding	£7.99
Caroline's Sister	£7.99
Too Good To Be True	£7.99
Destinations	£7.99
Dreaming of a Stranger	£7.99
Anyone But Him	£7.99
How Will I Know?	£6.99

TO ORDER SIMPLY CALL THIS NUMBER

01235 400 414

or visit our website: www.madaboutbooks.com

Prices and availability subject to change without notice.